To C...

Best Regards

Norm

7 - 5 - 02

D0762311

Like Whispers In The Wind

History-Romance
Adventure-Humor

Mystery
with Bat Masterson

Norman Dysart

This book is based on recorded and unrecorded historical events by Texas Panhandle pioneers who were friends of Bat Masterson, and also friends of the author's family.

Bat Masterson, born November 26, 1853, in Province of Quebec, Canada--Buffalo hunter, Indian fighter, surveyor, lawman, and newsman. Died October 25, 1921, and buried in New York.

Credit inside photographs: Mobeetie Jail Museum, Mobeetie, Texas, Panhandle Plains Historical Museum, Canyon, Texas, and Sallie Harris, Wheeler, Texas.

Credit Gene and Marceille Miller: Cover photo.
Credit Pat McCarthy: Cover illustration base sketch.
Credit Marissa DeBord: Cover art and saloon scene.

Maps based on historical landmarks.

Historical events, episodes and excerpts on last pages.

ISBN 0-9654503-3-3

Dysart Diversified, Publisher, Amarillo, Texas.

Copyright 1994 & 1996.

Printed in the U. S. A.

3rd printing, 2nd revision, 1999.

In honor of my Dad,
Carey Dysart,

who loved and lived the
Western Cowboy life.

Acknowledgments

Sallie Harris's, "Hidetown."
Pauline and R. L. Robertson's,
"Panhandle Pilgrimage."
Mrs. Homer Duval on her grandfather,
Emanuel Dubbs.
Marshall Cator on his Uncles, Jim and Bob Cator.
Tom O'Loughlin, on his grandparents,
Tom and Ellen O'Loughlin.
Ellis Locke on his grandfather,
Newt Locke, Texas Ranger.
F. Stanley, historical facts.
R. C. (Dick) House, who suggested this book.

To my wife, Vircie Dysart, and Carol Spann, Keith
Savage, Gene and Marceille Miller, Cathey Norwood,
Etta Lynch, and others ....And thanks for the memory
to all the oldtimers and their tales of pioneer days on
the Western frontier.

Index

Foreword

"Like Whispers In The Wind," the untold love story of Bat Masterson and Molly Brennan. The historical events of romance, mystery, humor, adventure, and violence is written in Western cowboy verncular.

Bat Masterson seemed to disappear for a short time in his early life. However, the three years he lived in the Texas Panhandle may have been the most exciting of his colorful career. He came to the Texas Panhandle to hunt buffaloes as a teen-ager, then scouted for the U. S. Army, and was soon caught-up in the "Battle Of Adobe Walls," June 27, 1874. After the conflict, he rode to a settlement called Hidetown, on Sweetwater Creek, in the east Texas Panhandle. Later Hidetown was called Sweetwater and finally Mobeetie (Mo-b-t)—Indian for sweet water.

High at the top of Texas, the settlement's closest neighbor was Dodge City, Kansas, 200 miles north. The vast untamed Panhandle was a hideout for outlaws and people seeking their fortune. Wyatt Earp was run out of Mobeetie, "The wildest and toughest of them all," for selling "gold bricks"—painted gold.

Not much was known about the Texas Panhandle until a little news began to trickle out in the late 1870's. The first buffalo hunters came in 1873, however, there was no law before 1879.

Mobeetie was a hellacious lustful town that boasted over 500 prostitutes. Numerous deaths occurred in the 1870's but few were recorded—all killed in gunfights.

In 1868, according to records, Gen. George Armstrong Custer, with the 7th Calvary, "Camped near the headwaters of Sweetwater River in the Texas Panhandle." Custer was on a military mission to wipe out a tribe of Cheyenne Indians, led by Chief Black Kettle. They were on the Washita, 35 miles east of Custer's campsite on Sweetwater. Seven years later, near where the 7th Calvary camped on Sweetwater Creek, Fort Elliot was established and named for Major Joel Elliot...killed in Custer's Black Kettle skirmish.

A Mobeetie gunfighter, claiming twenty notches on his gun, warned Bat Masterson, "Stay away from my woman!" Insanely jealous, the outlaw killed men, even threatened women who were friendly with, "The Rose of the Canadian," Molly Brennan. This was a challenge Bat Masterson could never pass up. And that's the way it was.

Ref. in back.

1 *Raging Bull*

From out of the west he come, his horse worming his way down a buffalo trail. The Adobe Walls battle was over but the Indian war-whoops would never fade away. Stuffing rags in bleeding arrow holes of a dying friend, begging for water, would haunt him always. Working the trail of the vanishing herds would soon put money in his pockets. Leaving Adobe Walls, the Indians had give him no respect after crossing the Canadian River... his horse was wrung-out; shoulders white with foam. The weather was hot and dry, his throat parched. He could have quenched his thirst up the creek but the hide-hunter settlement was in sight. An adobe building with an upper story, in among half-dugouts, and hide tents seemed odd. A saloon or a place to eat would offer relief.

Approaching the settlement, he saw a man standing by a hide buyer's lean-to. The old gray-bearded fellow stared at the big black horse coming toward him, then quickly stuffed his hide money deep in his pocket as he climbed onto his empty wagon. His team horses , an iron-gray and bay, hooked to an ancient butcher-knife wagon were chomping at the bits to go; he held tight team-lines, sizing up the newcomer.

No ordinary saddle-tramp, the handsome stranger sat tall in the saddle—young, well tanned, beard sparse, his hair long and dark—hat gray. Coming in close, his smile was friendly but his bluish-slate gray eyes flashed cold and fearless.

The man reined-up. "Howdy!" the old hide hunter

1

spoke, squinting his faded eyes. He peered from under his buffalo manure splotched hat...a shadow cut across his round weather beaten face—tanned and furrowed deep.

"Evening. Name's Masterson—Bat Masterson."

"Jist call me Zeb, Ol' Zeb Hunter they call me. New'n these parts?"

"Can't rightly say so," Bat replied. "I've been scoutin' for the Government, chasing Indians since August, but hunted in Kansas, and done some shootin' at 'Dobe Walls. 'Rode through here back in the summer...three or four tents staked on the south creek-bank—maybe a dozen hunters. Now I see hide tents and half-dugouts every-where I look. Back then they called it Hidetown—Hidetown, Texas."

"Ain't changed, still do," the old man said, chuckling. "Jumped up over night. 'Fact even jumped the creek. Ya know it's jist two miles out here where that Fort is but the Army made the squatters 'round the Post move. All 'em come here."

"Unusual," Bat mused. "What happened?"

"Nothin' much. They had to move on 'count of Bob Brennan killin' a guy for making a crack at his daugh-ter."

Gazing around, Bat said, "I'm looking for something that's a little body-bracing...see the Lady Gay Saloon down a ways...must be living quarters upstairs, there?"

"Is. Fanciest in town, and ah'll tell ya 'bout this town," the old man said. "We got saloons. 'Course Uncle Johnny Long's 'Mint' was here before anybody's...'got set up here after his freight wagons in Lyman's Wagon Train got caught by them Indians; few miles north. Then there's Walter Weed's Whiskey. He brought in a hun-dred barrels his first trip. And on down a piece is the Shores-Of-Hell. This place is boomin'. We got Bob

Brennan's blacksmith shop, Curry Brothers is puttin' in a supply store and Bill Kimball's puttin' in a livery stable. And we got the best hotels in the West...there's Tom O'Loughlin's, Ma Manlin's, and Mark Huselby is puttin' in one, too. Dogged Redskins burnt Tom out in Kansas so he come down here and put in this fine eatin' place. His hotel's got buffalo skins for rugs. 'Course the floor's dirt—soft dirt that is—but a good place if'n ya wanta bed down. We got saloons, fancy hotels, blacksmith shop, stores goin' in, and hide buyers thick as flies. She's boomin', man she's boomin'. This is the place, Bat—the promised land!"

"Buy you a drink," Bat suggested.

"Gotta do some fixin' on my wagon so's can get out amongst them hide critters in the mornin'. But I hafta tell ya this before ya go—there's a b-a-d man in this here town. I purt near nearly got caught up in one of his little shootin' scrapes having one at the Lady Gay few days back. This stranger, new in town, smiled and opened the door for that purty Brennan girl at Curry's store...next door to the 'Lady.' This gunslick, Dogface Melvin King, was settin' in the saloon and saw 'em. He didn't like what he saw. Been said he's killed up'ards of twenty men and booted outta the army for killin' 'nother soldier.   Well, here's what happened, I was standing at the bar, 'back to the door, looking in that big mirror. I saw this feller coming in the door to a standing spot between me and Hank Dittmos. Dogface he got up from the corner table to head off the stranger. He walks up to 'im and says, 'So you're the Sonovabitch that stole my horse!' 'Course Bat anybody knows them's shootin' words in this town, and kinda taken 'round here nobody talks to Dogface's wimmin. The stranger moved his hands and Dogface went for his Bowie knife in his belt. Like lightnin', the stranger grabbed Dogface's right hand. But

Dogface was jist as fast with his left and come up with his shootin' iron. Reckon 'was crazy, but I jist stood there. Hank Dittmos got splattered with blood and hit the floor to dodge the bullets. I got plumb tickled. Ol' Hank was so scared he laid there on the floor till we drug the dead man out. I thought ya might like to know, nary a man's come out winner that's took on that rattlesnake."

"Well, thanks," Bat replied.

Bat was not too concerned about the town bully. The old man wanted to let Bat know the overbearing guy had the town stirred up; a raging bull in the settlement.

"Yeah," Zeb rambled on, "Dogface takes soldiers' money with loaded dice. If they bitch he has his side-kicks pull their britches off and he quirt whips 'em. He accuses buffalo hunters of stealing his hides—hides he ain't never had in the first place. Another time a drifter smiled and tipped his hat to Molly Brennan there at J. J. Long's store. King saw it. Digger Dugan put the drifter six feet under the next day. Everybody thinks Molly is Dogface's woman but she hates his guts. And he gets smokin' hot and throws a fit ever time he sees that girl talkin' to her wimmin friends...the wimmin's husbands' then catch hell from Dogface—whips out that Bowie knife. Molly's burly Dad, he'll fight a circle-saw and King knows it, but since the Fort killin' Bob's sorta ridin' a slow hoss. There ain't another man that'll lay eyes on Molly when the bully comes to town."

People in the settlement were wringing their tail when Bat Masterson rode into Hidetown in the spring of 1875.

"Been in these parts long?" Bat asked the friendly oldtimer.

"For some time but did go up north to help Johnny Long. Like I say, he was in Lyman's wagon train in September and got caught by a bunch'o them Indians. Then he was in that bad December blizzard. His wagons was

4

loaded with that army stuff. We liked to froze our tails off."

"Yup, bad one but this warm weather will bring in many a hunter. The shaggie shooters will feel safe with this fort setting out here."

"Can bet on it," Zeb replied. "Hunters gonna be thicker'n flies 'round a bull's butt in August. Ain't never seen so dadgum many buffaloes in all my livins. One feller by name of Dick Bussel has done got over ten thousand hides—'nough to load a freight train clean to Kansas City." He chuckled, then added, "And that creek is full'o catfish and perch. Ah, this is it, the promised land."

"Good weather and plenty hides," Bat said.

"Yeah. Them weak-kneed dudes, 'scared of Redskins, been waitin' for the soldiers...when they start pourin' in, and ain't afraid no more; gonna be a dog-eat-dog thing. Killins' over who shot what."

"Saw it happen in Kansas—see you later," Bat replied, as he reined his horse around to ride off.

Zeb raised his voice, "Come over, my little home's 'cross the creek...half-dugout, that is. Do some sippin'n nippin; got some chawins, too!"

"Sounds good!" Bat yelled, as he spurred out. He left the old man scratching his head. Bat tied up at the Lady Gay, a two story landmark travelers could see for miles. Who'd give a hoot'n holler if the unfinished floor 'back of the bar was dirt and the tables were army packing crates? But the Lady Gay had more than Bat expected, more than any stranger expected—naked gal wall art, a big bar-length mirror, swinging bat-wing doors, and a dance floor.

Out aways from the back door were stacks of adobe bricks, along with some lumber and logs. The business was owned by Henry Fleming and Bill Thompson. Henry, talking with two or three buffalo hunters, glanced up;

5

he saw Bat coming through the door. Seeing an old friend in the sparsely settled country was like seeing a saint. Moving toward Bat, reaching out his hand, Henry exclaimed, "Damned if it ain't my old shoot'n hidin' friend from Kansas—Bat Masterson himself! How's it going?"

"Been scouting for the Government. Looks like she's booming here."

"Couldn't be better!" Henry exclaimed. "Sent my manager and bartender to Dodge City for supplies. You know my partner, Bill Thompson, he's in Kansas City hustling supplies too—women. I'm holding her down by myself. She's a boom town, hide-tents and half-dugouts jumping up by the dozens. We're all running over. I've got a full house and so have O'Loughlin's. The Manlin hotel has a full house too but nobody can remember when Ma swept the floors and changed the sheets. I'll tell you, Bat, big money for these hides will soon start pouring in, and your usual luck of rolling dice and shuffling cards—you can make a fortune."

Bat was all ears. "Aimed to move on but it sounds good. Figure be no more scouting for the Army," he said, tossing Henry a coin.

Henry tossed it back. "Guess you'll have to join the bunch sleeping under the stars, but Bat Masterson's spent many a night sleeping on the ground—the Grassland Hotel." Henry chuckled.

Hidetown settlement was running over with hunters but shaggie shooters were all over the prairie too. New hunters in town were running hog wild and crazy getting ready for the next day. The future looked good for the little community, however, Bat Masterson hated the stinking hide business. But he loved the sweet smell of money.

He unsaddled Coalie and threw his bedroll down in the lush grass to make for a soft bed. The horse could stuff his belly, too. Bat rolled over, dead to the world, he soon dropped off to sleep. But early the next morning he thought the giddyups and whoas would wake-up a dead man. He came out of bed with Zeb on his mind. The old buffalo hunter was all fired up about Hidetown but it wasn't all talk. People had gone hide crazy. Buffalo hunting educated but not book smart, he loved to hunt and was Bat's kind of man, but Bat thought he was stretching it a little about the big herds "back'n south."

Millions of buffaloes covered the prairie, but hunters by the thousands would soon wipe the animals off the face of the earth. Bat saddled his horse, took a chaw of "Brown Mule," and rode off to find Zeb. He reined around new businesses, thrown up tents, adobe houses, half-dugouts, and cellars too. The spring days were warm. He watched as droves of hunters went for the buffalo slaughter. Big wagon loads of hides were pouring in off the prairie and hide buyers were jumping through their tails to stay ahead. Charlie Rath's half-finished warehouse sat and nobody touching it. Bat could see why. Charlie was a big hide buyer but swamped with hides. Visiting city dudes were in awe, stood and gawked at the huge loads of hides coming in. The buildings for the most part in the settlement were thrown together and half finished, but enterprising Henry Fleming built a rock house that still stands today.

On his way to Zeb's place, Bat swung by Bob Brennan's blacksmith shop. The blacksmith meant everything to pioneers. Maybe not a doctor in two hundred miles, but the blacksmith came in with the first settlers...fix anything from seven foot wagon wheels to cowboy boots—hammer out branding iron symbols with such skill it would make any writer of script jealous. The trusted cowtown philosopher kept the harness and saddles patched up, and fixed the wagons...a good cobbler and horse doctor, too. No one was around the shop when Bat rode up.

The shop was nothing much. Bat didn't expect much two hundred miles from another settlement. Under a brush arbor shade was a home made forge, a few hand tools, and a cottonwood stump made do for an anvil-rest. His forge stood over in one corner, had sturdy iron pipe legs, and a little junk iron was stacked in another corner; that was about it.

Tall Jimson weeds behind the arbor blocked out the hot evening sun. Farther back, partly hid, was a half-dugout. Gazing around the smithy's shop, Bat noticed the grass was worn and mashed down. A pair of fire tongs lay in the dust under the forge and a shop hammer was left lying on the anvil. There was no wagon around, not even a horse. He figured the Smithy was on the prairie helping a buffalo hunter with an overloaded broken-down wagon. Bat had seen it happen, spokes in wooden wheels loosened up in dry weather, and get a hard jolt, they'd fall apart. He was ready to go, glanced the place over, spur-tickled Coalie's belly and the horse moved on. But suddenly the hanging rawhide door on the half-dugout flew open.

"Ah, ah, Mister, can I help you?" Someone called in a pleasant voice.

Bat reined around. A girl sixteen, maybe seventeen, walked toward him. Her good-looks, her pretty smile, and sparkling blue eyes could knock any man out of the saddle. She stopped out a-ways from him. Her long dark hair glistened in the sunshine.

"Ah-uh-Ma'am, yeah," he stammered. "Name's Masterson—Bat Masterson that is...yes'um, just kinda riding by, but-but what I'm actually looking for is-is a Hunter, Ma'am—a Hunter."

"Oh, there's plenty around," she said. "Shouldn't be

no trouble finding one."

"Well, yes'um, Mr. Hunter hunts—a hunter that is; I mean he hunts, too.

She cute-grinned him. "Well, Mister I just don't understand. He hunts too—two buffaloes and hunts hunters, too?"

Young Bat Masterson could handle his guns with the best, but this gal, with a figure he couldn't overlook, had the stumblebum mixed up and mumbling, wringing his tail. Timid and bashful around pretty girls, his shyness showed through. It's been said a beautiful woman can muddle a man's mind anytime always have and always will, but that conversation would give any girl a big laugh. He knew where Zeb Hunter's place was.

"Well, yup, Ma'am," he said, "name's Mr. Bat-uh, just plain Bat Masterson, that is. Just be riding on now, but I'll bring my horse back." He was making talk but it didn't make sense.

Had he planned to follow the herds to put money in his pocket; he couldn't even remember. Attractive and friendly, Molly Brennan snared him like a well thrown lariat. This is it, this was the place, the end of the buffalo trail for Bat Masterson. His head was set and his mind made up.

Bat rode on, thinking back, he had met-up with a green red-wheeled wagon about a year before east of Dodge City. Had a girl sitting on the spring-board seat between her dad and mother. Bat guessed her at fourteen, maybe fifteen. The kid waved as he rode ahead—met-up at Dodge City?

Coalie hit a little easy foxtrot. He suddenly pitched his ears forward; a running horse? Bat glanced up. A horse with a rider was coming down the street in a dead-run, but nothing unusual in the settlement; drunks did it all time. But the strawberry roan, a little bigger than usual for a saddlehorse, was well known in town. People stopped to stare. Suspicions were aroused. A man dashed behind the Shores-Of-Hell and peeped around the corner. He waited—a gunfight? The old Mexican hombre, deep in his siesta at Curry's doorstep, roused and set upright. A teamster ducked behind his wagon. The rider came in fast and reined in close to Bat, jerked the red roan up, but didn't say a word.

The stranger, wearing vintage khaki army clothes, dropped his reins over the saddlehorn. His gun-hands free, shadowed the six-guns on his hips. Still he never opened up. His stringy orange-red hair hung down under an old flopped-down army hat that half covered his beady eyes, A devilish sneer cracked his pock-marked face.

Bat had the red roan rider figured out; watching the blacksmith shop all time. Bat offered nothing. Was this Dogface Melvin King, the man Zeb had talked about that come down from Dodge City to show Hidetown how tough he was...had the town quaking in her boots; claimed he had laid a brand on Molly Brennan? Bat was a fun-loving guy. He could handle the bully's brand as easy as changing brands on a steer with a hot "running-iron." He loved to play the game.

The two saddlehorses stood fifteen/twenty feet apart at rest, flipping their ears, flinching their sides and tail-switching flies away...sneezing once in awhile. But the riders didn't move, sat stone-still in the saddle, staring eyeball to eyeball. Not a word was spoken—dead silence. The man peeping around the corner—the Mexican hombre—the ducking teamster, watched and listened. Could be they heard it said, "Ain't no son-of-a-bitch big enough to run me outta this town!"

2 *The Hunt*

The red roan rider reined around, gouged his spurs in the horse's belly and whipped out.

Bat was short on smokings. Tying up at the store, he saw a man hunkered down, dozing by the door. Bat spoke, "Howdy."

"Si, si, buenos dias." He looked up and down the street. "No bueno el hombre al rojo caballo."

The old Mexican seemed to be out of sorts. The red roan rider had no respect for the hombre's siesta. Spanish wasn't Bat's best talk, but he thought the old fellow had told him the man on the red horse was no good.

"Yeah, yeah, gracias, Senor."

Bat came to Texas for hide money. He'd find Zeb, he knew the country. Worming his way through stacks of buffalo hides he spoke and nodded to hunters. Men in wagons and on horseback too were pulling out. Wagons with bronc horses in the hitch had trouble getting off. The harness and rattling old wagons, the wild horses throwed a fit. Rearing up and kicking, they soon got the gentle horses stirred up too, then they all went crazy as hell. After weeks on the hunt the wagons would be back loaded with hides.

Bat watched. Everybody was in a hurry. Yelling teamsters and snorting horses, chaos in every direction. Ammunition, skinning knives, guns, grub, salt, and jugs of water were loaded. Hunters cracked their whips and wagons strung out. A gun went off, punched a couple new holes in a wagon, but the driver paid it no mind.

Unloading a big squirt of tobacco juice, he swung up in the wagon and yelled, "Giddyup!" Skinners' holding the broncs' bridle-bits let go and grabbed for the wagon when it went by. Losing his grip, a man slammed hard against the wagon-bed. Bat held his breath, mumbled, "Get in the spokes of that big iron-tired wheel, brother, and your hunting days are over"...'crazy, couldn't move faster if they were running for gold. The guy's sidekick reached for him, grabbed a handful of hair, and pulled him in. Floundering around, the half-squatted men bounced all over the wagon-bed.

The hunters often circled their wagons on the prairie and jokingly called it "Hidetown." But this place was for real. The wild, wild, West and all for the $2.50 hide of the buffalo. Bat Masterson had never seen anything like it.

Zeb rushed to get his wagon ready to go; however, Zeb's rushing was little more than a snail's pace. He called his team his four best'uns. Four horses was all the old man had, two browns, an iron-gray, and a bay. He was fussy about his harness and wagon. It wasn't the best but it had to hold together when racing with the Indians. Three horses were hitched to the wagon when Bat rode up. Zeb was working on the last one.

"Howdy, Podner," Zeb greeted. "I jist got the old bay simmered down. He throws a fit ever' time I throw the harness on him. Get off ya hoss, be ready in a minute."

"You're getting off early," Bat replied.

"Not early's I'd like, but the days are long and hot. These old plugs are always wrung out by sundown. Yeah, goin' down on the North Fork of the big Red...on south to McClellan Creek."

Bat came off his horse. "North Fork, huh?" A shrill scream burst out. Bat looked around then suddenly jumped! A racing team was headed straight for him. He

12

raised his voice, "What the hell Zeb, that a woman?"

"Get out of here you lazy stumblin' sons-a-bitches!" the woman yelled, laying the leather to the struggling four-horse hitch. Bat had never seen a Roman chariot race but thought this could be it. A couple of skinners jostling around in the wagon latched onto guns and grub. Bouncing over sagebrush and buffalo trails, the men tried to stay on their feet. They grabbed for the sideboards and held on. Dodge City was never like this, the wild and wooly Texas Panhandle. Men sopping up buffalo gravy had gone hide crazy.

"Yeah, that's Buffalo Bertha," Zeb drawled. "That old gal's tough as nine layers of rawhide and salty as the Dead Sea—gets her share of the hides, too. She never slowed down after the Indians raided their camp and scalped her Hezzie....And keeps her skinners warm in the winter," the old man added, grinning.

Bat had scouted the Panhandle, knew the country, knew too, in any direction from Hidetown there could be Redskin trouble.

"Out'n past the North Fork there's up'ards of ten million of them hide critters," Zeb continued. "I can use an eagle eye if'n ya'd go. Mine's sort of fogged over. Dust I reckon. Shot a big bull 'while back—thought I did—but the old sucker wouldn't fall. Pulled up'n my wagon, but no bull; shootin' at a big polecat bush. 'Course had a little nip before I went and might say it kinda kept me rockin'."

Bat said, "Could be fun, a little excitement, and I reckon as to how I could use the money, too. Zeb, gonna take you up on that but my saddle gun's going be a little light. I'll go get my big '50'."

"Don't hafta do that. Use Os's Sharps." Zeb turned. "Watch that old bay hoss. He's a kicker, got eyes in the back of his head. Kicked out the front-end once, wrecked the wagon, and he's got no use for strangers."

13

Bat said, "Well, not like having your own gun." He added, grinning, "Maybe I can bring down a polecat bush."

"Skinners done rode ahead. Jist tie ya hoss to that iron gray and ride a piece on this springboard seat; good ridin', mighty easy on ya butt if'n it don't leave it rubbed raw."

"Why not?" Bat replied, but he didn't buy that easy riding stuff. Zeb's springboard seat was nothing more than two poles rawhide-tied together that reached across the top sideboards. His wagon was no different than most, but "Solid Comfort" printed in big letters on the undercarriage caught Bat's eye. He soon wondered about the comfort, where was it? The springless wagon sent jarring jolts up and down his spine, but even so, nothing ...nothing could shake his mind off the girl at the blacksmith shop!

"Nope, Os wouldn't mind a bit. Right neighborly good feller. I reckon his name was Car, never knew, never asked. 'Course, might have been Oscar. Only been huntin' with me 'bout two months when he got his head peeled. This scalpin's gonna slow down when we get this fort in here." He added, "But the bad part is...all them buffaloes will be gone, too."

"Yup, buffaloes and Indians."

"If ya don't mind I'd like to go by and pay my respects to ol' Os on the way back. None outta the way."

"Don't mind at all. Ambushed?" Bat asked.

"Well yes, we wuz back'n south—where we're headed now— waitin' for the herd to come outta the river breaks and top out on flat country where a draw heads up. He hid, got set across the draw in a patch of shin-oak, and waited. I stayed on the other side; figured they'd top out between us. I hid the wagon in another draw then I got set. Here they come, the critters spreading out to graze. We could see for miles around us except in a deep gully behind Os. I think Os, he got wind that some of them confounded Redskins was hid in that gully. When I saw Os run for his hoss I run for the wagon, and laid the leather on them old hosses. Pore ol' Os didn't have a chance. Them Indians wuz on his tail like a duck on a June bug. But 'bout that time, thank goodness, some of these soldiers running all over the country showed up and they went after them rascals. Next day I saddled up and rode over to get Os. The wolves done chewed him up. Done all I could, put him in an old wolf den and throwed some buffalo chips over him."

"The skinners, what happened to your skinners?" Bat asked.

"Well, ya know they wuz ridin' hosses and never found 'em dead or alive; may still be running," he replied, chuckling.

Bat amd Zeb crossed the headwaters of North Fork and kept heading south toward McClellan Creek, the headwaters of the Salt Fork. Their second day out they came across mashed down grass and dung was everywhere; signs the buffaloes were close.

"Zeb continued, "If they ain't headed south, they's a big herd in these hills somewhere."

He gazed toward McClellan Creek. "Bat, I see something down there...them specks, that's 'em! Let's throw a camp and go for 'em tomorrow."

The old man's vision wasn't too good up close, but so far sighted Bat thought he could see the sunrise two days ahead.

"Believe you're right," Bat replied.

Early the next morning they broke camp and hustled out. Zeb said, nodding, "I'll take the wagon over yonder and leave it in that gully. These hosses go crazy when that shootin' starts. And Bat, them shaggies are moving

15

this way."

"Ain't polecat bushes?" Bat grinned.

"Nope. Big herd," Zeb replied, itching to start shooting.

"Yup," it is," Bat said, "but nothing like we've seen in the past. I've seen it and you have too, some of these herds around a hundred and twenty five miles long and twenty five miles wide, probably five million animals."

"Yeah, can really tear up cattle-drives, too, they say."

Bat pointing, said, "Zeb I'm tying my horse in that patch of shin-oak. 'Going to get set, got plenty ammunition, find a forked stick for a gun-rest; them gun-barrels get too hot for me."

Zeb set-up in a gully a little farther west. The herd was slowly moving up and soon thousands were topping out, pouring over the rise. An old bull hopping along, swinging a bullet- shattered leg, stopped, then moved on, struggling to stay with the herd. The guns were silent. The shaggies moved in gun-range then the big "50s" roared. The buffaloes started off in a trot. The hunters fired in front of the shaggies, and bullets kicking up dust at their front feet got them going in a circle. A shot in the lungs knocked the leader down then the next to take his place, and the next. The smell of blood seemed to confuse the buffaloes. They started milling around.

Bat and Zeb hunted buffaloes like most hunters, but they didn't understand the buffalo; nobody did. They watched the animals, at times when shooting was going on in the big herds, and animals falling like flies, others browsed around, seemed as if nothing was going on. Even the horny bulls carried on with the heifers in their usual prolific way.

Buffaloes often stampeded and for no reason it seemed. Herds would go over high cliffs and kill hundreds. Bat and Zeb didn't know what happened, the herd stampeded and disappeared in a cloud of dust. Already there were more carcasses than they could skin out before the stink set in. The skinners laid low in the gullies while the shooting was going on, but now it was skinning time.

Bat moseyed through the knocked-down buffaloes' kicking carcasses to be sure the animals were dead. A big bull had been shot. His hide would bring $3.50, a premium. Bat moved on. He heard a sudden shuffling behind him and swung his rifle around; too late. The snorting buffalo slammed Bat in the butt and threw him over his head. He lost his gun and come down across the bull's back, grabbed handfuls of hair and hung on. He knew, to let go, the big critter would smash him in the ground. But he lost his grip, went off over the buffalo's head, grabbed the bull by the horns, and held on. The bull set back on his haunches and spun around and around...spinning until Bat lost his grip and was slung out fifteen/twenty feet. Then, the buffalo lowered his head, snorted, pawed the earth, and come after Bat with blood in his eyes and foaming at the mouth. Something kept telling Bat to get out of there, things were beginning to get serious!

3 Skinning Time

The old denizen of the plains dropped dead at Bat's feet. A bullet was found lodged in his heart.

The hunters' hurried to skin the animals. The Indians were in the skinning business, too. The weather was hot, carcasses swelling and stinking; flies swarming. The buzzards circled overhead looking for a free meal. The sneaky coyotes came in close and the slinking wolves showed up, too. The job was going too slow. Bent on getting the work done, a Skinner asked, "Why not pull the hides off the carcasses with team-horses?" The hunters were always looking for a better way to do things.

"Good idea," Bat said, "a team or saddlehorse, but you know how horses shy at the sight of dead animals."

Ideas were kicked around. "Blindfold 'em with a piece of skin," another Skinner suggested. Everyone agreed it'd work. But the horses wanted no part of that skin business; they threw a fit. Finally the hunters jerked off their shirts, poked the horses' ears through the arm holes and brought it over their eyes. The team simmered down and the job moved along. A few days passed. The carcasses had swelled to a strut, the stink impossible, but the skinning was over. They pegged out two hundred hides to dry—hairy side down—and sprinkled on a little salt to keep the worms out.

As usual Zeb got to thinking he could handle more hides. But after they were loaded, no doubt, it was all his team could snake out of the hills.

"Bat, if'n we ride the flat country, stay out of the hills,

we'll make better time."

Zeb was right. Bat thought the Texas high staked plains, the Llano Estacado, was unusual country. The level ground usually falls off to rolling hills, but in places the terrain drops off to gorges over one thousand feet deep.

Bat replied, "Yup, skirt the rimrock high country, and if the Redskins show up we'll try to make the canyons. Now it's not going to be easy to move this load. I'll throw my lariat around one of the wagon standards and give the team some help. When this saddlehorse feels the pull on the saddlehorn he can move a mountain."

"Giddyup!" Zeb yelled, cracked his whip, and the wagon moved on. Riding Coalie, Bat went ahead, but soon he heard a horrified yell, "W-h-o-a now, whoa!" He looked back. Hides were sliding off the wagon on a downhill slope. Zeb was coming off with them, yelling, scrambling, flailing his arms, landing at the heels of the teamhorses'...desperate, he was buried in buffalo hides.

Bat burst out with laughter, yelled, "Stay with 'em."

The load piling off on the tongue-horses soon got them excited. Zeb was in real danger of kicking heels. But he held onto the team-lines. The bay snorted, reared up, and got his back foot straddle one of his trace-chains'. The darned old horse kept struggling until he worked the chain high-up between his back legs, sawing on tender flesh. He twisted and struggled in the harness. Soon all four horses went crazy. Zeb coaxed and cussed to simmer down the outlawed broncs. He busted their hips with team-lines, still yelling, "Whoa ya crazy bastards, whoa!" Disgusted, sweat was pouring off his forehead when Bat rode up. Bat grabbed the lead horses' bridle-bits to simmer down the team.

"A little trouble, there—eh?" Bat said, chuckling.

Zeb was still wound up on horse talk, "Confounded

19

old sumbitch! Don't know why he has to act up at a time like this —Redskins swarmin' thick as flies!"

The horses calmed down and the dumped-off hides were loaded. Zeb crawled back on the wagon and they were soon on their way again. Rambling on, Zeb soon stopped the wagon. Bat reined over.

"What's wrong, horses' give out?" he asked.

Zeb come off the wagon. "I jist wanted to pay my respects to old Os." He nodded toward an abandoned wolf den on a ledge. Buffalo chips had been stacked over the hole. With his hat off, Zeb bowed his head and stood silent. Soon he said, "Pore old Os, this is his grave, he wasn't afraid to die, real religious feller, fine Christian man, but he always wondered: if he got scalped, would he go to Heaven bald? Let's head 'em up."

The old grizzled man pulled his splotched hat down against his ears and crawled back on the wagon; another hunter's unmarked grave on the Texas high plains. The horseback-skinners had left early and rode ahead. Bat tied Coalie to the iron-gray and crawled on the wagon with Zeb. At sundown they pitched a camp on the banks of North Fork River.

On their way the next morning, not far from their camp, they found a spear-ripped buffalo.

"Well, the Indians were close," Bat said, "but it looks like they left in a hurry. We just missed a massacre; blood oozing, meat's still hot."

"Yeah, our massacre," Zeb replied. "I figure soldiers got on their tail. Reckon we're luckier than ol' Os, but it ain't too late. Let's get out of here!" he yelled and slapped the team with the lines.

Nerve-racking, the Indians were always on the hunters' mind. They jogged along, watching. Soon a string of horses showed up on the horizon ahead.

Zeb asked, shading his eyes, "Ya reckon thems'

Redskins—are they comin' this way—ain't soldiers is it?"

Bat was concerned too that they may have been seen; Indians waiting over the next rise? Bat said, "Zeb, strung-out, it's gotta be Indians, but going the other way."

The Indians disappeared in the distance. The team struggled, the wagon rolled on, bump after bump, jar after jar.

Bat asked, "About this Fort—'been out there?"

"Naw, and don't know much about it," Zeb said. "Nothin' 'ceptin' what this man by name of Johnny Long said—same feller I told ya about that got caught in that blizzard—'jist know what he heard. The Fort would be ready this coming month'o June, '75—didn't know much, have 500 white and 300 black soldiers."

Bat said, "They started to locate it a few miles west of here, on Cantonement Creek, but settled here on Sweetwater Creek."

"Yeah, working on it...be called Fort Elliot."

"Heard the same thing," Bat replied.

"Yeah, ya know," Zeb come back, "that man Elliot, Major Joel Elliot, was a big dog under that guy some people thought wuz crazy...big handle by name of General George Armstrong Custer. Few years back, in '68—'been told he camped on Sweetwater Creek couple miles up from Hidetown. A buffalo hunter camped up there found a me-dallion, a button of some kind that had a '7' or something on it—thought it was calvary. 'Don't know what they found but 'been told Custer reported to Washington he was in the Panhandle and camped near, 'The headwaters of Sweetwater River.' Not too smart, didn't know a creek from a river. Well anyway, it wasn't long until he went over east of here thirty five/forty miles and hopped out Chief Black Kettle on the Washita—Southern Cheyennes; jist about wiped 'em out, squaws and kids. And it riled up them Redskins. Custer sent Elliot and a few men out to finish off the Braves, but them Indian boys was smart. They wiped out Elliot and all of his men and you know what—that cussed Custer didn't have guts 'nough to go out and pick up Major Elliot and the dead troopers. 'Bout as crazy as the skunk that rides that old red roan hoss—'case ya ever meet up with 'im—got the blacksmith's daughter roped, he thinks."

"Yup," Bat said, "they tell me General Sheridan picked them up later. From what we've heard Custer and his 7th calvary troops did camp here on the head-waters of Sweetwater near where they're putting Ft. Elliot. Sweetwater springs are just a half mile or so above the Fort location. Yup, reckon you're right, Zeb....So he thinks he's got her roped, huh?"

"Yeah, what he thinks," Zeb replied, still with the Fort on his mind, "Well, 'bout this Military Post, it's gonna be two miles northwest of Hidetown on Sweetwater Creek, like ya say, right in there where them buffalo hunters found a bois d'arc charcoal pit...picked up a 7th calvary saddle-bag, too, didn't they?"

"Yup, heard it when I was scouting—'don't know if it's true. The troops like this good water I reckon, but don't think George and his bunch hung around too long—anxious to head-up Montana way and wipe out the Northern Cheyennes, too."

Zeb said, "They's a bunch them Injuns up'n there that'd like to clean his plow." He continued, "Well, Hidetown's movin' a mile northwest—half way to the Fort—and gonna sweeten up the name, too; be called Sweetwater. The Comanches call it 'Mobeetie' (Mo-b-t)—means the same thing—sweet water. But them crazy Cheyennes, they make fun of it...says Mobeetie means buffalo manure. Anyway, it ain't even gonna be on the creek." He added, grinning, "Hafta go a fur piece for my spring bath."

"Well," Bat said, chuckling, "spring has sprung, things are moving. A few days back I was north of town and saw an ox-train with big loads of lumber and other stuff."

"Yeah, ox-trains and wagons pulled by three spans of them big mules bringing in loads of wire and stuff like that. They're going to put in one of them telly-graph things at the Fort."

"Heard it too," Bat replied.

"Yeah," Zeb said, "hooked up with Fort Sill, Fort Reno, and Fort Supply, all in Indian Territory, and Fort Dodge in Kansas. These people coming in from everywhere, and them buffaloes wiped out—we ain't seen no mad Indian yet. They're goin' on a bloody tear like you ain't never seen in ya whole dadburn life."

"Can hardly blame 'em," Bat replied. "Just trying to stay alive, hang onto their hunting grounds. There's going to be scalping until the Indians are gone. The Army's here to beat down the Indian, kick him off the land he's always known, and stop the scalping. 'Been a Redman's paradise since God knows when, but the jig's up now."

Zeb replied, "I've heard it said, get the Redskins pushed out there could be six or seven thousand hunters in here. Maybe another year of good huntin'."

Bat nodded. "And '77 rolls around that will about wind her up. A few shot-up shaggies can be found around for a couple of years, but for me, it's all over."

"Wouldn't make it just one more?"

Bat paused. "Well, yup, reckon I would. 'Been at it all my life, hard to get it out of my craw, but you know there's some big changes coming to this country. White men are already settling on the prairie and the natives are about gone, herded to the Indian Nation. And the millions of buffaloes that once roamed a thousand hills will all but be forgotten."

"Yeah, sad, but it's coming." The old man mused, sort of getting next to him, "Just wondering what's ahead for an old ex-hide hunter."

4 Bull's Eye

It was late in the evening, nearly sundown, Bat and Zeb were almost home. Bat sat gazing at the sky as the wagon bounced along. "Zeb," he said, "don't believe I've ever seen a sky like that...look at them high thin purple clouds, sorta got a glowing pink around 'em—border."

Zeb replied, pointing, "that bright orange curving up from them pinks shooti'n' a streak clear to them hills back'n northwest. Hey Bat, what's them twinkling lights straight ahead?" Bat said, "Northeast it's Hidetown, northwest it's the Fort. But straight ahead—can't figure 'em out."

"They're west of old Hidetown and east of that Fort ...Hidetown's done been movin' out since we been gone!"

"Yup, believe you're right."

"Things are moving fast, like ya say," Zeb declared.

They pulled into Hidetown, jerked the harness off the horses and fed them. Bat said, "I'm tired, hungry as a bear, but don't have much appetite for more buffalo."

"We've got that cottontail rabbit we shot on the way in but I ain't much of a cook 'ceptin' buffalo," Zeb said.

"It can be 'possum or squirrel, but for now let's skip the buffalo."

"Rabbit, some water gravy and sourdough biscuits, that is if'n the rats ain't cleaned me out...outta water, too."

"I'll go to the creek and get some," Bat volunteered. "Do some washing up, too, but it's going take awhile."

"Bat, 'might move up the creek a piece...was a dead

possum in our dippin' place. Don't like possum hairs in my teeth."

The stars were out and the soft moonglow on the desert tan grass was like day. Bat could hear the beavers splashing up the creek, and an owl over in the big cottonwoods was night cooing. Sweetwater's rippling clear water sparkled fluorescence in the sand like a million tiny diamonds. A deep pool, half-circled by lillies and cattails, was full of bass and bluegill...a spreading cottonwood reached halfway across the stream. Bat shucked his clothes' to do a wash before he dived in. He could throw his blood-caked britches in a corner and they'd stand alone. Here of late they got plenty wear and well messed up, but a little sand-rubbing and water would help; even the smell. So he built a fire to dry his clothes. He stomped and pounded them in sand and water, rinsed and held them to the firelight but no good— still messed up. This wash was a bigger job than he expected. Rubbing with soap weed, milk weed, and tree bark didn't help much; the "buffalo" was hard to shake loose. Then, with a stick he beat them, and held them to the light again. He finally gave it up, figured it was the best he could do. He hung them on a green tree limb next to the fire to dry.

Molly Brennan was on Bat's mind from the day they left to go on the hunt until they returned. He was "chomping at the bits" to see her so this clothes wash was important, and his Saturday night bath, too. Scaling a three foot bank at the water's edge he glanced across the pool, back to his fire, ready to dive in. But out a ways from the fire two glowing yellow spots suddenly caught his eyes; weird, reflecting a burnt-orange from the flashing flames. Imagination? But soon the spots started toward him. Slowly coming, s-l-o-w-l-y moving up—moving up ...trapped without a stitch on, not even his gunbelt!

"Huh, the guy that claims he's got Molly Brennan roped and tied; crawling on his belly—slipping up?" Yup, Bat soon had the dirty skunk figured out...a dead shot at close range! Bat had no choice of escape. He flexed his wiry leg muscles, dived in, hit the water and went deep.

5 *The Doctors*

Bat came in the dugout door. "Confounded thing!" Zep fumed, trying to get his little old bachelor stove hot.

"Zeb, I believe I've got a few tadpoles here," Bat said, splashing the dirt floor with his can of water.

"Tadpoles, tadpoles!" Zeb blurted. "Pew-ee, got mor'n tadpoles. Got a skunk for sure, but ain't gonna have no tadpoles long—splatterin' the floor like a cow pizz'n on a flat rock! Don't mind tadpoles and frogs but gettin' shot by a polecat —pew-ee, that's something else."

"Yup, he got me but I did wash off some buffalo."

"Can tell it, can sure tell it!" Zeb declared. "I believe the skunk juice smells better; didn't hurt."

"Why you old goat, how would you know?" Bat guffawed. "You've inhaled so much of that sweet buffalo aroma your smeller's shot."

"Humf-p-ue-umf," Zeb snorted, determined to kill that snout curling odor. He rolled a Bull Durham smoke, struck a match on his britches suspender's button, and fired up. "Them cussed rats done got my hard-tack biscuits—p-u, hurts my eyes—but I was aimin' to make up a new batch anyway. 'Been thinkin' 'bout doin' some of that bathin' myself. Thought 'bout it nigh on a month ago...try and get around to it before summer rolls 'round. Man oughta take a bath once a year 'needs it'er not."

Zeb's whipped-out grub tasted larruping good to Bat. He was hungry but not surprised at Zeb's cooking; just good old common horse sense.

"Guess ya can bed down there," Zeb suggested, pointing to a couple of quilts piled in a corner. "Been nobody in that bed since Os got his hair piece lifted...oh, maybe a few rats and skunk'er two."

"Hot as it is, I'm moving out under the stars. Need the cool fresh air," Bat replied.

"Fresh air, fresh air! Who needs it?" Zeb ha-ha'd. "Stink ain't n'ya clothes. If'n ya hit that water again in the morning skunk odor'll be gone. But come to think 'bout it, Os did say there's some bedbugs in them soogans big enough to carry a man off. Don't reckon they bother me, it's them confounded chewing chiggers that chomps on me all night; guess it's chiggers, don't see to good— eyes been waterin'."

"Ah, Zeb, them bedbugs can't stand the taste of you any longer. Now, of course, if they were starving...."

"Whatever, chiggers or bedbugs, they's hungry."

Bat could hardly settle down. Molly Brennan was on his mind day and night. The next morning he grabbed his clothes and headed for the creek. He'd get rid of that skunk odor. When the sun broke the horizon he was already wallowing in the water. He rubbed on sand, mud, cedar bark, more soap weed, then dived under. Now by his own smeller he had the skunk odor whipped. Zeb would let him know if he smelled like a rose.

Walking in the dugout door, Bat said, "Well, Zeb, I think in another day this foul odor will be gone."

"Oh, Bat, you ain't never stunk better in ya whole dadburn life!" Zeb said, laughing. "Course I could use some help doctorin' that old hoss that got straddle of the chain."

Zeb's friends were always around when he needed help, but here of late the hunters were fighting-it on the prairie; a dog eat dog thing on the dwindling herds. Every man for himself.

29

Bat gazed out across the wide Sweetwater Creek bottom. There were buildings and half-dugouts still in use but Hidetown was a sad looking place. Plenty was going on but the buzzing hide business had slowed down at the settlement. There were still horses and mules in some of the old rail-corrals but horse lots were not crowded as in the past. Teamsters were moving big hay-like wagons in and out around huge stacks of hides from sun up until sundown. Each wagon was loaded with three hundred and twenty five half-dry hides and pulled by three spans of big mules. The proud teamsters yelled, cracked their whips, and headed for Dodge City. Hidetown was moving out.

Bat said, "Yup, old Hidetown is a gon'er—moving to Mobeetie. You think that rope you got there will hold the horse?"

"Yeah, hate to see her go, a ghost town, moving out fast, a bunch of 'em. A guy come by while you was at the creek hammerin' out the skunk juice...said while we wuz gone on the hunt they moved out in droves—even the Blacksmith's moved to Mobeetie."

"Don't say?" Bat asked.

"Do. Yeah, this rope will hold 'im, and guess we better get the old sucker doctored up. Good hoss but gets in trouble."

Down in the corral they lassoed the horse and soon had him hackamored. Zeb held the hackamore rein, and Bat took the long lariat and made a rope-like collar around the horse's neck.

"Now Bat, I'll hold him if'n you can get the other end of that lariat 'round his back foot at the fetlock so he can't kick. Pull it hard...back through the collar and get that foot off the ground—watch 'im, like I say, he's a kicker."

Bat was no greenhorn on livestock. All pioneers knew

how to work on their animals. Pouring castor oil down sick cows and castrating horses was not unusual work. To castrate horses, they threw them to the ground, rolled them on their back, and pulled their hind feet hard against their belly. But on the bay, Zeb only wanted to lift one foot so he couldn't kick.

Bat pulled on the rope, the horse bolted and jerked the hackamore rein out of Zeb's hand. Zeb just happened to be   standing with one foot in the coiled-end of the lariat lying on the ground. The horse broke away, the lariat jerked tight around Zeb's foot and his other foot shot straight up. Around and around the corral the bronc horse ran dragging Zeb by one foot; he yelled, "Whoa, ya old sumbitch, whoa!" Bat was broke up with laughter, but finally got the horse simmered down.

Still laughing, Bat said, "Z-Z-Zeb you plowed a pretty deep furrow through that horse manure—gonna plant a garden?"

"You guessed it, and use that old bastard for fertilizer."

With the horse's hoof pulled up so he couldn't kick, Bat asked, "Can't do much on three legs; got your snuff?"

"Couldn't get along out'n this country without that prairie snuff. Picked up 'couple balls nigh big's ya head."

"Huh, Zeb, that's pretty big snuff-balls. I reckon you've seen 'em bigger?"

"Well, 'purt' near nearly but not quite plumb."

Zeb's snuff ball description was quite clear to Bat. Maybe the old man did stretch it a little but the ten inch fungus balls was not unusual. Pioneers swore by it for doctoring livestock. The tobacco-like powder kept the flies out of cuts and stopped bleeding, too.

"Now, if you'll hold the rope Bat, then I'll see 'bout his old sore dong."

Always ready to give a hand, Bat soon asked, "What

do you think Doc?"

"He skint it up purty good. Ain't no good to him nohow since he's been 'cut'—jist a water spout. Got to get some snuff on there'er screw worms'll eat plumb to his belly. Yeah, them screw worms are hell on animals with cuts or knocked-off horns."

Bat replied, "Yup, a cut place or knocked off horn, green flies lay their eggs in the injury and screw worms hatch out. 'Seen 'em drill clear to the brain where a horn's been knocked off—makes 'em go crazy—got'er finished, good job, Doc."

Night was coming on. Back at the dugout, Bat could see Zeb was down in the mouth; not saying much. Maybe the old man got a few bruises doctoring the horse; could be it.

He finally come out with it. "B-a-d luck is dogging me."

"Yeah, how's that?" Bat asked.

"Looks I'm gonna hafta do some of that bathin' a month'er two before I aimed too."

Bat was surprised. "See no reason for that."

"Seems like I smell something since that old hoss drug me 'round the corral in that hoss manure."

Bat was still tickled over the incident. He laughed. "Seems like my smeller's picking it up, too...hey, where you going?"

Zeb raised his voice, "That hole of water!" He headed for the creek in the bright moonlight.

Approaching the water he started undoing his suspenders and pulling his britches down. He thought of his boots. Looking for a place to park, he sat down on a log by the pool, his naked butt hanging over. Struggling with his old boots, he paid no attention to anything else. Soon a couple of curious possums came by poking their noses around, sniffing, looking for something to chew on.

While Zeb's wet boots were giving him a heap'o trouble he got a glimpse of one of those possums at the other end of the log. Just a possum, he thought nothing about it. But about that time Bat thought he heard a scream. Was Zeb in trouble —just a howling wolf? Bat listened.

Zeb soon came dragging in the dug-out door wet as a drowned rat, and dripping water all over the floor.

Bat stared at him, grinning, "Wh-wh-what in the world happened to you?"

"Well, 'ever hear of getting attacked by a posse of possums? I was fixin' to get in the water, unbuttoned my 'spenders, jerked my britches down, then gonna take off my boots...set down on that log by the pool—got one boot off and one leg out—saw a possum at the end of the log, thought nothin' 'bout it. But another one of them confounded cusse's sneaked up behind me and stuck his old cold nose in the crack of my B V D drawers. 'Thought I was got, shot straight up off that log...purt near nearly lost my religion, said some b-a-d words goin' up—come down, hit the water, got re-baptized, and all my sins washed away."

Bat broke into a belly laugh; thought he would die. "ZZ-Zeb, how lucky can you be? A neighborly possum helped you do a year's bathing, put out a year's wash, got re-baptized, and all your sins washed away in less than a minute! Don't know about this, if I don't move out pretty soon they'll have to carry me out...dead from laughing."

Around sunup the next morning, before Zeb rolled out, Bat was at the swimming hole. If he could get the skunk odor whipped out he was heading for town. He came back from his dip in the creek and found Zeb already monkeying with his wagon and patching on his harness. Bat thought Zeb would never get through tinkering with his old worn out equipment. Get one thing fixed and something else would fall apart. But the old man worked miracles with what he had.

"I'm riding to that new town of Sweetwater," Bat said.

Zeb reminded, "Now that ain't what the Indians call it. Them Comanches knew what they was talkin' about when they called it Mobeetie, but them Cheyennes— don't know about them."

"Comanche or Cheyenne—sweet water or buffalo manure—take your choice, I'll know more about it when I get there. Zeb, I'll give you a hand on greasing them wheels before I go. You'll need some help?"

"Now Bat, dont'cha worry 'bout them wheels, I've done them things more times than ya can count."

"My horse is sort of lame. I want the blacksmith to take a look at him."

"Yeah, Blacksmith Bob they call him. Bob Brennan can do anything—blacksmith, cobbler. Look at that." Zeb raised his foot. "Bradded that old boot up and made it like new. 'Course, that hairy rawhide patch needs a hair-cut. Them Brennans, they's fine people; everybody likes 'em."

The Brennan on Bat's mind was special. He rolled a Bull Durham smoke, hit his britches with a match and lit up, pulled a draw, swung up in the saddle, and spurred out. He yelled back, "Adios, see you later!"

"Don't stay too long at the blacksmith's!" Zeb knew what Bat had in mind.

6 *Mobeetie*

Coming into town, Bat rode by an iron stake marker with the townsite's legal description--Section 45, Block A5, Houston and Great Northern RR Survey. Farther down were houses going up and holes scooped out for half-dugout homes. Men Bat had seen on the prairie skinning buffaloes, now they were here in town swinging hammers and sawing boards. The big money was in the hide business but the hunters knew the slaughter would soon be over. Land prospectors coming in had to have houses, too.

Loads of hides were pouring in off the prairie and money floating around. But when the old buffaloes were killed off nothing would be coming on. The little calves wouldn't last long with hungry wolves around. The buffaloes wiped out, the Indians were fearful of losing everything—their liveihood. The white man had the Indian where he wanted him. The Whites knew the natives had to have hides for wig-wams, and meat for food, but who cared? The buffalo hunters did what the U. S. Government had tried to do for years.

Bat rode by stacks of hides and farther down main street was a half-finished hide warehouse. A smear painted, blood-red sign hung over the front door—"Sweetwater Texas." Bat knew the sign would soon come down. There was another Sweetwater Texas down south. Hidetown first, then Sweetwater, and now Bat figured Mobeetie would stick. Saloons were opening up all over town. The O'Loughlin's, the Lady Gay, Ma

Manlin, the Mint, and Weed's Whiskey had all moved up from Hidetown. Other saloons had opened up, too. The Pink Pussycat's Paradise, Trader's Saloon, Bullhorn Tavern, White Elephant, Shores-Of-Hell, and Giltedge. Later came the Dirty Gerty, Ring Town, Happy Harry's, Cattleman's Exchange, Pendleton & Co, Buffalo Chip and the Cabinet. Then, not exactly a saloon was "Harriet's House—The Coziest Girls In Town." However, that was questionable with buffalo hunters, and cowboys, but who cared...where money growed, whiskey flowed, and wild women glowed.

What Bat had in mind was important, but like other guys who stayed on the prairie for months, they were gun-shy of girls. Molly Brennan was something special to Bat Masterson and he never wanted to say the wrong thing. And as he usually said, "What I need now is a little shot of juice to fortify my fortitude."

"Have one on the house," the friendly bartender offered. "Our first customer since we moved up from Hidetown. We're about to get squared up around here."

"Reckon as to how I'm sure much obliged," Bat replied. The bartender questioned, "Been 'round these parts long ...guess you can tell I've been gone?"

"Yup, few times. Henry Fleming or Bill Thompson around?" He eyeballed Bat hard and offered nothing. Thompson was in the saloon business, but running scared after he killed the Kansas Sheriff. "Know 'em?" the bartender asked.

"Know 'em well," Bat said. "Me and my brothers hunted with them in Kansas. 'Saw Henry awhile back in old Hidetown, but haven't been around these parts too much here of late. Name's Masterson—Bat Masterson."

"Oh, one of the Masterson boys out of Kansas!" exclaimed the bartender. "They've talked about you boys a lot around here; mighty glad to know you. I'm Bill

Sty, 'help out—they call me manager. Henry, Henry Fleming took Red...Red Day, the bartender, and went to Dodge for supplies. And might say Thompson went for supplies, too." He chuckled. "Went to Kansas City for some of them fillies—not the four legged kind—them young pretty things; blondes, brunettes, and red heads. Big opportunities 'round these parts...money, women, soldiers pouring in and hunters thick as fleas on a dog. Land promoters, gamblers, and cowboys coming in...the girls can get rich, nothing but a gold mine. I look for Henry back in a week and Thompson a couple; they own the place, you know."

"I'm camped down here at Hidetown," Bat said. "Rode in to see the blacksmith. My horse is lame."

"Yeah, Blacksmith Bob, a good smithy—boot maker, too. Fixes anything, and a good man...just moved up from Hidetown, too. He's out of Kansas, come down not too long ago...around the corner and down a piece."

"Happen to know anybody doing some hide loaning— stake a guy?" Bat asked

"Sure do, fellow down the street that owns the Mint, and J. J. Long General Merchandise Store, too...'call him Uncle Johnny. Not an old man, young, but has helped lots of people. A top notch guy that won't turn you down if he likes your looks. He's got the general store and you know how that goes...hardware, dry goods, groceries, whiskey, even girls, and heard it said maybe a bank one of these days. His oxen and mule teams freighted in tons of stuff for the Army; brought in the first batch. Yeah, right neighborly—town's biggest booster."

Bat replied, "Sure much obliged." He had his refreshments and headed for the door to find Johnny Long. But he couldn't figure out Bill Sty—acted strange—kept watching the door, shifting his eyes. "Going to the blacksmith, eh? I'll tell you, if you see a strawberry roan...well,

Bob's down yonder a ways," he whispered, and pointed.

On the way to the blacksmith Bat dropped by Uncle Johnny's store. The clerk behind the counter quick-glanced him.

"Howdy," Bat said, "looking for Uncle Johnny Long."

"Good morning." Sam Morris quit his chore and turned to Bat. Sam had never seen this man before, but kept his eyes on the guns he wore—fearless looking stranger—did he come to settle a score? It seemed the slender Englishman with iron-gray hair was not long out of the old country; reserved. "Mr. Long and a teamster transported a load of supplies to the Fort for the brig enclosure. It is for the misbehaving soldiers."

The talk of the Englishman was funny to Bat. Nothing like his old buffalo-hunter sidekick that slew the King's English. "I'll be back, but I do need a cinch strap for my saddle girth."

Sam asked, "Would that be an inch and three fourths?"

"Two inch width will do. I'll have the blacksmith brad it on. How much I owe you?"

"Mr. Brennan is quite crafty. He can place brads in it for you." Then Sam come down in a low whisper, "I would not stay too long...it will be four-bits."

Bat couldn't figure it out, what was going on in Mobeetie, a terror gripping the town? Was Sam Morris trying to tell Bat Masterson something, too—keep away from Bob Brennan's blacksmith shop; stay out of danger? The town was stirred up; people afraid to talk—trouble! Was the raging bull in town, the rider on the strawberry roan? "Just what to hell was going on?" Bat mused.

7 *Johnny Long*

Bat reined up at the Blacksmith shop. Down in the corral a couple of sorrel horses and a little brown mare were munching hay. A red-wheeled wagon was parked by the fence. Bat was thinking, "Yup, that's it, the same red-wheeled wagon I met-up with about a year ago, east of Dodge. Had a teen-age girl setting between her dad and mother on the springboard seat. The girl waved when I rode ahead." Looking the wagon over, Bat cracked a grin, "'Woman thought I was an outlaw, wouldn't look up." Dodge City was in sight, but that was a long ways for a wrung-out team. The overloaded wagon, pulled by two sorrel horses', had everything hanging on it from horse collars to chicken coops. A little brown horse and buggy trailed the wagon, and a rope-tied milk cow followed the buggy. The cute grinning girl that chided Bat in old Hidetown was that girl in the wagon—Molly Brennan!

Bob Brennan pulled a red hot iron from the forge about the time Bat rode up. Bob glanced up, "Don't mind, 'get this shaped up on that rocking-bolster while she's still hot." He made a fast walk to a wagon chassis a few steps away.

"No, no, don't mind at all," Bat said, coming off his horse. He knew what had happened to the wagon; he'd been there. Out on the prairie hunters often pushed their luck too far. Crossing deep buffalo trails and gullies with an overloaded wagon could mean trouble...wheels fall nart, rocking bolster split, or a coupling-pole snap—

39

anything, but every hide meant two or three dollars to the hunters.

The smithy beat and shaped the hot iron with such skill the old wagon soon looked good as new. He finished the job, wiped his hands on his britches, and came over to Bat. "Brennan, Bob Brennan." He extened a hand like a ham with a milk maiden's grip. He paused, "Haven't I met you somewhere before?"

Curly locks of black hair dangled across Bob's forehead. Little rivulets of sweat trickled down his cheeks; some off the end of his nose. He was short and stocky, very muscular, rather round face and was well tanned; a man with handsome features. His eyes were blue and clear; his smile friendly.

Bat offered his hand. "I'm Bat Masterson."

They sized each other up in a close handshake. Bat had him by a few inches in height. Bob sort of cocked his head, looked up, and asked, "Wasn't you riding that same black hoss headed for Dodge City sometime back—east of town—met up with you...ah, 'bout a year ago and you rode ahead?"

"Yup, that was me. And I see the stocking-legged blazed faced sorrels and the green red-wheeled wagon."

"Everybody from here to Dodge, to Mississippi, to Louisiana knows that green red-wheeled wagon."

The pioneers never forgot a wagon and team...Bat Masterson never forgot a pretty face. Beautiful girls and gambling were his weaknesses.

"I'd know that wagon anywhere," Bat declared.

"I'm trying to get set up here but it seems slow; just moved up from Hidetown. Yeah, that's the same hosses and the same wagon," Bob explained. "Just ride in?"

"Few days back, come off a hunt...camped down here at Hidetown."

"Old Hidetown she's 'bout a-goner," Bob replied. "It

40

won't be long until this country's going in for some big cattle ranching. The hunters are knocking off buffaloes by the thousands. It's unbelievable, hide men from east to west, and north to south are wiping out the herds."

"Oh, no doubt about it," Bat declared. "This place is booming in the hide business now, but when it's over it'll be cattle. I'm ready to head out on my last hunt but my horse has a slight limp. Like for you take a look at his hoof. May be just a bruised frog; left front."

Bat wasn't too concerned about the horse's hoof.

"Goodlooking hoss, stallion ain't he?" Bob asked, lifting Coalie's left front foot.

"Stallion and half thoroughbred—fast as the wind."

Bob dug and probed around on the hoof. "Just a bruised frog," Bob said.

"Well, I believe Doc Brennan's done a good job there."

"Could say I'd like to have a colt out of that stud," Bob said. "Know anything about his raisin's?"

"The guy I got him from was a horse trader, an old Western jockey in Kansas. The jockey said the horse came out of Kentucky. You never know, might have been stolen. The jockey went on to say there's lots of horses that come to Kansas and Missouri that's got that good racing blood but questionable ownership."

"I've heard that, too," Bob said. "It seems they lay a lot of it on the James Brothers."

"May be guilty," Bat come back, "but from Kansas to Texas it's talked nobody's covered more ground in the southwest, and stole more horses than Dutch Henry and Chummy Jones."

"Yeah, I've heard that too, heard it said they'll steal a hoss, or maybe a team, but they'd rather go for the whole herd. Good at the business. Let me trim all the frogs and rasp off the hooves, too; he's going to be O. K."

Another wagon pulled up at the blacksmith shop. Bob

looked around. He finished the job and let go of Coalie's hoof. The teamster stayed with the wagon but another man stepped down to the wheel-hub and onto the ground.

"You made it to the Fort?" Bob questioned the man.

"Yeah, did," the fellow replied, walking up.

"Uncle Johnny, this is Bat Masterson," Bob said.

Mr. Long gave Bat a firm handshake. "Well, the Masterson that left Kansas and come to Texas...'made a good showing at 'Dobe Walls. Texans in this part of the State will always remember Bat Masterson. Just ride in?"

"Yup did," Bat replied, "but been doing a little hunting here of late." Johnny Long, to Bat, seemed like an adventurous man with experience. He had an easy friendly smile, stood right at six feet, his skin was tanned, his hair and eyes were brown—eyes sharp. A crooked-stem pipe hung under his mustache. Bat got the idea Johnny Long loved the prairie land and would risk a lot to develop it. His dark eyes sized up Bat.

"Maybe a couple years of good hunting at best, but a no man's land now," Mr. Long said. "It's a dog-eat-dog thing, hunters running over each other. The Indians are getting in their licks too. They want to keep us out and the outlaws are trying to take over. The government will control the Indians, the Rangers will wrangle in the outlaws, and the prostitutes will take care of the lonely men. Fort Elliot out here has its problems, too. No brig yet, they keep the wild ones chained up. You know Bob, like that worthless soldier that comes around here shooting off his mouth...claims he laid a brand on that girl of yours—has that mangy orange-looking hair, beady eyes, and rides a strawberry roan. They say he's locoed."

Strawberry roan—Johnny Long, talking about the

guy on the strawberry roan? Bat listened—same guy that tried to bluff him the first day he rode into town? Bat had heard of a guy in Dodge City that said he was coming to Texas to show people how tough he was; made no difference to Bat Masterson.

"Yeah, I know him too well," Bob said. "Keeps Molly stirred up. He hangs around here and cocks that old army hat back—always bragging, badgering guys; nothing but a bully."

Uncle Johnny hitched onto what Bob said. "I know he come out of Fort Sill—killed God only knows how many men—knocked off black soldiers'—says: 'Cause I ain't gonna be under no black officer.' The funny thing, it's rumored at the Post Lt. Henry Flipper, a black man, will be stationed here. The military has got some good men and they got some doozies, too." Uncle Johnny turned, "Bat, this guy we're talking about is Dogface Melvin King—heard he got kicked out of the Army for killing another soldier. He's killed over gambling, horses, and women to name a few fracas he's been in. He keeps boasting around nobody moves in on him...on the women he calls his heifers. He pulls them crazy stunts there in Kansas, too. He dresses up in cowboy rigging, and goes out to meet the trail herds coming to Dodge City, and rides in like a real Texas cowpoke. Soon as he gets in town he starts shooting off his mouth and scares the life out of new settlers. The military would get him but I think he's got the Army brass buffaloed. Anyway, they claim they don't have any eye-witnesses to this stuff he pulls. Watch him, he's ambidextrous—dangerous as hell. He carries a Bowie knife in his belt."

"You mean they can't do nothing about even killing another soldier?" Bob asked, surprised. "Can't believe it."

Uncle Johnny shook his head. "No witnesses. Guess

the Army does their best on his kind—crazy and wild as a peach orchard boar...shoot a man in the back and laugh about it. Bob, I'm leaving this iron bar that needs more bending. They want it out here at the Fort soon as we can get it back to 'em. Can you handle it?"

"No problem, John. Got these boot heels to do for this fellow then get right on it; ready for you by sundown."

"Good, have it to 'em in the morning." Uncle Johnny turned to Bat. "Be in these parts long?"

"Spect to after I make this last hunt."

"Glad to hear it, this is the promised land. We need some good men, but no more gunslicks. See you later, Bob!" Uncle Johnny got on the wagon with his teamster and they drove off.

Bat eagerly watched for Molly. The loan he wanted to see Mr. Long about, and the horse's hoof, had slipped his mind. The shop forge was out of sight until Long's wagon pulled out. But the shop layout seemed to be the same as Hidetown...the forge, anvil, everything, except here—there was Molly at the forge!

Molly let go of the forge handle, the smoke cleared, and the coals glowed red hot. Bob said, "Molly, this is Bat Masterson. Bat if you don't mind waiting, I've got a little more to do on this old broken down wagon out here. Fellow's coming for it pretty soon."

Molly knocked Bat out of the saddle at Hidetown, and standing at the forge now, a smear of coal dust on her face didn't matter. Her good looks still come through...about five feet five, with shoulder length dark hair, beautiful sparkling blue eyes, cute dimples, and shapely generous breast. The young buffalo hunters on the prairie dreamed about pretty girls but that was about it. They knew more about the romantic ways of the buffalo than of women. But it was a good sign the

44

boys were hungry for romance when a forked tree limb looked good. Bat's head was set and his mind made up. He'd soon be giving up this hunting business. Molly Brennan set the woods on fire!

Bat loved the summer dress that Molly wore. The sun came through like an open door. She had good looks and then some more, but what he could see was no forked tree. She was just trying to beat the heat.

Bat blurted, "No, no, Bob, don't mind at all!"

Bob was already working on the wagon when Bat come-too. Molly sidled over near Bat and rolled her eyes, "Hi, Mister, I remember you at Dodge and Hidetown, too."

Bat Masterson wasn't long off the prairie, still trying to get it together on women, but once the handsome guy settled in he'd break the hearts of beautiful ladies. To Bat, Molly Brennan was a dream girl. "Howdy, Ma'am, uh, oh yeah, I did ride by the shop down at Hidetown. I want to get my horse fixed...'mean my cinch-strap fixed, and my horse is lame. Coalie's his name. Got a slight limp, too."

Her mother called from the dugout but Molly hesitated. Walking very close to Bat, looking up, and rolling her eyes, she said, "You'll be coming back for your cinch-strap?"

"Why-wh, yes'um, you bet!"

She turned and walked toward the dugout. Bat watched, kept his eyes on her all the way to the dugout door. It had slipped his mind he brought Coalie to Bob for a look at his hoof.

"I've got the lame hoss ready, Bat." Bob raised his voice, "Say Bat, I've got the lame hoss ready!"

"Oh yeah, yeah, just watching them geese fly over."

Bob knew there wasn't a goose in a hundred miles. Bat soon come down out of the clouds. "Got this leather strap too—needs bradding—how much I owe you?"

"Oh, I'll just put it on the cuff, but was going tell you, might bring him in later, left hoof's got a little crack, keep it trimmed, no trouble—frogs no problem, nothing unusual... but that old red roan that guy rides in here, he's got a funny looking frog—odd, right front. Never know it unless you see a track from just that foot—like in wet sand—frog on that hoof sort of makes a 'V'."

"Yup, that is unusual," Bat remarked, "back foot usually wipes out the front track; seldom see it."

"Yeah, bring ya hoss back when you come off your hunt and we'll take another look at 'im. You'll wanta pick up your cinch-strap, too."

"Much obliged for now." Bat swung up in the saddle; glanced up. Three horsebackers suddenly showed up on the rise just north of town. They sat in the saddle watching. One was riding a bay, one a brown, and one was riding a strawberry roan!

8 Snapping Turtle

"Hey, wait a minute!" Bob yelled.

Bat reined around, he was in no hurry. "Yeah, forgot to tell you how many holes I want in that cinch-strap—four."

"Sorta figured four," Bob said, "but I want to tell you, too, them horsebackers that ducked behind the hill out there—they're laying for you. This guy Dogface King likes to keep the settlement stirred up...got few friends, even some of our women folks are afraid of him. You'll never come up against one like him. He's as good with his left hand as his right. A coldblooded killer that'll trick you...go for his knife with his right hand, and when you pull-down you'll find out he's coming with his pistol in his left. He swears then you pulled-down first. I've heard it talked he gets by the law with it, too—where there is law."

"Much oblige, Bob," Bat replied, appreciated the warning, but wasn't too concerned. New settlers were warned not to be seen talking to "that Brennan girl."

Bat spurred out. Dogface and his sidekicks soon disappeared in the sand hills north of town. Bat knew they'd show up later...only a game, a game Bat Masterson loved to play—no fear of Dogface whatsoever. He headed for Hidetown.

Zeb, as usual, was tinkering with his old wagon when Bat rode up. He asked, "Well, Oldtimer, have you about got her whipped out? Looks like you're having a little trouble there."

The sun was sinking low. Zeb was working hard to

have his wagon ready for the next day's hunt—mon-keying with the chasis. The back wheels were blocked up with chunks of wood, and the front-bed was propped up with poles. Lying under the chasis, pushing and grunting, he bumped his head; almost cursed, "Confound that dang wheel! My big trouble is, the rocking bolster won't line up with the coupling-pole to take the king-pin."

Bat come off his horse. "Zeb you gotta have some help. Let me give you a hand." That was all the old man needed. Bat then asked, "Now what about the wheels?"

"Them back'uns are loose as a castor-oiled goose," Zeb grumbled. "Spokes 'bout to fall out. Spect we better soak 'em in the creek till they're tight as a fiddle string."

"No sweat, I'll roll 'em to the creek while you get finished up here."

"Hey, bring back a can'o water, too. Forgot, that can's got a hole in it. Jist get that old slop-jar there be alright."

That slop-jar business didn't set too well with Bat. But Zeb hadn't used it in his bedroom since 'way last winter. The old buffalo hunters didn't know what sani-tation was. Early day Westerners were far more apt to die from lead poison or the red man's arrow.

At dusk, Bat came in with the water. Zeb was still fooling with his wagon. He fumed, "Cussed thing, 'bout got'er."

The evening twilight was fast fading away...even darker in Zeb's half-dugout, but still Bat noticed some-thing swimming around in the pot-water. He started to throw out the tiny snapping turtle, but had a better idea. Bat Masterson could never pass up something like this. He loved a joke, a little fun. He lifted Zeb's burlap sheet, tossed the slimy thing in the bed, and went back out-side. "Zeb looks like you're coming along pretty good; about got'er?"

48

"Done been done if it wasn't for them confounded chomping chiggers. Can't get nothing done for scratching my chigger chewed butt. Wouldn't be surprised if they ain't swarming in my bed next with them humblin' hungry bedbugs."

Aside from all of his trouble Zeb finished up and had his wagon ready to roll. They ambled off to the dugout. Zeb's candle light in the half-dugout wasn't much but enough to whip out their supper on the small bachelor stove."

After supper, Bat said, "Moving out by the wagon. Nothing like sleeping under the stars these nights." He went out the door toting his bedroll.

Zeb soon shucked down to his B V D drawers, blew out the candlelight, lifted the sheet, and crawled in bed. Things were quiet. But the old man soon screamed, "Ow-oo-wee! Come here quick, Bat, I'm got!"

Every dog in the neighborhood heard the yell and set up a howl. Bat burst through the door boiled over with laughter, "Wh-wh-why, what's matter—rattlesnake?"

"It's them consarned bedbugs of Os's done and crawled over in my bed—crawled clear up in my-my clean drawers-er-er, they wuz clean, and chomped down on my-my...oh well, it's like old Bay's nohow—nothing but a water spout. Os told me there wuz some big'uns in there but 'didn't know they'uz that big. Guess I'll hafta be doing some more of that bathin' now. Makes two times in the water here of late. Gonna be scalin' off. Ripped my sheet, ripped my drawers. Well, I reckon 'could say, ripped my britches—messed up worse'n Hogan's goat!"

Bent over with laughter, Bat had convulsions. "Now, Z-Z-Zeb let me light the candle and see what the damage is."

"What the damage is? Shucks, I know what the damage is!" Zeb replied, grabbed his clothes and headed for the creek. Bat threw out the turtle.

Zeb worked hard to keep his wagon ready to go, but the buffalo hunters would soon disappear from the wide open country, vamoose into another world. But, as for Bat, he had a beautiful reason for hanging around Mobeetie.

When the sun broke the horizon the next morning, Bat and Zeb was at the creek looking the wheels over. Zeb said, "Be ready in the mornin'. Water have 'em tight as a drum."

"Won't shake apart," Bat added.

"Look who walked up!" Zeb exclaimed.

"Mawnin'," Zeb's neighbors, replied.

"Bat, 'want'cha to know these old Tenessee ridge-runner friends'o mine...Rip Nesbit and Baldy Beechnut. Tell ya guys 'bout Bat. He's outta Kansas and he's gonna light here in this town of Mobeetie. He's mighty handy with them Sharps, and so fast on the draw with that hawgleg, he can hit the first bullet before it hits the ground, with the second."

"Mighty fast," Rip drawled.

"Fast draw and glad to know ya," Baldy joined in.

Rip and Baldy glanced at Zeb—to Bat. Was Zeb hitting the fermented spirits again?

"Name's Masterson—Bat Masterson, glad to meet'cha."

Zeb continued, "Bat, these hillbillies ain't been huntin' but 'bout two years, but nary a hide man in this settlement can bust 'em out like these squirrel shooters. And if'n all them Redskin arrows was still stuck in their butts they'd look like porcupines."

"Ah come on, Zeb," Rip replied, "you ain't dropped another buffalo chip in your mulberry juice?"

"Bat you can bet they took on them Redskins...'course

50

now and then a little nip of that mulberry juice does sorta scare away them bedbugs. Me and Bat's gonna head out in the mornin'. If Bat don't mind, like for you guys go with us."

"Why not?" Bat replied. "I think we can trust these men with a gun. But as you guys know, some of these dudes on the prairie are just looking for adventure and I don't want to be around them. I've seen 'em hatch up more ways than one to get out of skinning. And they think every loping antelope is a Redskin...careless with a gun and dangerous as hell; sometimes worse than Redskins."

They knew Bat was right. "Goin' down south," Zeb continued, "figure they've drifted up from the Red to the Salt Fork."

"Naw," Rip replied. "Some guys come by last night and said the biggest herd in these parts had pushed back'n northwest ...up'n past the head waters of Sweetwater, clean to Red Deer Creek, and moving toward the Canadian."

Rip let go with a squirt of tobacco juice; dead aimed a grasshopper. He strained the juice through his longhorn mustache and gave the slug more chawin. His whacked of light hair hung down under his old black hat. Rip's barber, not a bad for another buffalo hunter.

"Yeah," Zeb come back, "them pore old critters don't know which way to run. Go first one way then the other, blasted every which way they go. Nope, no more of them big million-herds —history, thing of the past. 'Guess the hunters in south are moving 'em north, headed for the Canadian."

Soon Baldy joined in. "We heard about them five or six surveyors back'n north, on Wolf Creek, that got their heads peeled a few days back." Then he pulled his beat-up hat off and rubbed his onion slick head. He chuckled, saying, "And I don't need a haircut."

Baldy Beechnut might've got fat on buffalo meat and possum, but staying ahead in the hide business was hard work. The knees on his faded "duckins" were worn out, but like other hunters, it wasn't all from skinning buffaloes. Bat knew hunters that never denied part of that knee wear was kneeling time, asking for deliverance from the Indians. Their britches were always covered with blood and stuff, but the knees were the first to go. Bat had been hit in the face more than once by manure laden tails, slung around by a dying animal, with a generous amount splotched behind his ears. To get hit in the eyes, the stuff burned like fire. Buffalo hunting was a dirty stinking business. Few liked it, but the sweet smell of money made it worthwhile. Sure it was a dirty job but the guys did have pride. Baldy jerked his dirty faded shirt off and threw it in the creek for a quick wash. It wasn't much of a cleaning but did limber it up. Wet, he put it back on and pulled his hat down on his ears.

All hunters' were eager to get in on the kill—the last animal—the last shot. Bat's bunch was going to head northwest, but there could be a half-dozen wagons going, too, in search of the vanishing herds. The hunters' paradise was fast fading away; forever.

Bat figured there would be no problem crossing Sweetwater Creek, even though there was a downpour on the headwaters the evening before.

Rip said, "Bat guess you heard about the Mexican trying to cross Sweetwater during the head-rise yesterday just south where they're puttin' the Fort?"

"No, what happened?"

"Well, the Senor whipped his team into the raging water and right away the whole cheese went out of sight. Our neighbor friend found the guy hanging in a tree. Darn near drown, too, he told the neighbor."

"Of course the mules drown but what about the wagon—find it?" Bat asked.

Baldy spoke up, "Didn't find nothing, mules, wagon—nothing, even after poking down in a deep hole of water and quicksand with fifteen foot poles."

"Huh, the guy was lucky to get out alive, I reckon, but guess we'll know more about it tomorrow. Don't take long for the water to run down," Bat said, as he walked off to the dug-out.

9 *The Last Hunt*

Zeb struck out in the dark to get the teams ready while Bat stumbled around in the half-dugout hustling hunting supplies. He had been in this hunting business a long time, but this was it, his last hunt. He had mixed feelings about his last buffalo hunt but just the thought of Molly Brennan he had no reservation. The herds were dwindling down to nothing, and he could see the buffalo bordering on extinction.

Down at the corral, Bat and Zeb were fumbling around in the dark, trying to get the right set of harness on the right horse. Bat could have a problem finding his coal black saddle-horse, too, but he had figured that out a long time ago. He gave a bobwhite whistle and Coalie came back with a little low friendly nicker. Baldy and Rip faired no better in the dark, but soon streaks of light fanned out across the sky.

Baldy nudged Bat, "I want you and Zeb to know my nephew, Steve—Sister's boy—coming seventeen in the spring."

"Howdy, I'm Bat Masterson." The boy was only a shadow in the early morning darkness.

"Zeb Hunter, right glad to know ya—thought somebody was helpin' ya, Baldy."

"How do you do Mr. Masterson and Mr. ah-ah," the young voice stumbled.

"Hunter! Zeb Hunter's the name." He thought the boy talked as funny as the Englishman at Uncle Johnny's store. He figured the kid was well educated and book smart, but his kind of education didn't cover the rugged life of a western pioneer. Listening to Steve's talk, Zeb didn't think the boy had ever been out of the city. But Zeb would be first to admit the kid was no worse off than a buffalo hunter would be in a big city back east.

Daylight was coming on fast. Soon Steve said, "I wanted to fire at some of those wretched beast in this Godforsaken wilderness before it is all over with. We understand by the Eastern press that the great elimination of the worthless animal is in the last stage of completion."

Old Zeb nearly cracked up, he thought the kid was bordering on stupidity.

Baldy Beechnut broke in, "What he's trying to say, Zeb, is, he ain't never shot a gun and wants to go with us if ya'll don't mind?"

"Don't mind at all," Bat replied.

"Naw," Zeb added, "might need some help. Them red devils gettin' mighty mean since gettin' booted to the government promised land. I reckon we're ready to go—Bat I'll go to the dug-out and blow out the candle."

They strung out. Bat led the way on Coalie along with the skinners on horseback. Steve was with Baldy in his wagon, and the other wagon brought up the rear. Supplies for a three weeks hunt included the usual stuff, bullets, grub, keg of drinking water, knives, salt, and a sharpening stone. Flooded Sweetwater Creek that swallowed up the Mexican's worldly belongings had run down. They crossed the shallow water south of the Post ice storage pit and headed northwest.

Soon in Indian country, they watched for Redskins and anxiously looked for buffaloes. The tromped down grass across the hills was a sure sign a herd was moving west. The hunters trailed the herd tracks with a steady pace.

They soon run onto a shot-up buffalo cow with a baby calf. Suddenly the teams shied...a thrashing, shuffling in the shin-oak, and a crazed bull burst out of the brush. Stumbling, falling with blood shot eyes, blood running out his nose, and a bullet shattered horn dangled, but he tried to stay on his feet. Bat had seen this sort of thing before, the buffalo's head was eaten out by screw worms. There was no doubt the poor old critter had been chased all over hell and half the West—maybe shot a week before—even longer. The hunters threw a night camp on Red Deer Creek.

Bat usually rode point and led the way, sometimes a mile ahead of the slow moving wagons...always first to know if Indians or buffaloes were ahead. Indians or buffaloes, his thoughts were on Molly and he had always said, "It's dangerous as hell to day dream in hostile Indian country." And back in the Settlement there was that flaky King who kept everybody stirred up. Bat had never seen it but he'd been told how King loved to run over the boys around town. Anyone friendly with his women, he boasted, he'd "Mash 'em in the ground." And it wasn't a joke. People laughed when they saw the Sergeant and his sidekicks rub a Private's nose in fresh horse manure after the kid cut his eyes at King's girl friend. Bat was "chomping at the bits" to get back to Molly and maybe catch King in town. He'd play the game—the gunfighters game.

Moving out early the next morning, Bat spotted the herd, whirled his horse around and raced for the wagons. He yelled, "They're ahead, south bank of the river and angling southwest!" "Wadda ya think Bat?" Zeb yelled, excited. "Crossing the river?"

"River's too high! We'll circle left—try to head 'em off and take a stand in the shin-oak on that knoll—southwest!" he said, pointing.

"And come in on the fur side!" Zeb's scream faded in the distance. He laid the leather to his team.

"We'll head around the other way!" Baldy Beechnut yelled, and with a stinging whip, jumped his team to a flying start. The jolt flattened Rip Nesbit out on the floorboard. He came up grabbing and floundering around like a drunk.

In the mad race, Bat and his sidekicks soon took a stand, and got set. The herd moved up. The men had never seen such mangy shaggies, but soon the big "50s" roared, and animals began to fall. But skinny or fat it was $2.50 for the hide. The thinning herds were being chased from the Canadian River to the Red, and the critters could hardly slow down long enough to get a blade of grass in their bellies. Even the oldtimers were having second thoughts about the uncontrolled slaughter.

The Whites slaughtered buffaloes for hides only, but the natives wasted no part of the animal. Buffaloes and Indians gone, soon the oldtimers would be spinning hair-raising tales of the great hunts on the Western prairie. A few men got their start shooting shaggies but very few got rich. And they figured they earned every penny of it. It was the danger and hard work that went with it. However, guys like Bat Masterson, Zeb Hunter, Rip Nesbit, and Baldy Beechnut, they were not long for the hunter's way of life.

Baldy knew when the animals come in target range what was going on with his new sidekick, Steve. The hunters told the kid to brace up or the Sharps 50 would knock him on his butt—it did.

The big turkey shoot was over. Shot-up animals, kicking, gasping for air, struggling, scattered around in a half-circle, trying to get on their feet. The herd slowly started off down the river, but a pack of wolves triggered a stampede, and they soon disappeared in a cloud of dust. But the hunters had all the hides they could snake out of the hills, anyway. It rubbed Bat the wrong way to see hunters kill more animals than they could handle; leave unskinned carcasses on the prairie. The red man could never understand the white man's foolish waste.

The dust settled; a little bufffalo calf had been killed. The old shaggie shooters would never waste a bullet on a calf. They knew Steve had killed it. The calf skins wouldn't sell, hunters wouldn't fool with them; the wolves took care of the calves. Hunters only wanted adult skins and they really went for the big $3.50 bull hides.

Baldy was skinning. He slowed down. "I want'cha to look at these old boogers where they've been shot some time'er uther. Skin's full of screw worms, like a sieve; ain't gonna be worth much."

"Ah, Baldy," Rip come on, "them rich'uns in Europe will take anything's got hair on it."

Steve was tickled with his marksmanship. He ran down to look at the calf he had shot. Zeb soon noticed the boy walking around looking his kill over. "Baldy," Zeb said, shading his eyes, "that boy, he ain't got blood on his wrist, has he? His hands are snow white too."

"Naw," Baldy replied, "them's white cotton gloves with red wrists he's got on—'fraid'o germs. Don't know how my Sis raised seech a peculiar boy, but he's proud of them gloves."

Bat joined in. "I'll tell you one thing, if the boys on the spotted horses come around he'll be ahead of us; go out with clean hands."

The old prairie codgers could hardly take that glove stuff. Country boys wouldn't do it, wouldn't think of such a thing. Far-out country kids wrestled in the dirt, played marbles, and fought over pee-wees...whose marble was closest when lagging at the p-jinker line.

58

"Ah, Baldy, jist the way ya wuz brung up," Rip Nesbit declared. "Ain't all them people back'n east there sorta strange actin'; funny raisins'?"

Zeb added, "Reckon as to how they are. Bat you're right. This savage country ain't safe fur a boy that ain't never been away from home, gloves or no gloves—ain't safe for nobody."

Steve drug his kill up. Bat said, "Lets help the boy jerk the hide off."

After they helped Steve with his kill they gave him the job of watching for Indians. The hunters were fighting against time in hostile country. The weather was scorching hot, carcasses swelled to a strut, and the stink going to High Heaven. When the odor seemed unbearable they tied bandanas over their noses...looked like a bunch of hungry bank robbers gathered around the carcasses. The skinning was finally over, the hides stretched, salted, and pegged to dry.

Steve tugged at the cuff of his gloves, "I do not recollect the species of these wretched animals I detect on the hillside as appearing in my school textbook."

The hide men were polite and never wanted to show the kid up, but they had to turn their heads to wipe off grins.

"Some have departed," Steve added.

Baldy cleared his throat. "Boy, them's lobos, lazy lobo wolves, jist waitin' for somethin' to eat, but be doing their own huntin' before long."

"Well," Bat said—he hesitated. "That's it! I've fired my last buffalo shot. I come to Texas to hunt buffaloes, got caught up in the Adobe Walls battle and now....That's it!"

10 *Indians!*

Bat's sidekicks could see he didn't give up his buffalo hunting easy.

The hunters loaded each wagon with two hundred skins. It was all a four-horse team could snake out of the canyons. They soon strung out for Mobeetie, the skinners going ahead on horseback. Bat was riding Coalie and hung back to lead the way for the wagons. Coming out of the river bottom and topping the high bluffs, with steep slopes that stretched a mile uphill, was a hard pull on the teams. The teamsters headed the wagons southeast and soon came to Red Deer Creek. Rip and Baldy's wagon crossed the creek without a hitch. Zeb's bay horse, as usual, had everyone guessing; would he balk, ruin the whole day?

The Bay stopped dead still in his tracks at the crossing. Zeb coaxed and yelled. "Giddyup! Consarn 'im, why does the old sumbitch have to act up at a time like this?" A few come-on licks with his stinging whip and the stubborn old cuss pulled his share of the load. The wagons rolled on. The teamsters watched for deep buffalo trails and ditches and slowed down to ease across the rough spots.

The hunters were concerned for any delay, even the slow-down at Red Deer Creek put 'em on edge. Indians were always on the their mind; nerve racking. The Whites knew Indians hung out along Red Deer, but no Redskins had been seen. Wolves, deer, and antelope were everywhere, and a bear or mountain lion now and then.

The wagons crossed the creek and soon headed up the long grassy slope, to top out on high level country. Coming out of the Canadian River bottom, and then a few miles later, the hard pull up the steep slopes at Red Deer was killing on the horses; tame a team horse anytime. Zeb's horses give out halfway up and stopped. The wagon started rolling back. He quickly grabbed the brake and locked the wheels. The exhausted team had to "blow," but once rested, Zeb hollered, "Giddyup!" Bat topped out on level prairie, and then come Baldy and Rip's wagon. Bat slow-reined Coalie and waited for Zeb to come in sight. As soon as Zeb's lead team showed up at the rise Bat reined ahead.

"Keep it goin' hosses!" Zeb yelled. His lead team topped out; Steve was riding "shotgun." But the wagon was still on the steep slope; soon it stopped. The old bay horse on the back hitch balked again. The wagon started rolling back. Zeb quickly grabbed the brake and stopped the roll. He growled, "The old bastard don't care if it moves or not—jist standing there flipping his ears and switching his tail. Them browns and iron-gray can't do it without some help."

The old man glanced at the boy and raved on, "Damn it! I'd twist his ears but don't do no good on this old devil." He come off the wagon and hit the ground fuming, "Got another little scheme I pull on 'im once in awhile—never fails."

That kind of talk was strange stuff to Steve. He had never heard of such a thing...scheming against a horse—twisting his ears—educated, he wondered was there really bastard horses? Sitting on the hides watching, he could keep quiet no longer. He asked, "Could I be of service to you, Mr. Hunter? I would be glad to assist you."

"Naw boy, you stay up'n that wagon and gander over

them hills for Redskins...they liable to jump outta that grass. Got some little sticks here I keep tallowed up. I'll light 'em, drop 'em behind the old sucker's heels and give 'im the hot foot. Works every time; he'll move it out. Good hoss, but like some of us old coots, got a little stubborn streak." Zeb lit the sticks, they blazed up and he dropped them behind the bay's back feet. He popped his whip and yelled, "Come on Bay, move it out!"

All four horses tightened on the traces and moved the wagon up—up just far enough for the horse to get out of the heat; he balked again. The tail-end of the wagon was left over the burning sticks. The dry grass caught on fire and soon the wagon blazed up, too. Zeb was in one heckuva fix.

"Confound the luck! Ain't never had nothin' like it happen before!" He snorted, beating the fire with his hat. "Boy, jump down and grab that calf skin and go to beatin'!"

Thick gray smoke rolled from the wagon load of hairy hides, a smoke signal to Indians for miles around. Bat heard yelling and looked back. Smoke was pouring from under the hill. He whirled his horse around, dug in his spurs, and lit out for the back wagon—yelled at Baldy Beechnut and Rip Nesbit as he raced by, "Something's wrong back there!"

Rip and Baldy looked back. Steve had got off the wagon, climbed to the hilltop, waving and flopping his arms like a buzzard off a buffalo carcass. They ran for Zeb's wagon, too.

The men took their hats and grabbed green skins, too, to beat out the blazing wagon. The hide drainage down the steep angled wagon was a fire quencher, but things began to worsen. "Dang the luck!" Zeb yelled, "That blazing dry grass—she's a gon'er—can't stop 'er now!" Billows of white smoke rolled across the prairie;

nothing they could do.

Bat turned to Zeb, "What happened?"

Zeb explained, wiping his brow, "Ah"....Suddenly he froze. "What's that?" he asked. The old man had ears like a fox.

A band of renegade Redskins showed up at Red Deer Creek.

"Redskins, Redskins!" Zeb come on loud.

The Indians crossed the creek and whipped their calico horses up the slope, headed straight for the wagons. Comanche yells sent cold chills up and down the hunters' spine. No place to hide, nothing they could do, was the old bay horse going to be the death of the whole bunch?

"Cut the teams, cut 'em loose!" Bat yelled.

Rip and Baldy ran for their wagon. Bat dropped the trace-chains on Zeb's lead team and Zeb got the horses' on the back hitch. One brown and the iron-gray were gentle "riding-horses." Guns were going off and arrows falling around the wagons thick as flies. Redskin yells were bone chilling; closer and closer!

"Quick, take the gray!" Zeb yelled, grabbed Steve and shoved him on the harnessed horse. "He's the fastest!"

They cut the horses' loose but got nothing out of the wagons; not even a bullet. Zeb jumped on the brown, Bat swung up on Coalie, and they kicked out. The horses dug in their feet, heaving and grunting, they were gone; the harness rattled.

Bat topped the mesa, swung his saddle gun around and knocked a Redskin off the lead horse. But the Indians kept coming. The next horse went down, too, but they kept coming. The hard ride up the long steep slope had the Indian horses wrung out but they kept coming!

Bat glanced at Steve. "Kick him out! Lay it on him!"

Zeb knew the swinging ends of the trace-chains, which hook to the wagon doubletree, were dangerous to the rider of a harnessed horse anytime. But there was no time to secure them. Was the jig up? The savage yells were hell, but now the Indian horses' were slowing down; give out. Bat yelled at Steve, "We're gaining, keep it up!" The Indians hadn't give up, but the hunters were kicking dust in their eyes of the screaming Braves.

Without warning the iron-gray faltered; going down. Bat held his breath. Then a horrified scream from Steve going over the horse's head. Bat quickly reined-in, pushing in close to the stumbling horse, and reached far in the saddle for the boy—grabbing, spurring in closer, grabbing for Steve!

11 *Burying The Boy*

It was only luck that anyone survived the Indian raid. A flopping chain wrapped around Steve's horse's leg and rolled him. It soon shook loose and in a dead-run he caught up with the other horses. Losing Steve was most regrettable, but there was nothing they could do; sad, a great loss.

Coming home the moon was bright. The twinkling lights of Mobeetie soon showed up. It was a welcome sight, glowing lamps all over town, and every saloon in the settlement was open. But Bat was tired; though Molly was on his mind, he soon "hit the hay."

Early the next morning not a cloud was in sight. Sunlight began breaking over the horizon, drenching the prairie. Steve was on their mind; he was out there somewhere. His hunting partners would waste no time in finding him. But stuff was lost in the raid; they had to have a few supplies. Leaving O'Loughlin's cafe, they hustled on their way. Men were already at work tying pickets and nailing clapboard houses together. Bat and his cronies walked in Long's store; knocking was going on in the back. The hammering stopped. Uncle Johnny soon came to the front.

"Morning. You fellows had your coffee?" His smile was friendly and movement easy, but his had been a rugged outdoor life. He was with the Union Pacific Railroad surveying crew that spanned the great western wilderness. His civilian freight wagons transported Army supplies for General George Armstrong Custer, Gen.

Miles, and Col. Mackenzie. And he brought in the first supplies for Fort Elliot, including the only orginal Fort flag-pole standing today. As usual, Mr. Long stood relaxed with his right hand in the crook of his left elbow, and holding his old briar pipe with his left...not bothered by the heat, seldom lit anyway. He said, "Help yourself to the coffee, boys; what can I do for you?"

"Good morning," Bat spoke. "Uncle Johnny the Indians swarmed in on us yesterday. Dogged Redskins nearly done us in. Need some bridles and harness fixins— guns and bullets, some chawins, too."

"Yeah." Zeb nodded sorrowfully, "Bad part was we lost the boy. Got to have more guns—Sharps."

"The way these herds are thinning out a guy may have a hard time paying for a gun before long," Bat remarked.

Uncle Johnny knocked the ashes out of his pipe. "These herds are going down to nothing now. They're telling it around here Dick Bussell killed eight hundred shaggies in a one-day stand over north on the Canadian River. Seems to me somebody's stretching it a little, but he does have over ten thousand hides stacked and ready to go; what else?"

"Two loggerheads for old Bay's harness," Zeb replied, "and a hame-string. Arrow cut it purt'ner nearly plumb in two. Huh, ten thousand, lotta hides."

Baldy Beechnut bit off a chaw of tobacco, "Me and Rip's got extra guns but we lost a bridle and trace-chain."

"When the shaggies are all gone," Rip Nesbit remarked, "and the head peeling Redskins are herded to the Territory, us old prairie pie stompers will have to head back where we come from." He added, "Could cowboy on these new ranches, I reckon."

J. J. Long, a community booster, didn't see it like that. "It's great country for a guy like Bat here...young, full of of pizz'n vinegar, and ready to take on the world. Big future on these high plains for ranching and cattle. The promised land, all we need is more settlers and get rid of a few gunslicks."

"Think I'll hang around," Bat replied.

"I figure we'll have to keep our powder dry and guns oiled for awhile," Zeb said. "And Baldy we don't want to forget to take a shovel."

Mr. Long, working on their orders only heard mention of a shovel. "Shovel, say you need a shovel, Zeb?"

"Just talkin' to Baldy 'bout a shovel to bury the boy."

"Sorry about the boy," Uncle Johnny lamented. "These Indians are on the warpath now but their war whoops will soon be a thing of the past. Can't much blame 'em for fighting back, but killing that boy was senseless." He stepped over by a whiskey barrel, picked up a short board and handed it to Baldy. "This is not much but take it and mark the boy's grave."

Thinking of Steve, and concerned about their wagons too, the hunters hurried on their way. Up from Red Deer creek, where the Indians attacked, they found the wagons turned over and hides scattered all over hell and half the prairie. The boy's mutilated body, with his gloves on, was found near the wagons on the high mesa overlooking Red Deer Creek.

Digging Steve's grave, where he fell, someone was watching for Indians all time—the digging was hard. But the prairie flowers scattered around were beautiful. It was a mystery to the men why the Indians didn't take the boy's red and white gloves. And still with his gloves on, the saddened hunters folded the youth's hands over his chest, took a curry comb found under an overturned wagon, brushed his hair, and with his eyes closed, lowered his body in the shallow grave. They covered him over and set the marker. Somber and with respect, they placed prairie flowers on the grave...buttercups, Indian-blankets, sweet flowering horsemint, and cactus flower. With emotion, their eyes welled, tears trickled down Baldy's cheeks.

The three old hunters, along with Bat, stood together. They pulled their hats off, and when the mixed southern voices started humming—half-singing—"Shall We Gather At The River," Bat joined in, too. Baldy quoted a Bible verse and Zeb closed the service. He looked up to Heaven, "Oh, Lawdy, if'n this boy hunts buffaloes on that big prairie in the sky, keep his hoss from a'stumblin', and oh Lawdy kick old Bay's butt 'cause it was all his fault anyway. Rest the boy's soul. Amen," they all joined in.

Maybe the ten minute service was unusual on the high plains frontier but it made sense to the old grizzled hide men. Baldy Beechnut wanted it for his nephew, the best they could do. It was known only to God what pain and suffering the pioneers went through on the "buffalo trail."

12 *Dogface Against Bat*

The hunters were gathering up their stuff after the Indian raid at Red Deer Creek when Bat exclaimed, pointing, "The Redskins are hid in the hills over yonder and we better move fast!"

They hurried, and soon righted a turned over wagon. The guns and skinning-knives were gone, neck-yokes too, and the double-trees jerked off the wagon. But with what they'd gathered up, and with supplies they'd brought from the store, they soon had the wagons ready. They loaded the hides and was ready to go.

Zeb said, "Let's head 'em up, my prayer's been answered, the old bay hoss seems eager to pull his share of the load."

"Hope so," Rip replied, "let's get the hell gone!" The wagons quickly strung out. Bat led the way then come Zeb's wagon. Baldy Beechnut and Rip Nesbit's wagon brought up the rear. They gandered around, there would be no Indian surprises. Rambling on across level country, and then down sloping hills, they soon rolled into Mobeetie.

Mr. Long was standing in the door when Bat stopped off at the store. J J said, "Well, Bat, now that your back I figure you'll be needing some headin' money?"

Bat replied, "Evening, sir—well, yup."

Mr. Long handed him a hundred dollar bill. "Take this and head off them debts. All these hides you've got around here—not making you any money."

"Sure much obliged; can use it," Bat replied.

"I'll soon be loading out hide-wagons for Dodge City. We'll throw yours on too...'got lots of money tied up there." Mr. Long chuckled, "And besides, you may want to buy that pretty little girl a mint julep drink."

"Uncle Johnny you're reading my mind."

"Well," Mr. Long paused, "this Dogface King guy has been running around here since you've been gone; keeps pestering Molly. She tries to dodge him. He yells at her across the street that he loves her and all that kind of stuff—shoots off his mouth he's going to take care of her Dodge City buffalo hunter. Too, while you was gone he pulled another good one there at the front door. A friendly mule-skinner by name of Sid Stone smiled and tipped his hat to Molly. Dogface saw it. The bully ran up to Stone, pulled out that Bowie knife he keeps hid in his shirt...cut Sid's throat 'ear to ear. Stone was gone before he hit the dirt—'put him under last week. King is locoed, people ain't gonna settle down here as long as he keeps the town stirred up; keep moving on....Look who sneaked up—riding the red roan—looking your horse over now!"

He quickly spurred out. Everybody in town knew the red roan and who rode it. Bat wasn't fooled. Dogface Melvin King wanted to make it a big "happening" the day he gunned down a man that earned respect in the battle at Adobe Walls. The cold-blooded killer would gloat.

The Sergeant was blowing around town Molly Brennan was his woman in Dodge City. Maybe the boys in Kansas did have more to do with her "Baby" than her Mother would ever believe. Dogface was blabbing wild stuff about Molly and so was Bill Thompson. But who would believe it? Walking over boys at the Army Post boosted King's conceit. It was talked he had been kicked in the head by a mule and no one doubted it. He had the crazy idea he could build a fence around a girl in this rip-snorting town of Mobeetie, Texas. Maybe it worked around Fort Sill and Fort Dodge, but it would never work around Fort Elliot and Mobeetie."

"Uncle Johnny I've shot my wad, my last buffalo. I'm moving up in this world, but I don't have a job. I'm moving out of ol' Zeb's place at Hidetown to this place the Comanches call Mobeetie."

"Ah, don't sweat it Bat," Mr. Long replied. "You've got a job here at the Mint any time you want it, or over here at Henry's Lady Gay."

"It's all them winnings I'm missing," he said, chuckling.

"Well, I can see that, you're lucky at gambling."

Bat split the hide money with his skinners then he was on his way...moving to Mobeetie where money growed, whiskey flowed and wild women glowed!

"Bit'o Home And Heven," the sign read at the O'Loughlin restaurant/boarding house. Tom O'Loughlin was a hunter too, but still Ellen didn't much like it catering to those old smelly hidemen. She almost had to hold her nose when they showed up. But smell or no smell, she still welcomed them, and would do so even when they got their new hotel built—"The Grand Central." It didn't bother Bat. He had shucked his clothes at the creek and did a little sand rubbing to come out fresh and clean. The stinking hidemen didn't much care what people thought when they shied around them. They had hide money, it burned their pockets. They'd as soon sleep on the ground with the rattlesnakes as fight the bedbugs in the straw mattresses, anyway.

A cool breeze was blowing when Bat walked up to O'Loughlin's hotel and stepped on the loose boards; Tom's porch. Bat Masterson wasn't used to sleeping in a house. His bed of late had been the wide open spaces. The door was open. He raised his hand to knock, noticed

71

a little sign on a lamp table that said, "Welcome, come in." A woman soon came to the door; friendly and slender.

"Come in, come in!" she said.

Bat stood, sort of rolling his hat brim, and said, "Ah-ah, Ma'am, just wondering—reckon you could put me up for awhile —gonna settle down."

"Come on in young man," Ellen said. "Ya look like a clean boy to me...mind I look behind ya ears?" Hide men coming to the hotel with dirty splotched ears and manure caked boots was not unusual. "Gonna hang around long?" she asked.

"Spect too."

"Make you a good price," she declared. "Got new mattresses and nary a buffalo's slept on them straws in them new striped tickin's. Besides my bedbugs got no wings, and besides I drowned 'em all...soused them tickin's in the creek. Comfort like ya ain't never seen on the prairie!"

"Well, Ma'am how much?" Bat asked. Fumbling in his pocket, he mumbled, "Humf, bedbugs got no wings—sounds good!"

"Be twelve dollars a month—that is ya use the privy —slop-jar, two dollars more. Young man you lucked out, my new rooms got no bullet holes yet, and didn't have no rooms left till Digger Dugan carried off one of my customers. Shootin' scrape down at the Shores-of-hell put 'im six feet under. That red roan rider's bunch is crazy."

The Tom O'Loughlins, truly plains pioneers, lived in Kansas until the Indians burned their house down during a wild rampage down the Arkansas River. After the O'Loughlins had lost most everything, they set out for Texas where buffaloes roamed the prairie by the millions. However more trouble dogged them. The belongings they had left were loaded in the wagon and ready to go. But just before they pulled out a skunk came in the yard and bit their little two-year-old girl. The two boys, Willie and Miles were already in the wagon. But concerned about the little girl, at the last minute, they changed their minds... they'd leave her with Kansas relatives to be near doctors. But three months later they got the sad news; the little girl had died with rabies.

The O'Loughlins moved to Hidetown first, two miles southeast of the Fort, but soon moved back northwest and squatted on land halfway between Fort Elliot and Hidetown. A short time later they opened up their home as a restaurant/hotel. Tom, just off the prairie with a load of hides, met Bat at the front door. "I'm Tom," he said, and like a good neighbor, stuck his hand out, "glad to have ya."

"I'm Bat Masterson."

"Well, 'heard ya made a good showing at 'Dobe Walls." "Don't know about that, but I will say this, there was a bunch of them Indians. I'll be 'round and see ya later," Bat said, going to his room.

The O'Loughlin hotel had hide-covered floors. And they had some well known guest, too. Their registery lists pioneer ranchers, gamblers, gunsliners, and even horse thieves. Wyatt Earp, Billy the Kid, Dutch Henry, Clay Allison, Luke Short, and Ben Thompson, among others, were on the guest books. Tom went with Charles Goodnight to show him the way to Palo Duro Canyon from Mobeetie, one hundred miles southwest.

Ellen O'Loughlin's bedbugs had no wings? Bat got to thinking about that—never was a bedbug that had wings. Who did that jolly old gal think she was fooling? He knew drowning them wouldn't work, eggs would still hatch out. The O'Loughlins worked hard, she would mind the store for weeks while he was on the prairie shooting buffaloes.

Bat's was a first class room. For flooring he had a buffalo skin, and from the Fort a few pieces of scrap lumber. Snake heads poking up through knotholes didn't bother him all that much. Neither did scorpions and centipedes in one of the best hotels in town—in the West. He threw his bedroll and rain- slicker in the corner then left-out for the Lady Gay. This was his lucky day...found a place to hang his hat, and had only walked a short ways when he saw Molly coming down the street. Worming her way around the hitching rails and saloons, she then crossed the street to a new store just to walk on the wooden porch with a roof over-hang. She was on her way to Johnny Long's store, but met Bat in front of Curry's Supply store, next door to the Lady Gay saloon. She looked good to Bat in her blue summer dress. He took his hat off and bowed, always courteous to the ladies; respected them.

"Miss Molly, got something to tell you: I'm a full-fledged citizen—resident of Mobeetie, got a fancy room—live here."

She looked up, her pretty blue eyes sparkling, "Don't tell me you're running for mayor, too?"

"Nope," he replied with a big grin. "Got me a job. City surveyor, not much pay but lots of prestige; gonna stake off town lots."

"There wasn't a stake in this whole settlement when we came here. Wherever my daddy wanted to put Bob Brennan's blacksmith and boot shop that's where he put it. But after the killing out by the Fort the Army Brass made all the civilians move. Everybody moved to Hidetown.

Bat said, "Not much left of old Hidetown."

"We like it here, but"....She frowned. Trapped? She knew they were in trouble. Bat looked around. Dogface King was coming out of Curry's. He had murdered men

74

for talking to Molly right before her eyes. But Bat Masterson, a fun lover, he'd chap King's butt when he walked by. He took his hat off and bowed to Molly again, but never took his eyes off Dogface. Bat came in close — closer, why not burn the bully, show Molly affection? Dogface snorted, his face flashed red with anger, but walked on without saying a word and went in the Lady Gay.

Bat was in no hurry he wanted to talk, tell her about his surveying job, tell her how the town had made him the boss and Henry Dittmos was working with him. And each one was paid $10.00 in gold every night, but since Bat was the boss he got drinks on the town. Now Bat figured it was time to consume part of his pay. A little face to face meeting with King was what he'd been look-ing for. The whole town knew King didn't want men, even women, seen talking to Molly. Bat thought he was lucky to see Molly Brennan anytime, but this time he went out of his way to show her his admiration. He knew too he heaped coals of fire on the head of that stupid fool blowing around town he'd "Get Masterson, show him who's running this damn town!"

Bat looked into Molly's eyes. "Ah, what was you say-ing?"

"Going to Uncle Johnny's store." She quickly walked away.

The evening shadows were falling when Bat walked up to the Lady Gay's front door and hesitated. He watched Molly walk off. The bartender saw the stranger talking to Molly on the street. He cringed, he'd seen it before, he would tell the man, "Don't come in!" He'd seen it happen before, wouldn't give a dime for the stranger's life; hoping to hell he didn't come through that door. King sat at a table in the darkest corner.

With pleasant thoughts on Molly, Bat was in no hurry.

Dogface bellied up to the bar close to Hank Dittmos and ordered a drink. Looking in the big mirrior, he never took his eyes off the front door. Red Day, the nervous, handlebar-mustachioed bartender, knew what was coming, knew Dogface, knew what he would do. But he didn't know Bat Masterson. A few days back Red watched Melvin King kill another stranger seen talking to Molly. Red knew the jig was up for this one too— wanted to warn the man, but he was ready to duck out of sight.

Dogface had his usual two buttons open on his shirt, ready with the Bowie knife in his belt. Sloshing the whiskey, the shaky bartender shoved the drink at Dogface King. Bill Sty, the manager, was coming down the second floor stairway when he saw Bat heading for the bar, straight to the standing spot between Hank Dittmos and Dogface. Sty froze, mumbling, "This is it!" Dogface's devilish grin was enough to scare some men, maybe Satan himself, but this is what Bat Masterson had waited for.

"Just a minute there, Masterson!" Dogface snarled, shoved his drink and sort of braced up. "So your're the sonovabitch that stole my horse!"

Bat's bluish slate-gray eyes, cold and fearless, shot through King like a razor sharp stiletto...he froze, staring, glassy-eyed with fear; didn't move. Bat twitched his shoulder, King come alive and went for his knife— Hank Dittmos hit the floor to dodge the bullets—Red Day ducked behind the bar; soon Dittmos and the ducking Red heard a thud. Bill Sty, on the stairway, watched the killer. Dogface King had his right hand in his shirt bringing his Bowie knife out, his gun coming up in his left....Like lightening, Bat brought his .45 up and smashed it against King's temple, spun him around, knocking him senseless, turning his head, Bat knocked him to the floor.

Bill Sty said, "If I'd blinked I'd missed it all. The

sonovabitch must have seen stars when Bat connected with his pistol. King hit the floor like a ton of bricks and didn't move for a minute."

It was quiet, no shots were fired. Finally Red Day got up enough nerve to raise up behind the bar, his eyes staring out like a hoot owl's in a hen house. Dittmos was still on the floor, but finally raked up enough nerve to squint his eyes open. Dogface was lying next to him, blood spurting from a gash in his head. Ol' Hank Dittmos claimed he wasn't scared but he could hardly take the ribbing about his soiled britches.

Bat could have killed Dogface King and it wouldn't have done him much more harm. "Saved a little ammunition," Bat joked, "not even worth a damn bullet!" With that, he kicked Dogface's gun scooting across the floor. Slinking, afraid to stand, Dogface started crawling. Bat pointed him to the door with the business end of his .45. "Crawl you bastard, crawl!" Bat warned, and kicked his ass out in the street.

Bill Sty yelled, "Drinks are on the house!"

Night had come on and King left in the dark. He wasn't seen for weeks in Mobeetie. The rumors were going around town he was so flustered after Bat humblized him he went back to Fort Sill and killed another soldier, he said, "Just for the hell of it." The officers were after him, but he hauled out and soon started giving trouble along the Texas/Indian Territory border. Dogface Melvin King would never let Bat Masterson get by with the Lady Gay fracas. He'd wait for his glory, draw Bat out in a crowd. This was a tough town, but people were concerned, knew Bat was dealing with a dangerous insane jealous gunfighter. After King pulled out the town loosened up. But they were still talking it, low, "He'll be back—bloodthirsty—killed at least twenty men and that poor Molly's caught in the middle!"

13 *Ben Thompson*

Bat's surveying for the day was done. He strolled off down the street. Suddenly bullets kicked up dust around his feet. He stepped behind the Pink Pussycat's Paradise Saloon—nothing, just some stupid fool showing off. But on down a'ways a rukus was going on. Loud talk coming from somewhere. People started ducking all over the place. Suddenly a long-haired gunman burst through the front door at the Giltedge saloon, hit the ground reeling, one hand was dangling. He staggered around trying to stay on his feet. Hell-bent on getting a shot off, he splintered the saloon door. Bat figured it was all over, just a barroom brawl. He started walking. But soon a thin-faced mustachioed man wearing a full crown black hat burst through the door; his brace-of-sixes blazing. Bat recognized him. Mysterious Dave Mather exclaimed, "You thieving bastard try stealing somebody else's horse!"

The man on the ground thrashed around, snorted a few times, kicked up a little dust, but that was about it...a job for Digger Dugan. Bat had refreshments at the Lady Gay and headed home.

Along about daylight a knock on Bat's door woke him up. A little early, he thought, couldn't figure it out. Had he overerslept...Hank, ready to measure off more town lots? He jerked on his pants, slung on his gunbelt, cracked the door and eased it back. "Why, Zeb you old flea-bitten coyote!"

"Wouldn't load an old skinner with lead?" Zeb chuckled. "How's the 'partment—seems a mansion—skin for a rug and all!"

"Good, good. Yeah, almost covers my dirt floor—hold it! Snake there's coming out early!" Bat took the snake's head off with his .45. He asked, "Zeb how'd ya find me?"

"Well, down at Uncle Johnny's store met this lil' woman that runs this place. Bless'er heart, friendly, nice, jist like the lil' two hundred pound dumplin' 'left back home—said she rented a room to a nice young man ridin' a big black hoss; had to be you."

Tobacco juice trickled down the gully in Zeb's whiskers, but he was sanitary. If he missed a squirt at the snake hole he rubbed it out with his boot.

"They found a big herd down'n south past Salt Fork, toward the Red," Zeb said, stroking his dirty chin whiskers. "Bunch of us oldtimers gittin' together like for ya go with us."

"Sounds good, Zeb. How many wagons?"

"Five'er six. Good as you are we can round up a half dozen skinners for ya if'n ya'd go."

"Thanks Zeb but my old friend Billy Dixon draws a finer bead than I do."

"Now Bat, you know ya ain't never done nothin' in your whole dadburn life but shoot shaggies and done some scoutin'. 'Course ya ain't dry behind the ears yit. Big possibilities out'n here for you young ducks, but like I say, us old coots will soon be driftin' on, back where we come from."

"Tell you something, Zeb, got me a job in this town. Gonna be a civil engineer."

Zeb couldn't believe his ears. "Ya mean gonna drive one of them smokin' things right down main street—train?"

"Didn't get me, Zeb. Surveyor, a guy that squints through them transit things that sets on three legs.

Gonna lay off tracts of land, town lots, and drive stakes. Measure it off like the State surveyors do on square miles. It sounded good when Mr. Long called it civil engineer—carry-over from his days on the Union Pacific Railroad. Got me a helper, too—Hank Dittmos on the measuring rope, but none of that fancy three legged stuff."

"Did see one of them monkey's once back'n Alabamy wavin' and floppin' his arms like a buzzard off a buffalo carcass. Had a kid 'way out there holdin' a stick while he wuz squintin'."

Bat replied, "Indians are still knocking off these State survey crews but I'm going out to see how it's done anyway."

"Git ya edg-a-ma-cation, lay off lots for these town dudes —don't think ol' Bat can stay hitched."

"Figure it won't be dull as the job I had at Fort Supply counting Government mules," Bat said, chuckling.

"Mightnin' not be," Zeb replied, as he walked out the door.

Bat soon started staking off lots for settlers but surveying wasn't Bat's life ambition. He'd never pass up a job at the Lady Gay. Even so, he thought he had the bull by the tail with a downhill pull. This town was for Bat Masterson, money, land, and women. Mobeetie was famous for saloons and girls, more so than most western towns. The 500 girls on Featherbed Hill was enough to start a new town. Bat could see a big change in the settlement since the first day he rode in. The Saturday nights back then were all buffalo hunters. Now he rubbed elbows not only with hunters, but teamsters, ranchers, horse thieves, horse traders, soldiers, gamblers, gunslingers, prostitutes, shyster lawyers, and saddle tramps, too.

Rumors were going around town Sam Houston's

youngest son, Temple, was coming to practice law in Mobeetie. A few people liked the idea, but Temple got word there was no county organization in the Panhandle. By State law one hundred and fifty permanent citizens had to sign a petition to get county organization started. But there was some people in the Panhandle that didn't want legal law and order. Temple Houston postponed his trip to Mobeetie.

Bat dropped by the store. Uncle Johnny was beaming. "Looks like you done a pretty good job there, Bat."

"Yup, me and Hank's getting them town lots staked off."

"Well, 'wasn't exactly what I was talking about. Town's breathing easier since Dogface hauled-out."

"Oh, yeah. Uncle Johnny, I need some smokin's."

Late evening, around dark, Bat met Ben Thompson at the Lady Gay. The flickering candle was no floodlight in the corner where they sat. Ben came up from Austin to see his brother Bill, co-owner of the Lady Gay. Ben had old sidekicks in Mobeetie, too. But Bill was in Kansas City again on girl business. Ben wondered about that, knew the Kansas law was still looking for Bill since he done-in the County Sheriff. It was talked in Mobeetie Ben's gun kept Bill alive in that shoot-out. And now Ben wondered why run the risk, why venture out that way again? Ben Thompson could handle his guns with the best, maybe a good dresser too, but a man with any sense at all wouldn't let that kind of stuff fool them. It's been said he had the fastest gun in the State of Texas...understood too why so-called bad men shied around him. It was proved many times he would proudly take on any gun-slinger in the West.

Bat Masterson's was one of the fastest guns in the West, too, but he never was one to boast. He thought the fast gun honors should go to his good friend, Ben

Thompson. Ben liked the wide open town of Mobeetie—the town without even a shadow of law and order—even talked about moving to the settlement.

Ben laughed. "Now, Bat, since nobody else will open up around this town tell me about them loose screws in that hawgleg of yours. I think there oughta be a law against a guy wrecking a man's gun like that."

"Oughta be a law against a guy having such a damn hard head, too!" Bat replied, chuckling.

The lights were suddenly snuffed out across the room. Someone shrieked, "Terrible Tommy!" Yelling out in the saloons wasn't unusual but whose was the female voice?

Saloon patrons froze. Ben Thompson knew the voice, knew she was razzing him about his gun handling. He knew too she was screaming over a little incident that happened in South Texas. Had to be the old gal that jumped in to help her now-deceased lover.

She raised hell wherever she went, a female bully, had a big mouth, talked tough, buffaloed some men, but not the likes of Ben Thompson. She had heard of Mobeetie's wild reputation, no law, a good place to settle a score. Known gunfighters tried to avoid her, thought her gun-handling was nothing but a joke—looking for fame. She couldn't be ignored, she kept popping up. Ben didn't feel bad about the little shooting scrape she started down South. Her fingers on the gun just happened to be in the way when he blowed it out of her hand. The chase was over, so in Mobeetie, Texas, in 1875, she had her man. She sat in a dark corner with a gun leveled on the man she hated—the man in the lamp-light, the man that got her lover—no hurry, she set gloating...then suddenly shrieked, "You son-of-a-bitch I've tracked you all the way from South Texas for this and now Mr. Thompson, you're gon-na pay!"

A loud boom! Dirt trickled off the adobe walls.

14 *Strolling Sweetwater*

Bat shot out the lights, a deafening roar. A bullet from across the room zinged off the adobe walls. Bat and Ben holstered up. Ben's bullet-nicked sleeve would be no problem for the Chinese tailor; however, the scrambling customers who were knocked down and trampled didn't fair as well.

"Well...," Bat said.

Ben replied, "Bitch got what she deserved for spilling Henry's whiskey in my lap; burned like hell." Ben soon hauled out for Dodge City.

King hadn't been seen in Mobeetie since Bat knocked him senseless. Nobody would cry if he never did show up. His threats on one of the most admired men in town, "Gonna get Masterson," was keeping the town stirred up. He burned, knew Molly Brennan was in love with Bat Masterson and the Sergeant was hell bent on ending the love affair. Come right he'd try it but shooting off his mouth didn't shake Bat Masterson.

The natives had been here forever but the United States Army had the Indians whipped down. Buffalo hunters were still around but ranchers and cowboys were showing up every day. European syndicate land buyers were pouring in, too. They were men of wealth, men of dignity, bringing their high society "proper" ladies to see the wild untamed West...the land of naked running Redskins and countless buffaloes.

Mobeetie stood out like a castle in the sand. Not another settlement in 200 miles in the vast prairie land;

the exciting West. People from across the water were in awe. But for some, one night in town was enough, but for others it was an escape from the law; they settled in. The tanked up, fun-loving cowboys running their horses up and down the street, firing their pistols and yelling like Comanches, scared the life out of visitors. Weak-hearted dudes lost no time moving on, and to save embarrassment they left after dark.

The spring showers and warm sunshine brought out a myriad of beautiful flowers that covered the countryside...buttercups, fireweeds, horsemint, and many more. Dogwoods, water lilies, and violets were blooming on the creek, too. The Bob Brennans' always liked to think of Sweetwater Creek as a little bit of "Mississippi in the West"—a country of low land, trees, and flowers. Bessie and Molly loved the creek.

One pretty day Bessie said to Bob, "If you'll hitch Brownie to the buggy I'll take Molly and go to the creek. Poke-shoots ought to be coming out."

"Sounds good to me," Bob replied, "I could stand some fresh greens. Spring showers and warm days brings out poke-weed. Brownie's hossin' but be no trouble. No studs around, no Indians seen lately, or that Dogface; oughta be safe."

Bob's little brown mare was in season and he wanted a colt. He liked the horse Bat rode. Coalie was a good saddlehorse with racing stock blood and that's what Western pioneers liked.

Bessie and Molly struck out for the creek, a mile west of town. They kept south of the Fort, bounced over sagebrush and red bunch grass. There was no road, not even a trail all the way to the creek. They soon drove into a grove of big cottonwood trees standing along the creekbank; not far from the Post ice pit. Sweetwater ran south, snaked through underbrush and trees, then made a bend east, meandering twenty five miles to Indian Territory. The girls soon forgot about the rough ride, they were so tickled to be on the creek. Right away they stopped the buggy in the shade of a hackberry tree. Pouring across a beaver dam, and the crystal clear water rippling over white sand, it was music to their ears...rushing, babbling, winding through cattails, willows, and cottonwoods.

Coming out of the buggy, Bessie said, "Molly baby, we'll unhitch Brownie here and let her graze this good grass while we gather a few baskets of poke-greens."

Molly loved her mother but she was thinking now she had outgrown that "baby" stuff. She knew more about the "birds and bees" than her mother would ever believe. Her smile and beautiful eyes, it was easy to get any man's attention. They slipped the baskets on their arms and slowly walked through a forest of overlapping trees and vines; lots of chiggers, too.

The blooming undergrowth's sweet fresh smell was just like Mississippi in the spring. The creek was alive with birds and animals. Fun to Bessie and Molly, they stopped to watch the bright blue flying insects over the water. The darting "snake- doctors" didn't miss a reed. The playful beavers stirring up waves on the water had a croaking frog rocking on every lily pad. Bass jumped for bugs, redbirds flitted around in blankets of dogwood blooms, and as usual jaybirds screamed. Wing-fluttering quails woke up a squirrel that got in a few scolding barks. "Oh, my goodness, thought we was got!" Bessie exclaimed, frightened by a deer that jumped from the brush and high-tailed it down the trail. The excited girls loved it—hog heaven! Mississippi all over again.

Bessie filled her basket with greens, handed it to Molly and said, "I'll keep looking for more while you go empty this batch in the buggy, but be careful, don't booger Brownie!"

Molly was just a plain ol' country girl, really. She loved to go barefooted and feel the tender grass between her toes. In no hurry, she stopped on the way to watch a couple of rabbits working on a new family; forgot about snakes. But Molly loved wild life...maybe had a little of it herself.

She coaxed the little buggy horse, "Ho, Brownie, easy."

Brownie gave a quick jerk and raised her head, but like all horses, she loved grass and kept stuffing. Emptying her basket, she heard hoof beats; she glanced up. A black saddlehorse was coming in a run, straight for the buggy. Someone had cut Coalie's bridle reins and spooked the horse. Nothing unusual about cutting reins in Mobeetie-town. But it was hell to pay if you got caught; a gunfight, at least a fist fight. A cowboy that walked twenty miles for his runaway horse was usually out of humor. Molly stepped behind the buggy.

Coalie rubbed noses with Brownie and soon settled down. The stallion had horse-romance on his mind. The little mare was in a romantic mood too....And, well, Bob wanted a colt. Molly watched. She could hardly wait for the happenings, even forgot about getting the basket back to her mother. And all this time Bessie was wondering why in the world it was taking Molly so long just to empty the basket. Did her baby get snakebit?

Coalie nipped Brownie's withers and the mare squalled out. The good horse he was, he got on with Bob's colt business.

Bessie heard the squeal. "Oh, no, good gracious alive, something terrible has happened!" She jerked her dress up, gave a big leap, cleared the creek, and struck out running for the buggy. But she suddenly stopped and wheezed a scream, "Don't look, Molly, don't look! Oops, too late, Brownie's gonna have a baby."

86

Bessie was put out with herself, but for Molly...she got a big kick out of it. They got their greens and were soon on the way home. What Bessie's baby saw was nothing new to her. Bob always kept a horse at stud in Mississippi. Molly was no different than anyone else. She liked to watch the horseplay, too. Back then, she'd slip down to the breeding stall, peep through the cracks, and see what was going on. Her mother thought it was awful, told her it wasn't nice for little girls to do things like that. However, Molly got a country education, soon found out it wasn't swallowing pumpkin seed that caused women to have babies. She was just a normal teen-ager growing up on the outside and burning up on the inside.

Coalie followed the buggy. He still had Brownie on his mind when Bessie and Molly pulled up at the blacksmith shop. Bob and Bat came out. Bat, a little out of sorts, held the bobbed-off reins, but Bob could handle it.

"No sweat, Bat. I can splice 'em, brad 'em up and make 'em better than ever. Want 'em like they were or little longer?"

"Yup," he replied, his eyes on Molly.

"Yup, what?"

"Oh, longer, just watching that horsebacker."

Bob turned, didn't see a horsebacker in a mile—no dummy.

15 *The Surveyor*

Bat saddled up, rode down the street and reined-up at Johnny Long's store. J. J. and Henry Fleming were at the front door.

"Hi, Johnny—Henry. Looks like we're going to get a shower, all these thunderheads popping up."

"Could always use a shower in this country," Henry said.

J. J. replied, "Might bring in more settlers. Bat, been wanting to see you since you're the town's official surveyor."

"Oh, you bet. Me and Hank Dittmos drove stakes all day yesterday." Thinking of his job as official surveyor, mostly just a stake driver, he cracked a grin. "We're educated now."

"Well there's a guy from back east here that wants the official measurements on a little ten acre tract 'east edge of town; wants it officially recorded by the city surveyor. Here's some official looking paper and take this official cedar pencil; gotta sharpen it. Got your knife?"

"Yup. We can make that settler happy," Bat declared. "But Hank can't work...horse stepped on his foot. It's better though squished in his boot in a cowboy-poultice—fresh horse manure had to do, no cows around and buffaloes too far out. Where is this land the man wants?"

"In the town section, quarter mile east, but since Hank can't work pick up one of them little Indian kids that hangs around the livery stable to tote one end of ya measuring rope."

"Yeah, wondered about those boys, where they come from?"

Henry said, "Bat, they're orphans. Hunters found 'em fifteen miles north on the Washita in a plum thicket. Their mother was beat and left for dead; did die later. We know who's guilty, the hunters' do too. The boys are tore up, told us it was two men, one on a gray horse, and one was riding a red roan. The kids are sort of hiding-out around here now, just trying to stay alive; damn that Dogface!"

Bat shook his head. "These innocent kids, hate to see 'em go through that."

Uncle Johnny replied, "The kids don't like our kind of living, won't sleep anywhere but in the horse corral. I've been feeding the little half-starved things back of the store, hoping they'd take up with the Indians...Delaware scouts camped on the creek by the Fort. 'Kids are old enough to help ya."

Bat said, "Yup, I'd say the youngest is an 'eight past' and the oldest a 'coming ten.' Naturally the kids act strange around us Whites. But that oldest one, Tah, seems to like me."

Bat took the oldest boy to tote one end of the rope. He motioned to Tah he'd pull him up behind the saddle for the ride to the tract. But Tah shook his head, no. He carried the shiny half-gallon sorghum syrup bucket with the lunch Uncle Johnny had packed mostly for the kid's sake. But the boy surprised Bat. He wouldn't touch the hardtack biscuits or buffalo jerky, but went for the yellow lemon drops. Then he stuffed on a raw cottontail rabbit he caught with uncanny skill, like no one but an Indian could. Bat thought he hypnotized that old rabbit.

Bat couldn't get it over to his little Indian helper about the rope. The twisted lariat, kinks, knots, and all didn't mean a thing to the kid. Measuring off the prairie with a rope was crazy to any Indian...crazy as eating raw rabbit was to Bat. But Tah was a willing helper and too, Bat "felt" for the orphan boy. After Bat's official surveying he had the town dudes happy, his generous measurements. Anyway, who would check Bat Masterson's accuracy? The buffalo hunters didn't think about land measurements when they came to the Panhandle. They didn't care if it was laid off, staked off, or recorded. Wherever they squatted that's where they stayed.

Bat filled out the town's official papers and left them with Uncle Johnny. The town clerk/buffalo hunter had a cubby hole in the store for an office.

Mr. Long was puttering around the next morning when Bat came in. "Bat, you're getting good experience. Guess you're ready for another tract. You did give 'im a full ten acres?"

"Yup, you bet, ten and maybe more, and ready for another big one."

"Good, millions of acres around, glad you did. The guy's from the city and he knows nothing about figuring land. The clerk's back there now trying to figure out your measurements."

"Screwed up?"

Looking at Bat, Uncle Johnny cracked a grin.

"Good Morning," the clerk greeted.

"Howdy," Bat came back, wondering how he messed up. He wasn't afraid of losing the $10.00 in gold every night but it was those extra benefits; the drinks on the town.

"Got something down here can't figure out for the life of me," the clerk said. "These symbols, never seen anything like 'em; must be Choctaw."

"Choctaw or Comanche." Bat smiled.

"Done some puttin' down stuff in the courthouse records back in East Texas before I lit out for the Panhandle, but just ain't never run across anything like this. State puttin' out new stuff?"

"Nope, I'm responsible," Bat admitted.

"Figured you was sorta out of sorts." The clerk chuckled, laying the paper on his board-desk. "Got down here: Started at SB. Now where I come from that means sumbitch."

Bat broke into a hearty laugh. "Well, I'll tell ya, we started at a sagebrush."

"Just dying to hear about these other markings." The clerk joined in with a good laugh, too. "SB to BH to SD to BC and back to SB—don't reckon I'm getting onto this Panhandle civil engineering."

"It's like this, we started at a sagebrush, went to a buffalo head, then to a skunk den, and from there to a buffalo chip, then back to the sagebrush."

The clerk looked at Bat, amused. "Have to admit, makes sense. The State ought to make these official; never seen this logo. Bat you know there's no iron stakes here on the prairie?"

"Thought about that, too."

"Down on the creek sometime you might bring back some cottonwood staves and put one at each corner; it'd make the old boy happy. Here's another $10 gold piece. Good job."

Bat replied, "Thanks, not bad money." Chuckling, he added, "A hundred years from now people may be scratching their head over my surveying."

The clerk nodded, smiling. Bat watched one of his cottonwood staves take root. It soon grew into a big tree—a hanging tree, a Mobeetie landmark.

16 *Buggy Crisis*

The 4th of July coming up and the Lady Gay's move from Hidetown called for a big celebration...just a little something Henry Fleming and Bill Thompson hatched up. People were jubliant. "It's gonna be the biggest happenings in the settlement since we moved from Hidetown!" Henry exclaimed. Mobeetie loved to celebrate, drink to anything and bet on everything, the social life of pioneers for miles around. The settlement was a lonely far-out place, but the people were a proud bunch. The Englishmen from the old country were amused by the life style but they joined in, too. Cornmeal was scarce but the dance floor got a rub-down with cornmeal and the hairy side of a buffalo skin. The slickest dance floor in town—the only one in town.

But Henry saw right off that everything wasn't perfect. The sophisticated ladies of the European land buyers let him know right off they wouldn't get on the dance floor with those "Old smelly hide hunters and drunk cowboys." But Henry Fleming was a politican, he could handle it.

Bob Brennan was buying medicine for Bessie at J. J. Long's General Store when Bat run into him. "Guess you and Bessie's going to the big shindig tonight?" Bat questioned.

"Don't reckon as to how," Bob reasoned. "She's just feeling tolerable. Gettin' her some purgative now. You?"

"Yup. Figured to take Molly if you all haven't planned on something else; done some talking about it."

"Well, ain't talked to her Ma 'bout it," Bob drawled in his slow and easy way, "but understand there's a right respectable bunch gonna be there; big dogs looking for ranches. Be some goodlooking hosses and fancy buggies, too."

"Looking for a buggy myself, that is if Molly would like to go."

"No need'o that, use mine," Bob insisted.

Bat was as happy as a pig in a peanut patch...got the horse, the buggy, and the girl. He couldn't ask for anything more.

Bob was still at the store when Bat hustled on down to the Brennan home. Molly was currying the buggy pony.

"Uh-hi," Bat come on in his shyness, "Brownie's a pretty horse and your Dad is a right good guy, too...said to use his horse and buggy tonight, that is we go to the shindig."

Bat was learning fast in this courting business. He figured if he said the wrong thing to Molly it'd be like missing a "dead shot" at a buffalo. But the way he attracted women with his good-looks and manly charm he'd soon have the girls wrapped around his little finger. Molly had him excited.

"Oh yes, Mr. Bat, Brown—."

"Uh, just plain Bat."

She offered, "Oh, I reckon I'd just be most delighted if Mama'll let me."

Like most Southern girls, Molly was brought up to respect her parents.

Everybody who was anybody and a few undesirable nobodies would be at the Lady Gay. Henry Fleming and Bill Thompson was surprised the way people went all out for the celebration. They loved to celebrate—a round for the quick-draw winner—new settler, anything.

93

The town was isolated. New-comers had the feeling they were in a no-man's land. Dodge City was two hundred miles north and the Texas State Capitol over 500 miles south. "A helluva long ways by wagon," a Judge once said. The only State people Bat ever saw in the Panhandle was stake driving surveyors. But the Indians soon parted many a surveyor with their hair. Pioneers fogged to the Panhandle for the buffalo gravy, and now they were ready to celebrate. The night of July 4th, 1875, buffalo hunters, land agents, visiting ranchers, gamblers, European investors, cowboys, dance-hall girls, gunslingers, horse thieves, and military men made the party.

A new citizen in town, a Kentucky school teacher, wanted to join in on the fun, too. But the lady felt a little out of place. Back in Kentucky she read an ad in her hometown paper: "Wives wanted, Texas Panhandle Where Money Grows, Whiskey Flows, And Women Glow!" She lit out for the Texas Panhandle, be nothing but fun coming to Texas. She'd get a job teaching school in Texas—maybe a husband, too. But when she got to Mobeetie, to her surprise there was no schoolhouse within two hundred miles —but she got her man.

Bob Brennan wasn't fooled when Bat wanted to use his buggy. After all the Lady Gay was only around the corner and down a piece.

They left Molly's house at evening twilight. Down the road, on a little downhill slope, the buggy ran down against Brownie. The buggy-britching-harness tightened hard against her hips. Bat Masterson saw a crisis coming on. "Whoa Brownie!"

17 *July 4th Party*

Shuffling their feet, Bat and Molly almost broke a leg. An unsanitary buggy-horse without any consideration, any hesitation, relieved herself in the buggy floorboard. "The fragance is not there!" Molly giggled. That eased things. They relaxed with a big laugh.

"Nothing to it, really," Bat remarked. "Just nature at work....Whoa Brownie! I can handle it with a buffalo chip." They were soon on their way.

Out of town buggies, wagons, and saddlehorses crowded around the Lady Gay's hitching rail. They came from miles around, a good time and business opporunities was on their mind. It's been said, "The ranchers come to the Panhandle country looking for land, the gamblers come to take 'em by sleight of hand, and the girls come to roll 'em in the sand." And that's the way it was.

The noise died down when Bat and Molly walked through the Lady Gay's swinging bat-wing doors. The English girls stared and asked, "Could this be happening on the Great American Desert, this dashing gay-blade in the pin-stripe gambler's dress-up... tall, handsome, dark hair, and look at that mustache—his smile!" He had the ladies in a dither. And the girl in the pink party dress with beautiful blue eyes, wavy dark hair, and cute dimples; a prairie show-case, too. She had the guys locoed; men squirmed. An old southern buffalo hunter nudged his sidekick, "Ain't never seen nothin' like that'un. Purty's a red heifer in a patch'o daisies."

Henry Fleming ran the Lady Gay show. "Now listen

up!" he yelled, but the noise was too much, the party-goers paid him no mind. He pulled his old .45, blowed the rafters, and exclaimed, "Now everybody listen up. Got a band and want you to know about 'em! Guess you could call 'em the Duke Mixtures. Got a cowboy and a bartender on the fiddles, got a buffalo hunter and rancher on git-tars, and on the banjo and jug, got this jolly Buffalo soldier from out here at Fort Elliot...and, oh yeah, by the time he got here the jug was empty!" The crowd yelled and Henry went on, "And now on the pi-an-o that me and my podner, Bill Thompson, had freighted all the way from St. Louis...Slats Slattery!"

The whooping and hollering rung the rafters. Big stuff for Mobeetie, big stuff anywhere in the West. Most pioneer communities were lucky to have a fiddler and guitar picker for dances. But Mobeetie's motley bunch come up with an undreamed of band. The old meadow muffin mashers were fired up and ready to dance.

Henry soon got on with the program. He boomed, "Now, the six matchless musicians!"

A jovial buffalo hunter in the crowd yelled, "Would you call 'em Slat Slattery's Sleazy Six?" There was more laughter; they whooped it up.

Henry ignored him. "Everybody grab your podner and let's shake a leg!"

Bat and Molly never missed a set. She was only seventeen, and now she wondered how come she had missed all this excitement and fun over the years. Some dance-hall gals were oldtimers at sixteen, but she had been brought up to be a church-going girl. Bat knew she'd never been in a saloon before they came West. The Brennans' never made excuses about their religion. Molly was baptized back in a Mississippi creek by a visiting "hell fire and brimstone" preacher. But now the fun-loving kid had grown up, however she felt guilty as all hell when she walked in the Lady Gay saloon.

Molly's Mama knew she couldn't keep her beautiful daughter tied to her apron strings from now on. In this wicked place she cringed at the thought her "baby" would "go to the bad." Molly was popular, she had the looks and charm...put young men to scheming and old men to dreaming.

It was a fun night for Bat and Molly...a fun night for pretty blond Beth Barton, too. She always managed to be carrying on with Bat during the music breaks; a little too friendly, Molly thought. Beth was a "looker" too, beautiful green eyes with a little mischievous glint. She drew men's attention with her cute perky smile and chesty front. Her Jim was wimpy but strutted around like a little bantam rooster. He couldn't keep his eyes off Molly, quick glanced her when Beth wasn't watching. Molly knew the Bartons, knew she could hold her own with Beth anytime. The young Barton couple loved to socalize. Beth would never miss a party.

The smoke filled room was crowded with sot drunks, so polluted they couldn't hit the floor with their hats. A wobbling cowboy went down swinging and flattened out on the floor with a thud.

"Throw him out!" someone yelled.

Another shot back, "Throw 'im out hell—pour 'im out!"

The cowboy jerked a button off an English girl's dress and flaired it open, but she disregarded it, so drunk, too, she could hardly stay on her feet. The boy's sidekicks drug him out. Henry took charge.

"The cowboy just slipped on a cricket!" He bellowed, "Hit it Slats, everybody dance!"

Far into the night the boys kept swinging the girls. Henry finally went to the make-shift stage and exclaimed, "Now want'cha to listen up!" The noisy bunch paid him no mind. So as usual he pulled his .45, and blowed the rafters. "Time for the rooster to crow, shut her down Slats with a fast one!"

Dancing, Bat and Molly swung around close to people gathered at the front door. Some damn fool stuck his foot out and tripped Bat. He hit the floor and Molly piled down on top of him.

"Sorry, Molly," he apologized.

"It's O. K, I'm O. K, I saw him!"

Bat didn't wait to hear no more. "Stay here, I'll get that sonovabitch!" He jumped up, pulled Molly up, then rushed for the door. Bumping into Zeb, he asked, "Did you see him, get a look at him; know who it was?"

"Yeah, there at the door lamp. Pigeyed fool nearly knocked me down; Mangy Dogface!"

Zeb knew Bat's thinking, knew too the young guys played games even if it was smoking guns. Falling on the floor humilitated Bat, but of course this kind of stuff wasn't unusual in Mobeetie. Just don't get caught!

Dogface done a fast disappearing act, but here was Zeb spruced out like a country lawyer. His shirt was wrinkled, and his britches shrunk when he sand-washed them in the creek, but the best he had. Maybe his clothes did look slept-in, he could do no better. His fancy leather "spenders," and wide leather belt kept his pants riding high. The little gully of tobacco juice that usually trickled down his gray beard had been washed out to show a lush growth of white mane.

A crowd was gathered around Molly when Bat came back. The girls embarrassed him. They offered apologies. Bat Masterson didn't want sympathy. He wanted the guy that tripped him. The party was over. Bat and Molly groped in the dark until they found their buggy. Brownie was standing at ease, not like most horses' that paw the earth to go home after standing for hours. Bat said, "Molly, Baby, it's dark, but let me see if Dogface is up to his old tricks." He checked as best he could in the dark and added, "Don't think he's bothered a thing; nothing wrong." They got in the buggy and Bat pulled the lines; felt one snap in two. Brownie went in a circle. "Yup, he's been slipping around—one of his old tricks," Bat said, "The sleezy bastard cut one line almost in two and when I pulled on it, it come apart." Bat tied the rein together. They soon drove off.

Bat couldn't figure it out, how had he missed all this girl business? Out on the buffalo trail he dreamed about pretty girls, but now he had the real thing. The prettiest girl in town was setting by his warm side on the buggy seat—Molly Brennan! Ah, clutching in, her hot lips were like in hog-heaven! The buggy pony stopped. Bat went for his gun and grabbed for the lines.

"Bat, what's going on?" Molly asked, uneasy.

"Nothing Honey, really," he replied, relieving her anxiety. "The lines just came loose from the whip-holder and dragging the ground. Don't worry, we'll just let the pony take us home, take her time—lines dragging."

"Why not?" Molly asked. "It's been a fun night."

"Yup, beats shooting buffaloes!" Bat replied, chuckling.

Brownie stopped the buggy at the Brennan hitching-post. Molly's Mother thought of everything. Her "baby" wouldn't stumble over sagebrush with the lamp in the window. Bat kissed Molly goodnight, stabled the horse and went home. Romance was in the air, on his mind. The couple's burning flame of love was hot as a three dollar stove.

18 *Ranches*

Along about sunup it was a whistling meadow lark that brought Bat out of a deep sleep. His love for Molly was on his mind when he crawled out of bed. A new day, barking dogs, nickering horses, and people stirring around. He dressed, strolled down the street, and soon met-up with Jim Barton.

"Ah'll buy the morning coffee," Jim suggested.

"Morning, Jim," Bat replied. "Take you up on that."

At Weed's Water Hole, Jim continued, "Quite a shindig at the Lady Gay last night. You didn't miss a set with that good looking girl." Jim liked to pry. "Didn't know if you'd make it this morning."

Bat could see a little jealousy there but he didn't know why. The guy had a pretty wife.

"Yup, figured the other girls didn't want this old shaggie shooter with two left feet mashing their toes."

Jim wasn't too impressed, knew Bat was a good dancer. "Get this new house built me and Beth's throwing a big wing-ding fling on the 'Diamond."

"Hear you're bringing in Diamond Brand cattle."

"Few, from San Antonio...three thousand cows and a hundred and thirty bulls as soon as the government gets these renegade Indians cleared out." Jim and Beth were adding 300,000 acres to their South Texas Diamond Brand.

Jim Springer's ranch has been called the first in the Panhandle, but Charles Goodnight was figuring on a spread in Palo Duro Canyon at about the same time.

Then there was the T-bar brand, U-Bar's, Bugbee and others laying out blocks, too. Henry Cresswell had laid out 2,100,000 acres in the north Panhandle. And it was told, on good authority, that Wyatt and Jim Earp was figuring on a spread in the same area. Ranches in the Panhandle were soon running over 3,000,000 acres and stocked with over 100,000 head of cattle.

"Morning, fellers," George Jenkins greeted. He was ready to do some ranching when the Indians, surveys, and land titles were cleared. A big man, easy going, flowing iron-gray hair under his white hat, looked every bit the range boss. The trim on his handlebar mustache matched the horn-shape of his cattle.

Turning to George, Jim asked, "Bringing in some stuff now —hear you'll run 'round 75,000 head?"

"Few, ten thousand dogies, yearlings past, wanted to get started here in the Panhandle. I hear Cresswell's bringing in Colorado stock for the bar CC's; 25,000 head."

"It's a start on their hundred thousand," Bat said. "You stocking any new breeds like Herefords or Angus?"

George replied, "We'll run some later, but you know there's not a bovine living that can take this country like the Longhorns. It takes cattle with long horns to handle wolves and panthers. Horny more ways than one, too." He chuckled, and continued, "Take them bulls, horny critters can take care of fifty cows and still be looking for more young heifers. I figure it'll be Herefords someday."

"Yeah," Jim come in, "when the buffaloes are wiped out the wolves are going to be working on the cattle; kill a grown horse if they're hungry."

"That's right," George agreed. "Wolves, renegade Indians, blizzards, and twenty miles to water; not going to be easy."

"Oh, I can handle it," Jim bragged.

Jim was a cocky little guy that loved to talk big. He told it around that his extra high heels kept his boots from slipping through the stirrups. Bat and George knew that, and knew too Jim had high heels built up so he could look his pretty blond wife straight in the eyes.

Bat headed for the door. He turned, "See you guys tonight."

He stepped out the door and glanced around; anything could happen. Dogface was back in town. Shooting a man in the back was not unheard of in Mobeetie, Texas. A sudden shuffling! Bat went for his gun—relaxed, and soon holstered up.

"Hi," Beth's voice had a pleasant ring. Well educated, she knew how to handle words...and men. She stood by the building wearing a big smile.

"Why-wh, Mrs. Barton," Bat stammered. "Didn't expect to see you; looking for Jim?"

Bat had paid the little blonde doll only polite attention at the dance, but Beth was worth a second look anytime. Anyway, it was Molly, no pretty face was changing his mind, although the dance hall gals were working on it.

"No. Just call me Beth," she insisted. Moving farther back, leading Bat between the buildings. "You wouldn't dance with me last night."

Bat was easy-going, had lots of friends, but beautiful women—well, he couldn't figure it out. They sort of put him on edge; the prettier the tighter he got.

"You and Jim were doing O K, and there was George and Pearlie; you all were swapping out."

She rolled her green eyes and gave him a sweet smile. "Yes, but no one dances like the Peacock...that's what I heard them call you last night."

"Don't know if that's a compliment," Bat replied.

"Absolutely," she let him know right off. "Stood tall,

102

above them all, and dressed for the occasion. Seen nothing like it since I was in school."

The saloon door squeaked open but Beth was determined. She kept moving back. Prostitutes were usually hustling men on the street but Beth had something in mind, too.

"I suppose Jim's in there?" She nodded toward the saloon.

"Yup, him and George Jenkins."

"Talking about his bulls, I bet?"

"Well, yes."

"Gets his kicks watching his bulls; way he gets his education. If you ask me he's still in kindergarten."

Ranch women don't mince words when it comes to their horses and cattle.

Now, Bat was thinking Jim's performance as a lover was more like a gelding. The door squeaked again and they heard the same stuff—bulls. Of course ranchers talk about their livestock when they get together, but Beth thought Jim was more interested in his horses and cattle than in his wife. She felt neglected. She looked up with her glistening green eyes and a pretty smile that promised, "See you tonight, Prairie Peacock!"

Bat still didn't know about that "Peacock" stuff she'd hung on him. Seemed Stud or Stallion had a better ring. But Beth liked the handle, she thought the birds on their South Texas ranch were beautiful; their plumage unusual.

Beth went around the corner and Bat headed for J. J. Long's store with his head in the air. He couldn't figure out Beth Barton. But he did see King run out of the store, dodging around, jumped on his horse and whipped out.

19 *Rockabye Buggy*

Bat had business at his surveying office. "Hi J. J," he spoke, then added, "Gotta have some smokings; chawin's too."

"Been thinking about you, Bat. How'd the dance go?"

"Good. Missed you."

"Well," J. J. replied, in his slow and easy way, "like I've said before, used to never miss one of them shindigs, but since that Redskin messed up my leg with that arrow can't do much leg shaking now; just watch, that's about it."

"I was a little embarrassed, tripped and fell on the dance floor," Bat replied.

Mr. Long said, "Yeah, Dogface was in here blowing around, shooting off his mouth, said nobody was getting his woman; got diarrhea off the mouth. That's another thing he gloats over, is tripping people. I'll tell you, Bat, that guy's a damn fool, boasting like a kid. Ah've been kicking around in this old world quite a bit. Many a so-called gunfighter's just a yellow coward. Somebody'll get him sooner or later. Old Dogface there, never starts anything unless he's got the drop on ya. Sneaks around here, starts a big ruckus, but runs like hell when he sees Bat Masterson coming...got the town on edge, not gonna grow, new settlers move on. He knows it's coming, knows you'll take him on any day of the week; burns him up. He's out to get you this last day of celebration."

"Uncle Johnny, I've always said, I'd live to be a hundred and turn to an old gray mule. Once went back to

Dodge when I was scouting and a fracas was going on there. A guy was laid out with his throat cut. I'm thinking now this Dogface King guy was in that mix-up."

"You know," Uncle Johnny replied, "Dodge is sort of like this settlement, it's hard to remember any particular one. He treats me O K, but if it takes smoking guns to stop his kind...." Uncle Johnny paused, "Well, I know of one buffalo hunter 'turned town surveyor that's not aiming to be on the wrong end of that gun."

Bat walked out the door and glanced west. The sun was setting. It seemed the big ball of fire had rolled to a stop on the western horizon; soon sank behind the hills. In the northwest were beautiful jagged thunderheads. But back southwest swirls of white clouds, streaked with glowing pinks, was the only thing left of a summer shower. The clouds were unusual, but Bat didn't have time to gaze at the sky. He was in a cloud himself. Molly was waiting.

It was late evening, night was coming on when Bat and Molly walked through the swinging doors at the Lady Gay. Friends he hadn't seen in months showed up to make the last big day of celebration. The fourth of July revelry was going on all over town, in saloons up and down the street, and on Featherbed Hill. Horny hunters that hadn't seen a woman in months were shelling out. Everybody was having fun where whiskey flowed, money growed, and wild women glowed!

Bat had the right to strut a little. Dancing, he had the best-looking girl in town in his arms; beautiful, but good with a needle too. She dropped her party dress-front down to reveal a generous amount of hour-glass figure. To enhance the deep cleavage, she added a little lace here and there. Her needlecraft worked. She got men's attention and stirred green-eyed envy in the souls of women. Her attractive get-up shocked a few people, a little bold, yes, but she didn't play second fiddle to any girl in town. Since her mysterous friend, the beautiful Frenchy (Elizabeth) McGraw lit in Mobeetie, she was enjoying great popularity, too. Any self-respecting man would appreciate either lady.

Jim tapped Bat's shoulder. "May I have this dance, Molly?"

Bat let go of Molly and Beth fell in his arms. She pressed in hard against him, wasted no time, got his attention! "I love your thing in front," she said, staring in the half-dark room. "Way it hangs, stands out."

She come on to him in a loving sort of way. He stammered, "I-ah, yes'um, reckon so—you do?"

These girls were something else to Bat Masterson, but the ol' buffalo hunter was beginning to handle women as naturallike as he did his guns.

Slats, the band leader, swung into a new Stephen Foster song; Beautiful Dreamer. Was Beth dreaming? "Yes," she continued, "love it, stands out—unusual, nice size."

"Well, thanks." Bat couldn't figure it out. Was something wrong, something unbuttoned?

Beth touched him at the waist. "Beautiful gold chain and fob dangling from your watch pocket glistens; love it!"

Bat and Beth waltzed to Slat's music and never missed a beat but no one knew what was going on in the dim-lit smoke filled room; nobody cared. A good dancer, she loved dancing with Bat Masterson, a man-handling woman. Always there was girls around for entertainment in lusty Mobeetie. He soon got back with Molly and danced away into the night.

Dogface was back in town, sneaking around, with his old cronies playing the game; same old tricks. Pulling their dirty stuff it had to be dark before the full moon come up. A bur under the saddle is bad medicine any-time for a saddlehorse. But for a buggy-horse, Dogface King knew one better. It'd work on a gentle horse that stood at ease; it'd work on Brownie.

Bat and Molly strolled to the buggy. The big Texas moon had broken the eastern horizon and was flooding the prairie with soft moonglow. She raised her dress and lifted her foot to the high buggy step. Oops, something ripped.

It had been months since Molly and her Mother had seen a drygoods store. Uncle Johnny stocked a little stuff for the women, but if they ran out of clothing "fixins" there was nothing they could do...the West, a man's world. Molly busted her britches. Was it the "Pure Gold" flour sack bloomers Bat had seen on the clothes-line? The pioneer girls were proud of their flour sack drawers whipped out with needle and thread, but cornmeal-sack britches were down right miserable; chafed and chapped.

If Molly's bottom was bare it wasn't on Bat's mind. He knew Dogface was sneaking around; Molly did too. Bat wanted her mind on romance. He looked around, could find nothing wrong with the horse and buggy. The weird guy had more tricks than one he gloated over. For courting couples he loved to fill the buggy seat with the worse stinking thing he could find, like horse ma-nure.

On the way home Molly snuggled in close. Bat ho'd the horse, wrapped the lines around the whip-holder, put his arms around her, and laid on a few kisses. But she wasn't relaxed, something bothering, something chewing on her?

"Molly, Baby," he said, "everybody knows this guy is crazy that's running around here keeping the town tore up; insane, jealous, coldblooded killer. I love you and come hell or high water, not for King over my dead body, am I leaving you; not leaving town!"

Bat was no Romeo but regardless of how he said it she knew he meant it. "My dear, I know, but I wanta tell you somethin' —he's come back to kill you. I had a horrible dream, I know it sounnds crazy, but in a gunfight you won but lost."

He looked at her questioning. "Now what kind of talk is that—won but lost. Honey don't we all have dreams, good and bad. 'Don't believe in that stuff, sounds like a riddle; won but lost?"

"Can't forget it, the mystery haunts me, I dreamed...."

He broke in, "My Dear, let's get our minds off the nut. Cheer up Sweetheart, I'm not losing any sleep over King's threats; gonna be a meetin'-up. Riddles, bad dreams, nightmares, don't know about that, never bothered me."

She was worried, troubled, he pulled her in close and with his gentle power of persuasion she relaxed. Snuggling, her charms would make any ol' cowboy jump out of his boots. And soon she was having fun, too. The buffalo hunters and cowboys hungry for romance didn't fool around when it come to loving girls but crowded in the little buggy it cramped Bat's style.

The lovers couldn't get fixed. Molly squirmed and turned. Her wrapped around dress was pulling. She was in distress and as usual Bat Masterson was willing to help straighten things out. Shoving his hand deep in the buggy seat to lift her and free up the dress it just so happened he run his hand in the rip of her homemade underwear. The touch of her silk-smooth skin...ol' Masterson went locoed. He held her tight, her lips were luscious. She loved her Bat Masterson. He said, "Molly darling, this is it, this living and loving beats shooting buffaloes and kissing horses anytime."

He scooted over, scooted out, scooted up, scooted down, he couldn't get fixed. Courting in a little one-horse buggy flustered long legged cowboys. Long legs stretched across the dash rail was a shin-skinner. Soon the little buggy began to rock slow and easy; springs squeaking.

"Let me outta here!" Molly screamed, breaking loose, "There's mice in the buggy, mice in the seat, I heard 'em!" Bat burst out laughing. "Squeaky springs my Dear, just squeaky springs."

"Oh." She relaxed. They scrunched in tight again, the buggy rocked slow and easy—faster, the rhythmic springs grew louder, louder. Suddenly all hell broke loose.

"Whoa, Brownie, whoa!" Bat raised his voice, "That damn King is driving nails in his coffin!"

Another Dogface King trick. Stretching his legs across the rail, Bat kicked the buggy horse in the tail. She went wild, snorted, gassed up, reared and bucked like a bronc. The mare soon kicked out the dashboard. Bat shoved Molly to the floorboard to miss the flying hooves. He grabbed for the lines on the whip-holder but they were gone, dragging the ground.

The horse dug her feet in the ground, jerking the buggy, and hit a dead-run. She swung the thing around the corner so fast it balanced on two wheels. Bat reached for the lines, but they were dragging under the buggy. He leaned far, grabbing, sweeping his hand back and forth with no luck. The lovers were in trouble, big trouble. The mare headed for home with the old buggy swinging back and forth on two wheels all the way. Racing full gait she soon plowed her feet in the ground at the Brennan hitching-post. The sudden stop lifted the back wheels off the ground. Molly, shaking with fright, leaped out and made a dash for the house—outhouse.

Bat knew the trick, knew it had been pulled in

Mobeetie before; pure devilment. He unharnessed the horse and found what he expected—cockleburs tied to the harness-crupper, the part that goes under the horse's tail. And the kick drove hunderds of needle-sharp burs into the mare's most tender parts.

20 *Rattlesnake Bed Mate*

The next morning at about the crack of dawn a knock on Bat's door woke him up. Not all that early but after partying all night he could stand more sleep. Was old Zeb wanting another hunting partner?

"Yeah, who is it?"

"Lt. Baldwin and Captain Arrington—Texas Ranger."

Lt. Baldwin and Capt. Arrington? Everybody in Texas knew of the Captain...his reputation as a Ranger, knew too he was usually looking for outlaws! Bat had scouted with Lt. Baldwin but why did he bring the Captain?

"Just a minute!" Bat yelled. He slipped on his britches and buckled on his guns. It sounded like the Lieutenant but Bat took no chances. He cracked the door.

"Bat Masterson himself—good to see you!" Lt. Baldwin gestured, "Captain Arrington, Texas Ranger."

"Ah, Lieutenant, it's been too long; come on in. Captain, glad to know ya. Yeah, Lt. Baldwin and I go back a long ways."

Capt. Arrington said, "Bat as you know this Panhandle country is still wild and untamed. The outlaws are drifting in here and raising all kinds of hell with the hunters...'got 'em stirred up, even got the renegade Indians wrung in on this horse stealing—running wild along the Indian Territory border. The ring leader rides a strawberry roan."

Lt. Baldwin spoke up. "The Army wants to know, too, what's going on...the trouble along the border, get

111

to the bottom of it, maybe move in a few troops. It's like the Captain said, mixed-up affair, the outlaws and renegade Redskins are in cahoots. You've done some good work for the Service in the past. 'Thought you might do a little more scouting...same pay as before, seventy-five and usual fifty dollar bonus."

Bat could handle the danger part, use the extra money, and still have his surveying job. "I'll take it," he said.

The Captain added, "The such as Dutch Henry and Chummy Jones are running hog wild in these parts?"

"What I heard," Bat replied.

"Run into 'em or Redskins do what you have to do."

"Be on your way pretty soon?" Lt. Baldwin asked.

"Yup, right now," Bat replied. His visitors soon left. He gathered up his rain-slicker and bedroll then hustled over to see Uncle Johnny. And he had to get word to Molly, too, but Molly and her Mother would be asleep. Molly danced into the wee hours of the night and her Mother always waited up for her "baby." Uncle Johnny would let her know, she'd be in the store.

"Uh, Uncle Johnny, got any jerky? I-I mean, would you tell Molly something?"

J. J. chuckled. "Going to feed her jerky?" Mr. Long got a big kick out of kidding Bat. "You know it's a long hard ride and I'll help you any way I can. Looks you're ready to go. Here's your hardtack and jerky; saddlebag of stuff."

"I don't understand, got my grub and stuff ready."

Uncle Johnny smiled. "Well, the Captain and Ranger Newt Locke rode in together; old friends of mine. They're fearless officers, pack big guns, and they'll go after any outlaw alive. Told them I couldn't think of a better man than Bat Masterson to help 'em out a little. Molly will understand."

"Much oblige," Bat said, and rode off.

When he left going southeast the sun was breaking over the hills. He rode by old Hidetown. People had moved out but thousands of hides were still stacked on the creek-bottom. Hunters were out on the prairie but going farther to find the vanishing herds. Sixty million buffaloes were about wiped out and the Indians would soon be corraled in Indian Territory. Hidetown was no longer a bustling community, nothing much left, but there was Henry Fleming's rock house. To Bat, it stood like a monument and still stands today.

Old Zeb was still holed up in Hidetown, (now called Sweetwater) but hadn't got out yet; still in bed? Fighting bedbugs all night, Bat figured; late for any buffalo hunter. His team was in the corral. Bat let him sleep, rode on, held southeast and soon come to Bronco Creek. There was no tres on Bronco creek. The stream was clear and grass grew wild on the banks but the water was no good; gyppie.

Fat lazy lobo wolves slinked around patches of shinoak. They feasted on the thousands of buffalo carcasses the hunters left scattered across the prairie. Bat glanced up. Buzzards living off of buffalo, too, circled lazily overhead. The sun was bearing down, Coalie's shoulders were white with foam, but Willow Creek's good water wasn't too far.

Coalie shied around the prairie dog holes that dotted the prairie; prairie dog towns were rattlesnake country. Coalie hated the snakes. A rattler's "buzz" and the horse would break into a wild bucking pitch. The tough little prairie dogs often dig their holes to water, maybe a hundred feet deep. Bat would never run his horse through a prairie dog town even in daylight. Night herding Cowboys hated them—like suicide racing their horses through the almost straight down holes. Horses with broken legs was the usual thing. The rodents inhabited a region that stretched from the Gulf of Mexico to Canada. Bat kept riding, twisting and turning in the saddle, gandering, always alert, watching for outlaws and Indians.

A cottonwood tree loomed ahead, then a small grove of willows came in sight. Willow Creek! At the creek, Coalie dunked his nose in the water up to his eyes. Bat come off the horse tired and thirsty. He never thought of laying on his belly to quench his thirst. The Indians would love to spear-nail him to the ground. He took his hat off, creased the brim, dipped it in the water and swigged it down again and again.

The sun was sinking behind the purple hills and the coyotes howling when Bat pulled the saddle off Coalie. The horse was wrung out. Bat laid the saddle blanket on the damp sandbar for his bed and the saddle for his pillow. With the rope around the horse's neck and the other end tied to the saddlehorn, it'd give Coalie the full thirty five feet free to graze. No hobbles here. Coalie's tug on the rope had saved Bat's life time after time. Make no mistake about it, when a man lays down to sleep in outlaw and Indian country, wild animals and rattlesnakes, he'll think twice; will he wake up the next morning or will he have to move out in a hurry?

Along about daylight a stirring around the campsite shook Bat out of a deep sleep. Hard to rouse out but something had woke him up. Something was going on around the camp. Was it a wolf, a horse thief, a rabid skunk? He suddenly broke into a cold sweat, fear paralyzed him. He heard the deadly buzz of a rattlesnake. He slowly opened his eyes.

The snake had his head poked up through the saddle hand-hold five inches from Bat's face...stone still like he was froze there. The snake found a warm sheepskin saddle-liner in the cool of the night. Bat didn't move, hardly breathing, but he could see the snake from the corner of his eye. Just a blink, a sneeze, a cough, and Bat Masterson could kiss this old world goodbye.

21 *Pigeyes Looney*

Coalie had been Bat's life-saver many times but never at a time like this. Bat slowly, very s-l-o-w-l-y, puckered his lips and gave Coalie his usual bobwhite whistle to let the horse know it was time to saddle up. Coalie, as usual, came on with his little low nicker, threw his head up, jerked the rope, shook the saddle, and the big rattler ducked back under it. Bat had no love for rattlesnakes. He laid him out with a handy stick and saddled up.

Deep in country that straddled the Texas-Indian Nation border Bat watched for outlaw hideouts. The murderous thieves that were holed-up in isolated gypsum caves were stealing horses in Indian Territory, and giving Texas hunters pure hell, too. Pioneers called it a no-man's land. Ten miles east, beyond the hills, was the Indian Nation border. Reining up at the North Fork River crossing, Bat noticed fresh horse tracks coming out of the water. Three horses were headed south. Huh, an odd track in the wet sand—King? Bat kept heading south, too. Salt Fork lay a long hot ride ahead. The horse could take it, but the saddle seat got hard.

Following a trail, Bat soon splashed his horse through the narrow Salt Fork stream and reined up. Tracks at the river crossing indicated the three horses were still headed south. Looking ahead out a quarter-mile or so he saw two horses standing by a tree. Urging Coalie on he noticed it wasn't the horses' he'd been tracking. Could it be an old buffalo hunter's camp and his team-horses?

116

Bat rode in closer. The skinny horses were rope-tied to a horse-high cedar tree, the ground bare, no wagon, no teepee, no sign of anything but the horses. Behind the cedar a small gypsum bluff poked up ten/fifteen feet high with a cave at the base big enough for a man to walk in. No buffalo hunter. Bringing Coalie in for a closer look, next to the tethered horses, Bat wondered about the stacked rocks that half-hid the cave entrance; what was behind them?

"Woof-woof!" Suddenly a big shaghound shot-out from under the tree and came at Bat. The dog slid, plowed his feet in the ground at Coalie's back feet...froze, growled; snarling viciously, he showed his fangs. He soon moved around— threatening, and suddenly nipped Coalie's hocks. Coalie jumped and Masterson almost lost his seat. A little coaxing and the horse simmered down. Bat eased up but still gandering around trying to figure things out.

"That's 'bout damn fur 'nough. Stop it rat there!" a raspy voice called out, coming from behind the cedar.

Slowly turning his head, Bat was soon looking down the barrel of a buffalo rifle. A mangy looking guy stepped from behind the tree. "What'cha damn business, nohow?"

Bat just happened to stumble across the man, but thought he had him figured out; a horse thief that had been run out of Kansas. And now he was part of the trouble along the border.

"Just passing through, headin' south," Bat said.

"Ain't headin' nowhere till we do some talkin'. Ain't one'o them thar Texas Ranger's air ya?"

"Surveyor, laying out ranch-land between the Canadian and Red River; hang out at Mobeetie."

"Humf, heard of that damn sinful place, killins'n all. Git off ya damn hoss. Reckon ya look all right; gonna have a drink."

"Name's Masterson, Bat Masterson. Didn't get yours?"

At first the man acted like he didn't hear Bat. But he suddenly perked up; something rung a bell. Squinting his pigeyes under his old black hat, the little dirty weasel looked Bat over from "head to tail." The old man's close-set eyes were sunk-in deep under fox-like bushy eyebrows; a picture of the devil himself. He slurped tobacco juice and drug his sleeve across his salt-and-pepper lice-laden beard. He spewed. "Any ya damn business, Looney—Pigeyes Looney."

Bat thought the old foxy bastard was a little smarter than he looked. Bat got a whiff of foul odor that curled his nose. He glanced around, snorting and gagging, asked, "Been in these parts long—'believe something's dead around here?"

They started toward the cave with Pigeyes backing, walking sideways, watching every move Bat made.

"Reckon 'can say I have if any ya damn business," he snarled, and offered no more.

They moved past the cedar. Bat soon discovered the source of the foul odor.

Pigeyes squirted a load of tobacco juice. "Thought that old dawg drug 'im off."

Bat tried to shift the conversation. "Wondered about the Indians, giving any trouble?"

The question seemed to insult old Pigeyes. "Naw, that crazy sumbitch layin' there asked the same damn question...wanted to know if'n I'se doin' any hoss swappin' with them Redskins, or this friend of mine that rides a red roan. None'o his damn business. Went on to say somethin' 'bout stealin' hosses; didn't like what he said. But I wuz neighborly, offered him a drink; turned me down flat. Hell, ain't no sumbitch too good to drink with old Pigeyes. Wait here, git us lil' snort of redeye juice."

Now Bat knew the red roan rider had been the old man's visitor. Pigeyes backed all the way to the cave, never taking his eyes off Bat. Bat had the feeling the old man kept his eyes on him while he was inside, too. Bat looked at the dead man on the blood-splattered rock slab; drilled in the face with a high powered rifle. Half of his face was missing. Pigeyes soon come back. He shadowed his six-gun with one hand and offered the rusty tin cup to Bat with the other.

"Straight whiskey," he sneered, "ceptin' added a little hoss piss to make it go further."

The stink around the place was impossible and Bat was glad to let Pigeyes know what he thought of his whiskey.

"No thanks, don't care for your whiskey."

The old man exploded. "Hell, I said, ain't no sumbitch too good to drink with old Pigeyes!"

Gunshots echoed against the gypsum bluff.

Texas Cowboys on the Dodge City trail in borrowed dress-up clothes for picture making. Carey Dysart, center, father of the author.

The Battle of Adobe Walls 50th Anniversary, June 27, 1924. Only Andrew Johnson (No. 1) who fought along with Bat Masterson in the conflict was present. Bill Tilghman (No. 2) was shot and killed three months after this picture was made. The author (No. 3)

Photo courtesy of Panhandle Plains Historical Museum, Canyon, Texas

Mobeetie early day leading citizens. Front row L-R, Newt Locke, Texas Ranger; Emanuel Dubbs, first Texas Panhandle Judge; Johnny Long, Pioneer Merchant; Back row L-R, Joe Mason, ex-Dodge City Deputy Sheriff; Captain Arrington, Texas Ranger; Cape Willingham, former stage-driver.

Photo courtesy of Panhandle Plains Historical Museum, Canyon, Texas

Fort Elliot Army scouts that includes Delaware Indians anc Whites.
Photo courtesy of Panhandle Plains Historical Museum,.Canyon,, Texas.

Mobeetie Texas Post Office 1878.
Photo courtesy of Panhandle Plains Historical Museum, Canyon, Texas

Johnny Long's "Mint" saloon.
Photo courtesy of Panhandle Plains Historical Museum, Canyon, Texas

J.J. Long General Merchandise Store.
Photo courtesy of Panhandle Plains Historical Museum, Canyon, Texas

Bat Masterson
*Photo courtesy of Panhandle Plains Historical
Museum, Canyon, Texas*

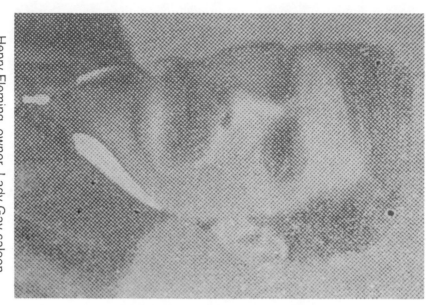

Henry Fleming, owner, Lady Gay saloon.

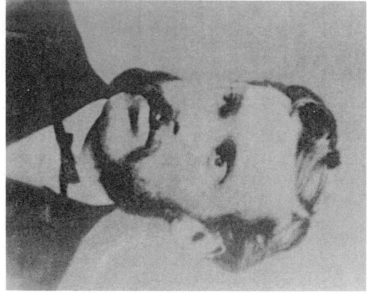

Major Joel Elliot, Fort Elliot namesake. Officer under Gen. George Armstrong Custer, killed in battle of "Black Kettle", 35 miles east of Mobeetie. *Photo courtesy of Mobeetie Jail Museum, Mobeetie, Texas*

"Cook Drug & Medical Co."Mobeetie peddler, Mobeetie Texas.
Photo courtesy of Mobeetie Jail Museum, Mobeetie, Texas

Tom O'Loughlin Grand Central Hotel.
Mobeetie, Texas

Mary Long, wife of John J. Long.

Mark Huselby, pioneer Panhandle rancher. *Photo courtesy of Panhandle Plains Historical Museum, Canyon, Texas.*

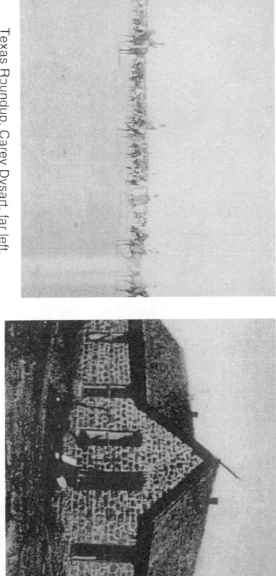

Texas Roundup. Carey Dysart, far left.

Henry Fleming rock house built in 1875, still lived in today. Oldest in the Panhandle.
Photo courtesy of Sallie Harris, Wheeler, Texas

Mobeetie Jail Museum

STREET SCENE LOOKING SOUTH

Mobeetie street scene 1870's looking south. Note yokes of oxen.
Photo courtesy of Sallie Harris, Wheeler, Texas.

Temple Houston, son of Sam Houston. Mobeetie citizen, lawyer.

Billy Dixon, scout/buffalo hunter. *Photo courtesy of Panhandle Plains Historical Museum, Canyon, Texas.*

Robert Ealey, Mobeetie barber.

Charles Goodnight, Panhandle pioneer rancher. *Photo courtesy of Panhandle Plains Historical Museum, Canyon, Texas.*

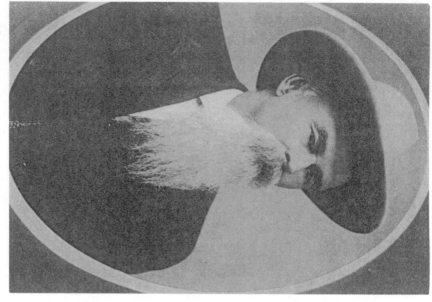

"Cap" Arrington in later years.
Photo courtesy of Mobeetie Jail Museum,
Mobeetie, Texas.

Tom O'Loughlin, Mobeetie businessman and
buffalo hunter.
Photo courtesy of Mobeetie Jail Museum,
Mobeetie, Texas.

Elizabeth (Frenchy) McGraw, Mobeetie
dance-hall girl.
Photo courtesy of Panhandle Plains
Historical Museum, Canyon, Texas.

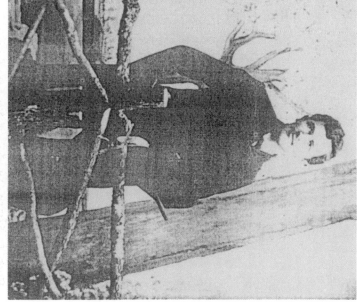

Mickey McCormack
Married Frenchy McGraw
Photo Courtesy of Panhandle Plains
Historical Museum, Canyon, Texas

Fort Elliot visitors, with bottles.
Photo courtesy of Mobeetie Jail Museum, Mobeetie, Texas.

Delaware Indian scouts campsite near Fort Elliot.
Photo courtesy of Mobeetie Jail Museum, Mobeetie, Texas.

Pioneer John Kesler, with horse and buggy.

"Shores of Hell" Saloon

Lady Gay Saloon

Mysterious Dave Mather, Mobeetie gunfighter.
*Photo courtesy of Panhandle Plains Historical Museum,
Canyon, Texas*

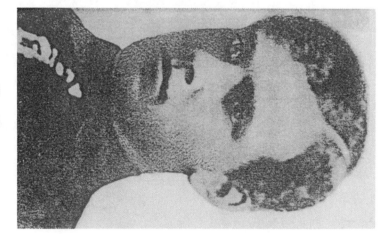

Clay Allison,
"The Wild Wolf of The Washita."
*Courtesy of Panhandle Plains
Historical Museum, Canyon, Texas*

"Crossin' The Sweetwater," depicts Custer and the
7th Calvary in the 1868 Black Kettle Campaign
Courtesy of Kenneth Wyatt and Mobeetie Jail Museum

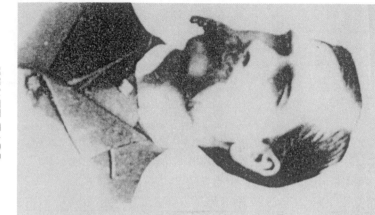

WYATT EARP
A friend of Bat Masterson, run out of
Mobeetie twice for trying to buy a ranch
with "Painted Gold" bricks.
Photo Courtesy of L.O.C.

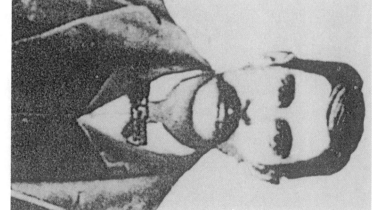

DOC HOLLIDAY
A friend of Wyatt Earp and
Bat Masterson, Doc was a frequent
Mobeetie gambler from "Down South."
Photo Courtesy of L.O.C.

LOUISE HOUSTON
BORN 1885 — DIED 1887 IN MOBEETIE
DAUGHTER OF
SENATOR TEMPLE and LAURA CROSS HOUSTON
GRANDDAUGHTER OF
GENERAL SAM and MARGARET LEA HOUSTON
DIED OF CHOLERA INFATUM
SHE WAS LAID OUT FOR BURIAL BY
MRS. JOHNNY LONG AND BURIED IN
THIS CEMETERY SOMEWHERE NEAR THIS MARKER.

King ordered a drink and waited, watching in the bar's long mirror, as Bat Masterson came through the doors.

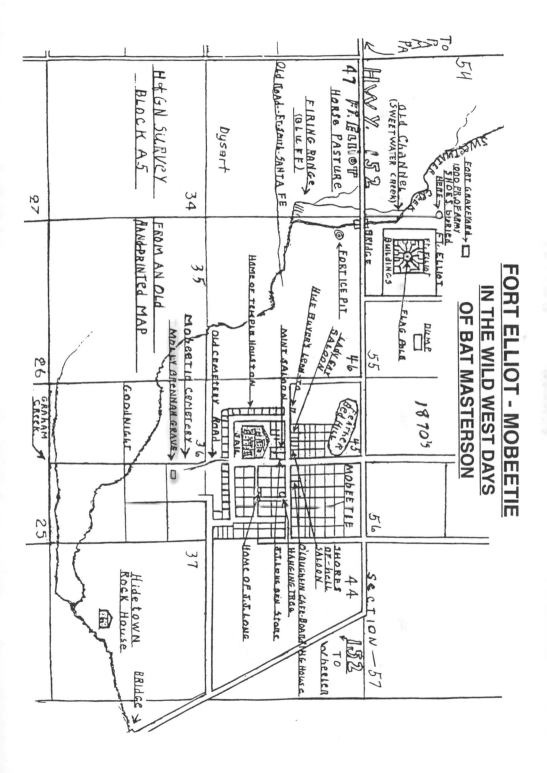

FORT ELLIOT - MOBEETIE
IN THE WILD WEST DAYS
OF BAT MASTERSON

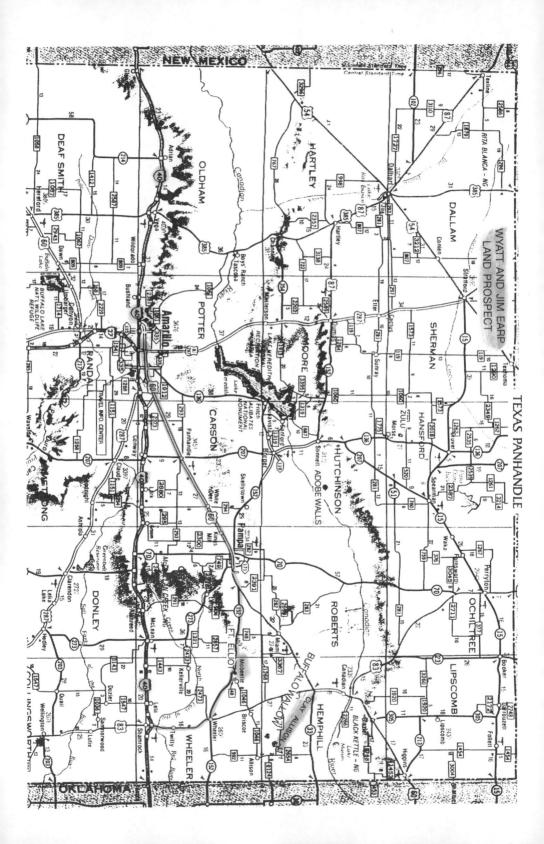

22 *The Hanging Tree*

Bat jogged along. Pigeye's hideout soon faded in the distance. The two horses Bat led was nothing but skin and bones; he thought they'd fall apart. But caught with them a hunter mad as all hell, with a loaded gun, looking for his stolen horses, death staring him in the face, he wouldn't ask questions. Bat watched and twisted in the saddle. The weather was hot and sultry, wavy thermal mirages appeared but soon faded away. He stayed with a dry-dusty buffalo path. He hoped for water at the end of the trail that'd cool his parched throat; his horses were thirsty, too. Coalie shied, side-stepped a coiled rattler in the trail. Bat urged him on. A few scrawny trees loomed away in the distance. Water? He kept Coalie in his slow-easy foxtrot and came to a spring hidden in salt-water grass. Water trickled to a stagant pool, inched along to soon peter out in the alkali sand. Bat paid no mind to the buffalo meadow muffins splashed in the water. The horses shoved their heads' in up to their eyes. The brackish water was gyppie/bitter, famous for diarrhea, but a starving man wouldn't think twice before he swigged; it was wet.

Swinging back and forth in the saddle, Bat's was a lonely world. Glancing up at the curlews circling over-head, he hummed a tune to Coalie's little easy get-along. Molly and her haunting dream was on his mind—a gun-fight he won but he lost? A mystery, a riddle, didn't make sense; he couldn't figure it out. But it was no time for dreams. Two horsebackers were coming in a fast lope.

Buffalo hunters? Bat made sure the Bays' lead rope was clear of his guns. He reined Coalie to a walk. The horsebackers reined-up, stopped out a ways. Bat slow-rode toward them. Their reins hung over the saddlehorn, gun hands free. Now the hunters had their man...that low-down son-of-a-bitch that stole the bay horses and left their friends out there to die! Bat reined up too...a deadly "meetin'-up? A split second, it'd be over? Moving up he eyeballed them severely; desperate men! "Howdy," he said.

A black bearded man riding a black horse rode in close, looked the horses over, back to Bat, to his side-kick, and back to Bat. "Bout these hosses your're leadin' here—our friends set down on Buck Creek to do some shootin', had a couple bays like them that strayed. They hoofed out two weeks ago to find 'em but nary man's showed up yet; ain't seen 'em?"

Staring, the man on the dun horse came in closer, deep frowning, daggers shooting from his eyes, shadowing his guns, trying to figure out Bat. He wasn't cool, seemed to be the "nervous kind," and that concerned Bat. "Maybe one of 'em," Bat replied, ready, his eyes shifting from one man to the other. "I'm Bat Masterson, scouting in these parts for the Army and State, looking for renegade Indians and these guys raising hell with the hunters—dodging the law."

The buffalo hunters listened to what Bat had to say and eased up. "I'm Blackie and that's my friend Jock." The dark haired man nodded to his sidekick.

These men were lucky to be alive in this Godforbidden land of desperadoes, hostile Indians, and miles from good water. Their jitters, Bat could understand.

"Well, there's a cave back in past that hill 'side of a little bluff, on a rise," Bat said, pointing. "May be where you'll find one of your men. That's where I found the horses."

"Anybody else 'round?" Jock questioned.

"Shaghound."

"Any idea who's the hoss thief holed up there?" Blackie asked, determined.

"Looney, Pigeyes Looney."

"Was? Heard of 'im...bloodthirsty, drill you if ya won't drink his rotgut whiskey and blow your head off if you swig too much. Say you're from down south?"

"Nope, Mobeetie."

Jock was shocked. "Mobeetie, don't think I want no part of that place, killings and all—and that Dogface guy!"

"Simmering down. Take these hosses, I figure they're your friends. Gotta head on."

"Might be on the lookout for a band of Redskins 'saw going over that rise," Blackie said, pointing east.

"Adios!" Bat yelled, and spurred out.

He went east staying north of Red River. Buffalo guns boomed in the distance. Bat was ready to tell anybody if they expected settlers in this part of the world somebody would have to shake out the devil first. He kept going east. The Indian Nation-Texas border was close, but nobody knew for sure where the line was. The no-man's strip along the 100th meridian had been hassled over for years...been to Washington and back a dozen times, but still wasn't settled.

Swinging back north, Bat topped a rise. In the valley ahead was a grove of trees. Wagons, buggies, and saddlehorses were scattered around through the cottownwoods and men running around like crazy. He "ho'd" his horse. What was going on? He slow-walked Coalie on down, reined in among the wagons, but not a head turned. The crowd soon settled down. A dozen men had gathered around a wagon near a big tree. People seemed hell-bent on watching what was going on. Bat come off his horse and sidled up to a "hayseed" with long stringy hair; had a rank beard. His old tattered hat shoved down on his head had him dog-eared. The belly-band off a set of harness wrapped around his hips made-do for a belt; the strap-end hung to his knees.

"What's going on?" Bat asked.

The man didn't seem to hear, didn't look around, and kept his eyes on the happenings. His pregnant wife and three kids stared; looked Bat over. The guy glanced Bat's way. "There's a-gonna be some hang'ns soon as the Shar-iff finds his hangin' ropes. Reckon as to how a-body stole 'em. There's gonna be some law'n order 'round these parts. I reckon there ain't been no hangin' nigh on a week. And reckon might say gettin' mighty tame 'long this here bo'der. But makes no never mind to me, I'm headin' west nohow—Colorado."

"Horse thieves?" Bat queried.

"Hoss thieves, cattle rustlers, robbers, killers, reckon there ain't nothin' they ain't done 'ceptin' two say they ain't guilty. I reckon as to how the main'est one on an old strawberry roan from Fort Sill, he got away." Slim, leaning against his old green faded butcher-knife wagon shifted from one foot to the other, and squirted tobacco juice like it was going out of style. He added, "That there guy he ain't no Shar-iff; jist what they call 'im."

The "Sheriff" sent a couple of men over to a tree with four noose-ropes. They threw the rope-ends over a big limb, then four bronc horses were brought out. An outlaw was slip-knot-tied on each horse then the nooses were dropped. The Sheriff boomed. "Either of ya got somethin' to say?"

"I ain't guilty," a shaky voice came from one.

A .45 roared. The bronc horses threw the accused men as high as the rope-limb. The horses went wild, ran

123

over the scrambling guys on the lead ropes, knocking them down. The broncs broke through the crowd and scattered people like a covey of quail. Two of the men were cut down and hauled to Mobeetie and buried in boothill cemetery. A stone marker was set at each grave.

The hanging happening was over. Bat soon headed north for Salt Fork River. At the river, three sets of fresh horse tracks showed up in the wet sand. One track, right front hoof, was different—odd, seldom seen, wiped out by the back tracking hoof. Dogface was not far ahead. All the tracks soon disappeard in the water—up the river or down the river? Bat was guessing up the river. But there was no other sign, no campfire, nobody in sight. Bat figured Dogface was at the hanging to save his part-ners-in-crime, just sneaking around, but the sight of the hanging ropes changed his mind; he never showed up.

Bat quenched his thirst at the river, throwed a camp, and eat a little jerky. Hid out in the river brush, on a sandy bank, behind a big log, he throwed his bed-roll down. A loud pop a'way in the night roused him. A shot or limb snapped? Drowsy, he raised up with his gun in hand and looked over the log. A moonlit night, he watched and listened. A faint light flashed. Going through the brush not far away was a shadow. He took no chances, he fired his rifle. Suddenly hooves pounded the earth. Horses—Dogface and his gang hauling-out? Bat watched and listened—nothing. He soon drifted back to sleep.

The next morning Bat rode through the brush to see what was going on during the night; did he get his man? No, just a buffalo. He felt sort of stupid, and more so than ever after he figured the faint flashing light was nothing but a lightening bug. But Bat Masterson stayed alert to stay alive.

He crossed Salt Fork River the next morning and kept heading north. At North Fork he headed west up the winding stream. The river was almost dry, the weather was droughty.

Up the river a ways he saw horse tracks coming off the river bank headed west, too. A hundred Indians coming out of Indian Territory and going back to their old stomping ground? Looking at the many tracks, Bat found no sign of the odd hoof print. The natives had been herded to the Indian Nation, but they loved the high plains of Texas...going home. That Indian Nation stuff didn't make sense to natives getting kicked all over hell and half the West.

Bat followed the Indian movement up North Fork, reined up about fifteen miles southwest of Mobeetie, and studied the tracks. Another bunch had joined the Indians coming up the river. Bat had the Indian savvy. A big pow-wow had been going on. Something was blowing in the wind. Could it be the Comanches, Cheyennes, and Kiowas cooking up bad medicine for a last ditch stand? After getting clobbered at Adobe Walls, Bat doubted it. He whipped out for Fort Elliot.

23 *The Preacher*

About the time Bat left the Army Post the evening shadows were falling and darkness coming on. He rode into town, stabled his horse, and started walking. It was only a short distance down the street to his room. His legs were stiff and bowed, a pig could run through them without touching hide nor hair. Within ear-shot of the O'Loughlin boarding house he heard strange sounds, strange for Mobeetie. He stopped to listen. Music, gospel music. Ah, some circuit riding preacher had found this place.

At home, Bat always came in the back door off a hard day's ride. But this kind of backyard carrying on was unheard of in this town. A couple of smoked-up lanterns hanging on posts shed some light but hardly enough to make-out people sitting on split logs and nail kegs; three or four had parked on the back doorstep, too. A buffalo hunter, a cowboy, and two dance hall gals were hunkered down on the grass. Bat didn't shove by to the door. He liked the singing, hadn't heard this kind of music in years. Anyway, he thought it would soon be over with.

The singing stopped and a weird looking man came out of the shadows. Part of the guy was missing. Half of his hair and one ear was gone. He stepped up by the lantern. He would have been run out of town but the ex-hide hunter was their kind of man. "I'm Parson Pounds. Can't blame you if you look at me like I'm a freak. Sometimes I wonder why I'm still walking this earth, too. This old hide hunter thought it was all over when the Indians got me and started butchering...whacked off my ear and tore at my scalp. I prayed not to live but to die." He read some Bible verses. "Thank God I lived, and I'm here to tell you there's hope even for the souls of the savages that cut me up. Everybody sins. Anybody here that don't do no sinning?"

A drifter that had slipped in and set down on the log shot his hand up. The Preacher caught it. "Young man, you must live a clean life. Not many saints around these days. Tell us how you do it."

It could be seen it was the boy's first "preach'n'meetin'." He glanced around, eased up off the log, thought of his hat, jerked it off, and nervously rolled the brim. "Well-er, I ain't killed nobody yet."

"Good!" the preacher said. "Now you old sinners you know you stand around these high wagon-beds and buggy steps hoping to see these pretty wimmin with well turned ankles. What vile and vulgar thoughts. Sinful! You're doomed and damned!" But suddenly he sputtered and spit out a flying cricket. "And doomed is that damn bug!"

Bat knew there had been some missionary work going on in the settlement to get this motley bunch out. Most of them would be back in the saloons raising hell in thirty minutes.

The service was over and as Bat watched he wondered if any of his friends had come to this unusual get-together. From out of the shadows here come church-going Johnny Long leading the way with Mary on his arm, followed by Tom and Ellen O'Loughlin. With his hand out, Johnny walked up to Bat. "Well, Bat Masterson, never expected to see you in a preach'n'meetin'."

"Never expected to be here, and never expected to see this in Mobeetie," Bat replied."

Ellen said, "Only the Good Lord knows what's in the

127

poor boy's heart. Too bad that pretty little Molly's not here. She was coming but her Mama's just feeling tolerable. But we feel so good, don't we Mary? Two 'ladies of the evening' come."

Bat sympathized with the preacher, knew what he'd been through. "I rode a hard sixty miles to get here on time."

Affable Uncle Johnny looked at Bat and smiled. Bat knew J. J. didn't buy a word he said. The women knew, too, that shady ladies hung-out around the O'Loughlin saloon and Johnny Long's Mint. Then Uncle Johnny flashed a guilty grin at Tom like they knew they'd been caught.

"Yes, Bat," Mary added, glancing at Johnny and Tom. "Molly couldn't come but we did get some of those poor soiled doves from the dens of iniquity to come. Two of them were here at the Wednesday night Shores-Of-Hell prayer meeting, too."

Bat looked at Johnny, to Tom, back to Mary and Ellen. He couldn't believe his ears. "Oh, yes," Mary continued, "that man, Clay Allison, rode his horse down main street with nothing on but his hat, boots, and gunbelt shooting out windows. Of course Ellen and I didn't look, but he was riding a pretty horse. Then down there somewhere he slipped on his clothes, rode back down the street, and invited the whole town to come to the prayer meeting."

"Ah, uh, you mean at the saloon?" stammering Bat, asked.

"Oh yes, to atone for his sinful ways before he left for New Mexico. A miracle happened! A cowboy that didn't know how to pray led the prayer. It's all over town how sweet his voice went up to Heaven."

"He must have had religion years before," Bat suggested.

"Oh, but that Allison fellow is a religious man. He likes to start his services with a loud joyful sound. He said, 'Now Cactus Joe will lead us in prayer.' That poor boy looked up for the Spirit to put words in his mouth, but nothing come out."

"Then Joe never prayed?"

"Never prayed—oh yes he prayed!" Mary quickly replied, "When bullets hit the floor at his feet it's amazing how quick that boy went to the Lord. He jumped up and shouted, 'Praise the Lord and pass the hat!' A beautiful prayer don't you think, Ellen? Even asking donations for the Lord. And now we're praying that your two friends here will soon see the light, too. We're so glad you made it. Must have been a terrible hard ride. We're so proud of you, and we know dear Mama Masterson would be proud too, to know her poor lonely boy is trying to live the righteous life. God bless you and may all your troubles be little ones."

Mobeetie was a tough town with six-gun law, a hangout for every gunslick in the West, but that didn't bother the old butchered up preacher; he told it like it was. Outlaws had souls too, even the ruthless Redskins. Nobody knew where the old preacher come from or where he went. He left town the next day with his three dollar hat collection riding his old gray mule. His saddle was worn out, his Bible too, wrapped with saddle strings that held it together.

Early the next morning Bat went to Fort Elliot and gave the officers details on the border situation, how the buffalo hunters were catching hell. But he was soon back in town.

"Hi, Tom," Bat spoke as Tom O'loughlin left the store.

Bat, coming in the door, J. J. asked, "Find out anything —trouble along the border?"

"Yup, the buffalo hunters are catching it down there

from horse thieves, including Dogface, and others dodging the law. The Redskins are peeling scalps on every far-out hunter in the hills, too. Now, how's Mol—I-I mean how's my job?"

"Oh yeah, needing our surveyor. Town's growing by leaps and bounds. Need a bunch of lots staked off—well, that is, two."

"Sounds good. Uh-uh, Uncle Johnny, about Molly...."

"You bet. Old Dogface rode in late yesterday. Molly come around the corner there and he grabbed her hand. Not afraid of the overbearing bastard, she slapped hell out of him. He won't give up—can't get over it."

"You mean he's back in town now? Can't believe it. What do you mean, 'can't get over it...won't give up?'"

"Well, yeah, he's back, but it had been a while since he'd been seen. Back yonder before you come along he thought he had Molly roped and tied. 'Don't know why he unloads on me but the bully comes in here blowing around, 'Gonna show Masterson who's running this damn town.' He's crazy, got the whole town stirred up— the way he likes it. He's slick, knows how to dodge you. And here of late he's been shooting off his mouth he knows all about the border trouble, too."

"Never seen him but he's been there; tracked 'im to the letter."

"Well, he beat you back, and you was on his tail all the way, huh—tracking him along the border, down in that part of the country; how did you know it was him?"

Bat replied, "Yup, did, dead giveaway, I...."

"Just a minute, 'get this guy, wants huntin' stuff."

The customer wanted to visit but finally Mr. Long came back, still wound up on King's devilment. J. J. cleard his throat, "Don't know how he gets by with all the stuff he pulls. He watches for new settlers then figures out how to get to 'em; usually cheating at card games. When his hand is called he whips out that knife. If I know Bat Masterson, the stupid Sergeant can throw away that knife—gotta be stopped."

Curiosity was getting the best of Mr. Long. He still couldn't figure out how Bat knew he was on King's tail. He continued, "So you found out he was down on the Territory border and tracked him. Yeah, how do you know it was him?"

"Yup it was him, dead giveway. I...."

"Just a minute, another feller here wants huntin' stuff, too."

Bat waited around, finally jumped on his horse and spurred out for the blacksmith shop. On his way he met Molly coming down the trail. He wanted to get off just to hold her hand and make small talk. But usually hand-holding on the streets of Mobeetie was with gals hustling business.

He said, "Molly, gonna celebrate, taking you to the Lady Gay tomorrow night!"

"Can't wait," she giggled.

"Got some laying-off land to do now; surveying out west. Yup, gonna celebrate!" He swung on his horse and spurred out.

He could handle the surveying, nothing to it but driving a few stakes, and that "surveying" still sounded good to Bat. But now Molly had a problem—so thrilled she forgot why she was going to the store.

Around the first bend, past a patch of sagebrush, Bat met up with an old grizzled Western horse jockey. The boss had two wranglers whooping and hollering to keep 150 "calico" horses rounded up; horses of every description. Tradin' hosses he called them. Most Western jockeys, old cowboys past their range riding days, went from town to town dodging Indians with trading horses. They always kept a few good horses, but it was mostly stock ready for the boneyard—locoed, blind in one eye, wind broke, in-bred and crazy or could never be saddle-broke. But the old timey jockeys were good traders, schemers that knew every trick in the book. An old gray horse might just turn into a beautiful iron-gray overnight. A bottle of "bluing" would do the trick. Or an old speck-led-face black would turn to a beautiful coal black with a bottle of shoe polish. But no one was ever fooled by a "smooth-mouth." Everybody, including Bat, loved to haggle over horses. Sometimes a cowboy spent hours over a trade and soon hated himself for making the deal in the first place. Bat jawed with the jockey too long. His staking job would have to wait until another day.

He rode into town and came in back of the Dirty Gerty saloon, on his way to the Lady Gay. The town goof-ball yelled, "Oof," and threw a tin bucket under Coalie. The bucket bounced up, hit the horse in the belly, and scared hell out of him. Coalie snorted and broke into a wild-bucking pitch. Bat "pulled leather" to stay in the saddle. He burst out, "You crazy little bastard I'll get'cha!" Flailing his quirt, he went after Goofy Oofy. The snickering half-wit dodged around outhouses and saddle horses. Bat soon lost him. A Dogface trick. Bat headed for refreshments.

24 *Bat's Reservations*

Walking in the Lady Gay, Bat exclaimed, "Billy Dixon, best rifle shot in the West! Haven't seen you since we flushed out old Graybeard and Kicking Bird." Chuckling, he added, "And how about that crazy Medicine Man, Old Coyote Droppings?"

"Ah, come on, Bat, the best rifle shot in the West?" Dixon, a man of the prairie, young, handsome, long dark hair, replied, "My friend, you've been out'n the hot sun too long. Sit down, buy ya a drink, and let's forget about Old Coyote Droppings."

"Where you been hiding?" Bat asked his old scouting partner. "Oh, still banging around 'Dobe Walls, getting off a few shots. You know, like a bunch of others 'round here, everybody's loaded and the town's booming, but what's next? As you know Bat, this huntin' thing is about over. What have you been up to?"

"You're right," Bat agreed. "Mobeetie's booming now and money's floating around; what's next? Well, I've been picking up a few 'gold wagon wheels', doing a little faro dealing here for Henry."

"I was in Dodge awhile back," Billy said, "saw a St. Louis paper with a write-up about Mobeetie: 'Mobeetie, where money grows, whiskey flows, and wild women glow—the wildest town in the West'—a haven for every outlaw running loose.' Went onto say fifty million buffaloes had been killed and Mobeetie, known as Hidetown, too, was in the middle of the whole shebang."

"Fifty million? Don't doubt it," Bat replied.

"The write-up said, 'The biggest slaughter of wild animals ever known.'"

"Don't doubt that either, but here's one you will doubt, I'm the town surveyor; civil engineer!"

Billy laughed. "You've always been the darndest guy to kid and pull jokes. Now, tell me you're driving stakes with your .45 settin' on your horse. Still got him, that coal black stallion you traded for after we clobbered Quanah Parker?"

"Yup, still got him, and I do get off sometimes to measure off a spot of ground," Bat said, grinning broadly.

"Everything's fair and square, I bet?" Dixon chided. "Bat Masterson, civil engineer; can't believe it."

"Wouldn't say everything's square. Measured off two sides of a section (square mile) west of here and rode into town to grab a bite to eat. While we were gone a shower came up. Found out later the rain had shrunk the measuring rope and now the section is fifteen yards shy on two sides."

"And thirty acres short," Dixon declared, laughing. "And will be a hundred years from now, but who cares with the millions of acres laying around? But I'd say it's legal grounds for getting fired; lose them $10.00 gold pieces."

"Gold pieces? It's them refreshments on the town. Reckon you're right but I'm not worried. Nobody's around to check this old civil engineer. How'd you come in?"

"By the Fort. Rode in by the Trader's Saloon, whipped around back of the Dirty Gertie, and some fool kid threw a tin bucket under my horse and darn near got bucked off."

"Happened to me too. This guy that comes around here—been seen in Dodge too—puts that half-wit up to that."

Billy said, "Yeah, if that's the same guy I'm thinking about, he's always shooting off his mouth; rejects hang around him."

"Name's King," Bat replied, "stays hid out, got the town stirred up, killed a hunter 'too friendly with his woman', he said. And cut a stranger's throat that opened the door at Long's store for Molly Brennan—blacksmith's daughter. I've mauled him a time or two."

"Yeah," Billy come back, "sounds like that same Army Sergeant—says he is—but been told he's a corporal. I saw him in Dodge City once. He carries that Bowie knife hid in his shirt. Better watch out crossing swords with guys like Bat Masterson; walking on thin ice, I'd say." Dixon grinning, looked at Bat. "It's coming, bet my life on it—hope I'm around."

Bat and his old Adobe Walls sidekick walked down the alley, and stopped behind the Buffalo Chip saloon to catch up on old times. "Let's wait right here," Bat said, "the goof-ball at the Dirty Gerty might show up around the hitching-rail." Along about sundown Oofy made a dash for the outhouse. "Let's go!" Bat exclaimed. They ran for their horses', bumping against people, knocking them down. A man come off the ground swinging his six-gun, but the scouts had already spurred out yelling like Comanches. Soon they had their lariats swinging at Oofy's outhouse. Roping a wolf is cowboy fun, but roping an outhouse with someone in it is side splittin'. They swung, roped and jerked the scrap-wood-pasteboard-one-holer throne over, and strung out down main street. Screaming, Oofy rolled out the door. His britches caught on a nail-head left sticking up by the drunk that threw the thing together and jerked them down to his knees. People down the street heard screaming and wondered what was going on. Here they come, the kid's naked butt winging dry sand like a moldboard plow; yelling and laughter was loud. The boy's britches let go of the nail near the fun loving crowd. Never looking back, he streaked off down the alley. Still laughing, Bat hurried on to Molly's house.

Saturday night and Molly was in a natural lady's tizzy, afraid she wouldn't be ready when her beau come. Bat was everything to Molly, and even her mother thought she was getting up in this world sparking a city officer, the surveyor. But her mother had no love for Dogface. His language was dirty, smarted off to Molly at the blacksmith shop and Bob walked in. Bob was easy going, Dogface knew him, knew too another guy was pushing up daisies in boothill cemetery for making a crack at Molly. Dogface had his bluff in on most people but not Bob Brennan. Bob let him know right-off he'd make a gelding out of him in a hurry—with his fire-tongs.

The Saturday night dance was the place to go in the frontier towns, but any day of the week Mobeetie's excitement was enough to stir a man's soul. Walking in the Lady Gay's door Bat and Molly hardly noticed the gunfire down the street. But inside Slats Slattery's band was tunning up for the dance. A little rendition was going on, piano banging, banging like it never got on it's way to Mobeetie in Johnny Long's freight wagon.

No other frontier town had music like the Lady Gay. A piano was unusual. People gawked at Slat's white/red striped shirt, red suspenders, and red armbands. The slim comical dude cocked his sailor straw hat back on his head, pounded the ivory, sang a song or two and let the music roll, laugable in Mobeetie but people loved it. Molly was in hog-heaven swinging on the arm of the man she loved. But she didn't have him alone. The girls gathered around ol' handsome Bat to giggle and take on over the funny little hat he had on...as much out of place in Mobeetie as the rigging Slats wore. But Bat wore it on a dare from Mark Huselby, a friend, who had brought the derby all the way from England and gave it to him.

Saturday nights the dusty walls of the Lady Gay shook with fun and laughter. A dozen saloons down the street were full-up too and so was Featherbed Hill; a red light at every shack, a saddlehorse at every hitching post. Henry Fleming didn't forget his friends, he kept a special table for Bat and Molly. Right off they started holding hands and juicing it up with a few kisses. After awhile Billy Dixon and Ben Thompson walked in; a couple of guys tough as rawhide and smooth as silk. Billy's fame spread after he knocked an Indian off his horse at 7/8 mile, and everybody in the West knew of Ben Thompson's skill with a pistol. Ben was on his way home from Dodge City and stopped back by to see friends in Mobeetie. And he might catch his brother in town, too. But Bill was out of town, still running scared since the Sheriff was killed in their Kansas squabble.

Dixon and Ben, a little wobbly, swaggered up to Bat and Molly's table. Full of fun, laughing and cutting up, Billy slapped Bat on the shoulder. "Why, you old flea-bitten coyote, we thought you'd leave the hard work for us, you know, like you used to do, remember?"

"Can't say as I do," Bat replied. "I thought the skinners done all the work." Bat turned to Molly. "Pay no mind to these guys. Now, my friends, tell me about this hard work you're volunteering for?"

Ben grinned. "We'd been glad, even tickled to got a horse and buggy and brought Molly to the Lady Gay for you."

"Why, you old mangy lobos!" Bat exclaimed, chuckling, "Wouldn't trust you studhosses far as I could throw a bull by the tail. Now, let's have one."

Henry was helping out, had two young gals on the way with refreshments. And the fun loving guys had al-

137

ready hung a name on them—Violet the virgin and Mozell the moose. After a few shots of whiskey and Slat Slattery's wild music, nobody cared what was hung on them. The guitar picker's singing—well, that ol' boy could call the cows from the backside of the pasture. The big Fort Elliot possum-eating negro soldier blowed the jug, and was a "banjo picking fool," too; always grinning, always jolly, and rolling the whites of those big black eyes. They loved him. The cowboy fiddlers sawed it out, unusual country musicans, the guys could entertain anywhere. Everybody dancing, having fun, after a few drinks the old buffalo hunters thought they were the best dancers, ever.

At the end of a lively tune Slats jumped up and yelled, "Is everybody happy? There's a-gonna be a thirty minute break while the men whip out for the corral and the ladies head for the little house on the prairie!"

Slats got a big laugh. Soon the saloon cleared out. Bat and an old Kansas friend strolled out in the dark; not far. The outside hanging lantern didn't throw out much light anyway. Well, in the dark, after they paused, Bat soon felt a light squeeze on his arm; got a whiff of perfume, too.

"Excuse me a minute, please?"

"Whi-uh-ah, Beth Barton," Bat stammered, "didn't know you was here."

"See you later, Bat." His friend thought it was time to haul-out.

Beth was a conniving little gal, knew what she wanted and went after it. Though common play for the gals in lusty Mobeetie, men respected the girls; Western pioneers, too.

"We came in late, heard ranchers were here looking for land." Her voice was soft and pleasant. She moved closer.

"How are things going at the ranch—have you got them new bulls—where's Jim?"

"The Indians killed three of our cows last week," Beth said. "Jim's in there talking bulls. Bulls, bulls, all he thinks about." At this moment she didn't care about four-legged bulls, and like the ranch woman she was, got right to the point. "I've said it before and I'll say it again: he watches his bulls and stud-horses trying to improve his own miserable performance, but never rises to the occasion; disgusting. He's at the bar." She stood on her tiptoes and threw her arms around Bat... determined, an unquenchable burning desire for passionate love. Beth was no prostitute. Maybe a little devious, but just a nice girl. Yes, looking for love in lusty Mobeetie.

Now Bat had brought Molly, he had some reservations; put on a brave front. But it's been said, a tender loving woman can knock a man of steel any time. It's so, always has been, and always will be. Wringing his tail, Bat was ready to throw away some of those reservations. He stammered, "Well, I'm-uh here...." Someone came out the door, coming straight for Bat and Beth. It was Jim, headed for the pitch dark too, feeling his way, to "water his horse." Danged if he didn't stop close enough to splatter Bat and Beth when he whipped out. Things got a little tense. Jim soon wrung it out and headed back for the saloon. Beth got uneasy. As soon as she saw him walk in the door she gave Bat a shove and ran for the door, too. Now ol' Bat felt a little—well, like he'd been hit in the face with a sack of fresh mule manure. Bat knew Beth wouldn't give up easy. She'd be back. Wasn't wild, just had a screwball husband. But Bat Masterson was a neighborly guy, help a friend anytime, especially a pretty girl. Beth walked in the Lady Gay behind Jim and raised her voice, a show of great concern, "Honey I've looked everywhere for you!"

"Ah, had to make it to the corral," he said. "Let's dance."

Molly and her friends soon dashed in the door, too, through a cloud of bugs swarming around the light. When Bat walked in he came in for a little more joshing. Billy Dixon and Ben Thompson were waiting for him. Ben said, "Billy, did 'Loose-screws Masterson' tell you about his gun?"

"Don't reckon I've heard that one," Dixon replied.

Bat gestured, "Billy, I was just trying to save a little ammunition. There's some damn hard-headed people in this town."

Ben laughed. "Our old friend here got in a little scrape with this hard-head that's blowing off around town. Bat loosened the screws on his gun when he bopped him over the head. Billy, tell Bat how to use that thing, which end, when he's playing games, especially if the guy rides a strawberry roan!"

The boys were having fun and the girls joined in. Billy turned to Molly. "Did Bat ever tell you about singing to his horse, lobos, and buffaloes? That's why there's not many left on the prairie; ears couldn't stand it."

Bat let him have it good naturedly, "Billy, it's like this: Molly has to listen, always Molly on my mind."

"Give us one more little sample, Bat." Ben laughed.

To everyone's surprise Bat stood up, slightly wobbly, straightened up with effort, and belted it out, "I'd lay it all on the line for my sweet Molly anytime!"

Things got quiet for a minute. Then the ladies burst out with loud applause and the men hooted and hollered. Bat glanced toward the front door. Four men stood crowding the entrance. Something was up. The music started, he danced with Molly in perfect time but kept his eyes on the door. Had ol' Dogface slipped in to challenge Bat Masterson? Molly pressed against him, tugged

140

at him, nudged him, but he never turned his head. He strained to see through the crowd. Stretching his neck, looking straight ahead, he leaned this way, that, determined nothing would stand in his way.

The music stopped and Bat made his way toward the door. Molly held on, squeezing his arm, uneasy, apprehensive; was this it, the gun fight he won but he lost? Whatever, come hell or high water, she'd stand by her man; his eyes hard on the door. Ben and Billy, reading the situation, moved up flanking Bat, hawking the crowd. Molly dropped back with Mozell and Violet. Clearing the way, people pushed back. The door blockers throwing a threat—Bat's game! Friends knew he had no fear, none whatsoever of the killer that was keeping the town tore up. Now, just humiliate the hell out of him again. Bat Masterson would do what a man had to do.

Four men standing in a semi-circle had the door blocked; Dogface and his sidekicks. Dogface, wearing an old army hat, right hand in his unbuttoned shirt, stuck his foot out and braced up. Bat came in slow, cat-like and cautious within arm's length of the sneering bastard.

"Masterson, let go of my woman!" Dogface blurted.

People scrambled for the door, ducked under tables, and froze behind the bar. Dogface's right hand gripped the Bowie knife in his belt, and shadowed his six-shooter with his left. A devilish grin wrinkled his pock-marked face, and scorn blistered his beady eyes; he feinted. Bat kicked his braced-out foot and threw the guy off balance; he come out with his knife. But Bat's gun-barrel got him on the temple and spun him around. Reeling, moon eyed, he stared in space, half-out, he turned his head. Bat let him have it on the other temple and knocked him down. King hit the floor on his hands and knees, groping for his gun and knife.

"Crawl, you sonovbitch, crawl!" Bat said, calmly.

King, afraid to stand, started crawling. Bat lifted him off the floor when he kicked his ass out the door; the second time in as many months. But Dogface Melvin King would be back to play the game, the gunfighters game, but damn serious business, too. Dogface hit the dirt, hoots and hollars went up, and the Saturday night fun was winding down. But contempt could be seen in the eyes of the man who swore he'd get Bat Masterson.

"Calls for another drink!" the bartender yelled.

25 *Scouting North Fork*

Bat and Molly slow-walked the buggy pony home. Molly had more fun at the Lady Gay than she'd ever dreamed of, but she couldn't understand Bat Masterson. Relaxed, she thought he was made of steel, acted as if nothing happened. It was her second time in the Lady Gay and still she had reservations about going in saloons. Back in Mississippi, in their small town, when the little church doors swung open, her family was there. But the swinging church doors in Mississippi was a long ways from the swinging doors at the Lady Gay saloon in Mobeetie, Texas. Tonight she shrugged it off. She was eighteen now and snuggled on the buggy seat by the man she loved.

Bat reined-up the buggy horse at the Brennan hitching post. Dark, it was dark as a sack of black cats, and a way after midnight. Not even a candlelight around the Brennan house— unusual. Molly's mother had a habit of leaving the light in the window; had she forgot it? Lights out, no moon, and with a beautiful girl, who cared? The old buggy pony stood like a statue; not even a sneeze.

But buggy horses had no sympathy for lovers on the horsehair seats. A horse that stood for hours at the hitching rail was ready to go home. Cramped on the small buggy seats, trying to make out with his girl, and a buggy horse raring to go, was nothing but a cowboy's nightmare. Stopping off on the way not many horses would stand at ease...pull up, back up, twist in the harness, fill the air with horrible odors, and keep trying to go. Then any old cowpoke would swear, "That damned old horse ruined everything." A disappointed girl-friend in a cooled off manner would soon let her boy friend know, "It's time you take me home!" But the boys got there just the same. Why not on the ground, but grassburrs were no bed of roses, either. Lucky, no grassburrs around Molly's house.

Bat got out of the buggy and Molly come off in his arms. Relaxing and rolling in the soft buffalo grass was lovers' fun anytime; the Western way to romance. And she loved his romancing ways. Cuddling and coddling, he kissed her again and again. Suddenly a beam of light hit them in the eyes.

Bless her heart, of course Bessie wondered about her "baby," but why did she have to fire up that old lamp? A warm summer night, the windows open, and the curtains pulled back, the light hit the lovers square in the eyes. Molly gave Bat a shove and they jerked upright. Bessie ambled over to look at the old Seth Thomas clock on the wall. "Oh my goodness, after midnight, and away past time for my baby to be home." She knew how to put the damper on things. Bat walked Molly to the door and kissed her goodnight.

Dogface left town after Bat worked him over the second time here of late. Nobody expected to see the Sergeant around. People loosened up. Molly was so sweet and relaxed now...so sweet she had Bat thinking he was in love.

But there could never be love in the heart of the old American Natives for the white man. The Panhandle country had always been their home, but now the once-proud Braves were humblized, shoved off to the Indian Nation. The Whites said it was just a time of transition, but that never made sense to the Indians. They were slipping out of the Indian nation and back to the Texas

Panhandle. They loved the high plains country (3600')
with the prairie as level as a floor. In the past thousands
of buffaloes grazed the lush buffalo grass. Spring fed
creeks of good water that cuts through deep canyons
and rugged country made ideal campsites. The Army
Brass asked Bat and Billy Dixon to scout southwest to
see what the Renegades were up to.

Settlers and investors were looking for ranches but
the Redskins raids were scaring them off. Really it was
pitiful, the Indians were only looking for the vanishing
herds to have something to put in their bellies. But now
there was no such thing as the great herds. The buffalo
was about wiped off the wind-swept prairie. The Indians' livelihood was gone. What could they do? The white
hunter wasn't concerned about the squaws and kids.
What if they were starving? Buffalo hides were worth
money. The Indians were still having their scalp dances,
too, and slaughtering cattle brought in on the range. Of
course the Whites didn't like it, raising hell all the way
to Washington. Something had to be done—"Get rid of
them damn Redskins, now!" The Europeans would jump
through their tail if they got wind the natives were
swarming back to their old stomping ground. The
oversea syndicate buyers were big land investors.

Along about sun-up Bat Masterson and Billy Dixon
headed out southwest. If the Indians were drifting back
to the Panhandle the scouts would find it out. No question, the Whites lost cattle, the Redskins sneaked in,
killed cattle, then slipped back to the Territory and were
seldom caught. Renegade bands were wiping out far-
out Ranchers.

Bat and Billy hit North Fork River about ten miles
southwest of Mobeetie. Not a big river here, the head-
waters were only twenty miles farther west. But big rains
had put the river on a high rise, churned up quicksand

that would swallow a horse before the rider could leave the saddle. A few horse tracks were found in the river-bed, but further on more and more showed up in the wet sand.

"Wadda ya think, Bat?" Billy asked, "Something blowing in the wind—bad medicine?"

"Don't doubt it," Bat replied. "Same bunch I tracked up the river joining up with another bunch. Things are too quiet, not even a mangy buffalo around!" They watched, twisted in the saddle, and looked up the river, down the river.

Suddenly chanting Redskin warriors were closing in on the scouts! Spent arrows and wild gun-shots were coming close. And Indians were pouring in, jumping their horses off five foot river banks. Bloodcurdling yells put the cringing fear in the two white men.

"Let's get the hell out of here, Billy!" Bat screamed. "To damn many Indians for two men!" They dug in their spurs. It seemed the Indians were coming out of the ground, out of the sky; from everywhere. A warrior jumped his old gray horse, flying through the air, off the river bank and landed right in front of Bat and Billy—hit the ground and rolled. The scouts horses' leaped high to clear him. Outrunning the Indians, Billy said, "Looks like we got out of that one—horses' got a few arrow nicks!"

But soon the scouts heard a new burst of yells. Suddenly a swarm of Indians showed up coming down the river headed straight for the scouts! Redskin fun, yelling, chanting, two scalps in the bag! At full gait, hell-bent on taking scalps, they soon hit quicksand. Horses' went down, horses piled on top of horses...struggling, floundering around, sinking, going deeper in the sucking sand. The Indians quickly jumped from their mounts to solid ground. There was danger ahead but the warriors left behind were coming up fast; bows bent, bullets whiz-

146

zing, and lances drawn!

With his usual humor, Bat yelled, "Billy let's haul-ass, things are beginning to get serious!"

26 *Dr. Bat Masterson*

Bat and Dixon stayed with the buffalo trails coming out of the rugged hills to finally top out on high level country. Soon Billy exclaimed, "Look at that, a burned out wagon!"

"Yup," Bat replied, "looks like a family's had it—bodies scattered around like firewood; all stripped naked. Danged if I ain't seen that old green wagon before! Yeah, at a neck-tie party there on the Territory border. Slim and his family was headed for the Colorado gold mines—going it alone, he said. I couldn't see taking the big risk—anybody. 'Told him I'd never set out across this unsettled country like that."

"But you know, Bat, some do and I can't see why when they've been warned about the Indians; disgusting cruelty!"

"They didn't have a chance," Bat said, "but from the looks of things the family put up a fight; the woman with a handful of hair and the man cut and slashed all over."

The horses were gone, the wagon set afire, and the harness cut up; the clothing and bedding was missing. The wagon tongue was propped up with the neckyoke with the end raised six feet in the air. The man hanging by one foot on the raised-end dangled...scalped, sticks run under his skin and the ends set fire. The tortued woman lost her new baby, and Bat wondered what happened to the other kids. It wasn't too unusual, the scouts had seen this kind of thing before. Many disappeared in the rugged wild country and was never heard from again.

Skeletons are found until this day on the prairie and the mystery of what might have happened lingers on; skulls caved in—bullet holes. To ride off and leave the dead seemed thoughtless and cruel, however there was nothing they could do. Soon they rode on, the sun was getting low, and about time to "throw a camp."

The Indians lost the Adobe Walls battle and now they were mad as all hell, burning, hitting the Whites any way they could. And they would until they were chased off the plains. Bat and Dixon had friends among the Indians, scouted with them, hunted with them, and it was hard for anyone to understand the extreme cruelty the natives dished out. Just as the Indians couldn't see why they were rounded up and kicked off land they had lived on since God knows when.

At sun-up the next morning Bat and Billy broke camp. Jogging their horses along they soon saw lots of horse tracks. A sure sign the Redskin renegades had left the Indian Territory and drifted back to Texas.

North, was the Canadian river breaks, but the scouts swung back southeast toward Mobeetie. They were crossing level country and could see for miles. Far to the northeast three wranglers suddenly showed up with a big herd of horses. They swung the herd around the scouts and kept pushing hard. But one wrangler in the bunch split off, loping his horse, come straight for the scouts. Still away out there, Bat had him figured out, and turned to Dixon, "Know who that is?"

"Don't know's I do," Billy answered.

"Yeah, you do. Seen him around Dodge City—in the 'Dobe Walls scrap, too—Dutch Henry."

"Yeah, it is him," Billy replied.

As Dutch rode in closer Bat lowered his voice, "Heard the Army screwed him in some kind of deal; don't know if it's true, but got the reputation: 'best horse thief in

149

the in the West'—. ain't choicy, steals anywhere he can get 'em...just happened to be around 'Dobe Walls when the Indians swarmed in and got caught with the rest of us."

Riding in close, Dutch reined up, and said, "Well, you guys looking for something?" He seemed to be "in the saddle," knew what he was doing; bold and cocksure. He didn't run when he saw the scouts, but he soon figured out who he was talking to. "Dogged if it ain't Bat Masterson and Billy Dixon, the 'Dobe Walls hide hunters—still at it?"

"Nope." Bat didn't offer much. "See you're still in the horse business."

"Yeah. All broncs, wild as deer, rounded 'em up on Wolf Creek. Reckon 'better catch up with the herd." Dutch reined around and spurred out. He had no hankering to deal with these hide hunters.

Trying to make Mobeetie, the scouts moved on. "Billy, I know a lot of people that would like to get their hands on Dutch Henry."

"Yeah, you know when we were hunting out west they liked to got him there in Dodge. Did got four of his sidekicks. Your brothers got in on that, didn't they?" Billy asked.

"Yup, they did, and four out of five wasn't too bad. But, you know, he got some gun lead, too...got over it, and since then he's been running hog wild; wild as a peach orchard boar."

The scouts dropped off the high level country down to the rolling hills. Dutch was still on their mind. Billy said, "Bat he's got nothing to be afraid of in this no-man's land. Yeah, loose as a goose and free as the mountain air. Heard he wiped out Manny Dubbs, a hunter, set down north of Dodge; stole all of his horses."

"Yup," Bat replied. "Stole 'em right out from under

Dubb's nose. Dutch don't go for just one or two but the whole herd. He'll steal your eye-teeth if you don't keep your mouth shut. He's making it hard on ranchers settling along the Canadian. Huh, rounded 'em up on Wolf Creek. You can bet that's a big joke."

Dixon said, "It looked like they had a bunch of sorrels—army stuff. You reckon he raided Fort Elliot; that would be side splittin'?"

Bat shrugged. "Possible. But I'd bet Dutch Henry won't be going in Palo Duro Canyon. Charles Goodnight is putting a spread together down there and told him if he ever caught him in the canyon he wouldn't come out alive; just stay north of the Palo Duro. He knows all about Dutch. Charles Goodnight is as salty as the Dead Sea."

Dixon nodded. "You don't fool with them crusty old codgers like Charlie Goodnight, especially a Ranger that helped do-in a great warrior like Pete Nocona. And don't forget, his son was a good warrior, too, but we raked Quannah over pretty good at Adobe Walls, didn't we?"

"Did," Bat said. "Dutch Henry knows Goodnight's not afraid of forked lightning. And Dutch was more than glad to seal a pact with the Colonel...even sealed it with Dutch's possum blossom wild grape wine. No sir, the Colonel won't be bothered."

On the head-waters of Sweetwater Creek, Bat and Billy saw more signs of Indians. The renegades had come in closer than expected. The scouts were thirsty, had had a hard day's ride. They swung a ways south by Jim and Beth Barton's place to swig from springs bubbling cool water. Dixon had old buffalo-hunting sidekicks there; going to cowboy for Jim when he brought in cattle. Cattle were moving in, the unmerciful slaughter of the buffalo was on the last pages of America's frontier history. The buffalo hunters were a dying breed.

Nobody at home at Barton's place, but the scouts

tanked up at the spring anyway. Not far from Fort Elliot, and no Indians around, they figured they were safe. Suddenly, yells—Comanches! The scouts quickly swung their saddle guns around. But it was nothing, really...just two drunk cowboys yelling and racing for the water hole, too...fanning their hats and reeling in the saddle; their bridle reins dragging the ground. Jim called them cowboys, but no cowboying yet; no cows. Sot drunk, Bat and Billy thought the boys had made every saloon in town. Billy Dixon had spent days on the high plains "shootin'n skinnin" with these buffalo hunters.

Jim Barton was down around San Antonio looking for cattle, his cowboys said. Come spring, 1876, and warm weather, he'd trail cattle to the Panhandle. Jim was gone and Beth wasn't around, either. "Out chasing coyotes," the boys said, "loves to try her skill at roping coyotes." It was fun and an escape from boredom on the lonely prairie. Billy and his friends had old-time hunting days to talk about so Bat struck out for Fort Elliot...said he'd report on the renegade Indians.

That was Bat's story but Billy thought Bat had something else in mind, something prettier, more desirable to look at than the mugs of those old hide hunters.

Bat had rode about a mile and topped out on a rise. A way in the distance a horse was racing across the prairie over one rise after another. Was someone in trouble? Bat spurred out for the runaway horse, come in close and stopped; he watched. Beth Barton was chasing a coyote. The hard-riding gal on the fast horse was no greenhorn. She could handle a rope, but the old tail wringing coyote was pretty darn smart, too. Looking back, looking up, he ran around sagebrush and shin-oak...laying low, up and running, turning, dodging her loops. Roping the flea bitten critters wasn't easy. Bat had tried it and he admired her skill. Many a good horse has been wind-broke by cowboys trying to prove they could rope the coyotes and wolves. It's fun and all cowboys love to try it.

Without warning, Beth's horse went down. He came up without the rider. Was she in trouble? Bat gouged in his spurs and raced toward her.

She raised up and looked around. A horsebacker was coming in a dead-run. A conniving gal, she knew who was riding the big black horse. She flopped back down. The young Westerners' loved to romance in the soft prairie grass and Beth was the loving kind. She hoped for this but could hardly believe it. Bat brought Coalie in fast, reined-up, jumped off, and ran to her.

"What happened, what happened, are you hurt? Where, what's hurtin' worse?"

"It's my leg, my thigh," she moaned. "It's killing me. Will you do something and quit horsein' around?" In his ignorance, she let him know how she felt; he was slow.

Bat thought she was in real pain but his training on first aid wasn't much. However there had been times when he helped his dad pour castor oil down sick cows by the quart; about it. He had heard some big names for body parts, too, but didn't remember any of them. And he didn't see Beth's mischievous grin, either.

"Wh-wh-what'cha want me to do first?"

"Rub my leg, quick. It's killing me!"

"Which one?"

"They're both broke. Rub 'em, rub 'em—higher, and quit being so rough!"

Bat couldn't figure it out. Two broke legs, in real pain, and bad off! He rubbed the calves of her legs more like giving a yearling a shot of blackleg serum but that wasn't enough.

She lost patience. "Dammit, I told you it's higher!"

He put his hand on her knee. "Yup, that's it, knee's

153

broke."

"No, no, it's my thigh!" she said, scooting toward him.

Men trying to give first-aid the first time are clumsy as a cub bear playing with his ying yang, but Bat was getting an education on a beautiful thigh.

"That's better. My hip, it's killing me. Ah, it's this rig I've got on."

Relaxed now and laid back in the soft grass, then with a little "got'cha" smile she jerked her split-tail riding skirt open. His eyes bugged out—in shock, he turned his head. A quick glance, he turned back. "Ugh," he said.

Naturally riding without a saddle clothes were no problem. But coming out of the saddle, the women's clothes could hang-up on the saddlehorn, but not Beth's. Except for her boots she was bare from the waist down. Beth rode with a saddle but some girls love to ride bare-back. However, high withers on a horse can be wrenching hell on a man. Bat stammered, "I-I reckon, yup, you're hurt bad, real bad off—something is broke."

"Really, it's my pelvis," she suggested, scooting closer. "I caught it on the saddlehorn coming out of the saddle."

Bat was no doctor, not even a rubbing doctor, but the least he could do on the saddlehorn injury was try. He knew the pain of raking over a saddlehorn, too. She was hurt, needed a doctor bad. Somebody had to do it....Dr. Bat Masterson. But she had ol' Bat wringing his tail. At a loss, stuttering and stammering around, he mumbled, "This doctoring could be more fun than shooting buffaloes—even roping coyotes." Soon he heard a low rumbling; pounding hoof-beats! "Dixon! It's Dixon!"

He jumped up and pulled up a spewing Beth. She blurted out, "That fool knows how to hurt a person but I'm not giving up that easy."

Beth was a nice lady, loved her romance, wasn't satisfied —disappointed, of course. Billy Dixon was her good friend, but now in her fit of passion she hated him; would like to tear him apart. But soon she wondered why she said all those nasty things about him; it happens. She had promised she'd catch Bat in the tall grass...she did.

"Is she hurt, Bat?" Dixon hollered, coming in closer. "Is she hurt bad?"

"Don't know. Bring her horse up!"

"I'm O K," Beth said, as Dixon approached. "Just knocked the breath out of me when I went over his head. He stepped in a badger hole and now a perfect day is ruined!"

"Had the same thing happen and felt the same way," Dixon said, leading her horse up, lending a little sympathy. "Them badger holes are dangerous." But Beth's and Dixon's thoughts were running in different directions.

Beth settled down and Bat boosted her on the horse. She leaned over in the saddle and whispered, "Be another time wait and see." A tear glistened on her cheek. She quickly spurred out and yelled when she turned in the saddle to wave, "Better luck next time, Bat!"

"Don't know what she meant by that," Dixon mused. "Oh, hoped her horse would stay out of them badger holes."

"Probably." Bat hid a grin and mounted up.

27 *The Ghost*

Mobeetie was in sight. The scouts rode in a silent world, each consumed in his own thoughts. Squeaky saddles and horses' hoofs swishing through the grass was the only sound on the prairie; jackrabbits jumping up everywhere. Suddenly the horses bolted, a wing-flapping, cackling, flock of prairie chickens took to the air; a kangroo rat ran for his life and ducked in his hole. The chickens, looking for a place to alight, flew low over a couple romping mountain lions but soon disappeared in the distance.

Dixon shifted his butt in the saddle. "Up'n Dodge awhile back 'run into a couple of your old hunting buddies—Jim and Wyatt Earp; 'said they'd be down before long."

"Been expecting 'em," Bat replied. "They'll like it here, no U. S. Marshal, no sheriff, no nothing but a haven for horse thieves, whores, a few bank robbers, land tooters, and crap shooters, plus a few red-men and dead men."

Dixon grinned. "And where money grows, whiskey flows, and wild women glow."

"All of 'em coming?"

"Nope, just Wyatt and Jim. Virgil's in Arizona—maybe Morgan...still holding you a spot for Arizona."

Light streaks were fanning out across the sky from the sinking sun when the scouts rode into Mobeetie. They were tired, but with the very thought of Molly, Bat soon forgot his hard day's ride.

The next day, at the Fort, Bat and Dixon gave the officers more news on renegade Indians; the natives were drifting back to the Panhandle. The scouts soon rode back to town.

Dixon dropped off at the "White Elephant." Bat rode to the Lady Gay. He walked in, exclaimed, "Manny Dubb's ghost?"

Dubbs laughed. "Bat Masterson, right as two rabbits!"

Bat grabbed Dubbs hand, slapped him on the shoulder, and said, "I would've sworn Emanuel Dubb's bones were bleaching out'n the breaks of the baldies!"

"I thought the jig was up too. And as you know, my wife's cousins, the Shiller boys, were scalped at 'Dobe Walls but guess I was lucky."

Bat shook his head, not believing. "Manny Dubbs, just can't believe it. I rode east, swung a ways south after the 'Dobe Walls scrap and run onto your campsite. A helluva mess, skinners hanging and cut up, sticks run under their skin, wagon burned, no horses around, so I 'figured the Redskins done you in, too."

"Well, here's what happened: Our hobbled team horses had grazed out a ways, so 'round sun-up I rode out to get 'em. Since I was out there 'just looked around for shaggies. Soon I heard yelling going on behind me, glanced back and saw about a hundred Redskins swarming the camp. The screaming bastards saw me and the chase was on. I lit out for 'Dobe Walls and a bunch of them crazy devils stayed on my tail till I got nearly there. About a couple hundred yards from camp my poor old horse dropped dead. Don't know why I done it, thought I had to save my saddle, so I jerked it off and run the fastest two hundred yards ever run in my life—totin' that darn thing, too. I made it to the saloon there at 'Dobe Walls about four o'clock in the morning and banged on the door till they let me in. How did I miss you—big country I guess, and the scrap with the Indians—everybody looking out for himself; a lot going on at 'Dobe Walls about that time. Yeah, the Redskins wiped me out—wagons, teams, guns—everything. What have you been up to, taming wild women or bragging bullies?"

Bat grinned. "Reckon a little of both. Me and Dixon's been scoutin' for the Government back southwest; circled out northwest too. Redskins are still hanging out in the river breaks, drifting back to the Panhandle; coming out of the Territory."

"Hitting their old stomping grounds, eh? Tell ya one thing, they've dealt me misery...hate some of them bastards but reckon in a way can't blame 'em—here a thousand years before I come along."

"Yup," Bat agreed, "they've been here thousands of years, but they're smoking hot now. The buffaloes are about wiped out and the natives are scratching to stay alive. The Army's going in there on the head-waters of North Fork, then Salt Fork, and farther south to Palo Duro Canyon—run 'em back to Indian Territory. They're still trying to round up the renegades that raided the John German family on the Smokey Hill River in Western Kansas; remember? Killed four of 'em. The Army thinks the Redskins are hid out here in the Panhandle holding the other kids; four girls. Hey, me and Dixon run into one of your old sidekicks out on the prairie; Dutch Henry!"

"Dutch Henry, Dutch Henry!" Dubbs fumed. "Would I ever like to get my hands on that guy. Missed him by a day after the 'Dobe Walls scrap. Did you hear what he done to me?"

"A little, just what happened?"

"Well, I homesteaded some land up north of Dodge—aimed to do a little farming. Along about that time Dutch come by with a herd of horses...had some goodlooking stuff. I bought a couple of the best he had and thought a lot of 'em. I hadn't put up a corral yet so staked 'em out with my other horses. Didn't want nothing happening to 'em so just threw my bedroll down close to the whole bunch. Along about daylight something roused me...saw a moving shadow so 'figured it was my skinner haying the horses. Guess I just dozed back to sleep; couldn't been more than a few minutes. Then something struck me—them new horses. I jumped up, and be hanged, they were gone. That confounded Dutch had done stole 'em back!"

A pioneer that couldn't laugh at his misfortunes didn't last long in the West. "Manny, that's one for the book. Heard he done some double dealing; slick as a greased weasel."

"Slick, man, that ain't the half of it. That cussed skunk not only stole the new ones but had the gall to get the other ones I had, too."

"Can't believe it," Bat said, chuckling, "took 'em out of the country?"

"Yeah, left me stranded way out there five miles from town. Didn't even know which way he headed. I wasted no time, 'hot footed it across the prairie, and when I got to town found out I wasn't the only one in the community that had horses stolen. I joined up with a posse that your brothers got up and we went after them dang thieves."

"Knew they were in on it but didn't know much about it —scouting for the Army at the time," Bat explained.

"Yeah," Dubbs replied, "Dutch and his sidekicks raided many a settler around Dodge City, and even been down in here. He dealt me misery and wiped out other homesteaders, too. But we soon found out which way they went. Cowboys coming up from the Panhandle here saw 'em headed south, for Texas. We got on their tail and soon posseized four of them bastards. Dutch got shot-up but he got away."

Bat said, "I heard you'd brought your family down here in the Panhandle. Gonna do some staking-out?"

"Yeah, did," Dubbs said, "thought it'd be safe here, this new army camp out here. But let me tell you something, Dodge City—never like this wild place. Back yonder, about a year ago, while the town was still going a mile southeast of here, I rode in innocent as a lamb. You know it's nothing much unusual around here, but I dang near got killed the first day I was there."

"One way to welcome a guy; how'd it happen?"

"Well, we were camped out a ways from old Hidetown, up the creek four or five hundred yards, so thought I'd ride in to see some old friends; buy a little stuff, too. I rode up to Decker's Shores-Of-Hell saloon and got off my horse. No more'n hit the ground, Decker and a guy by name of Collinson burst out the door in a blazing gunfight. My horse bolted, bullets flying around, hitting the ground at my feet, had me dodging every which way."

"Any damage done?" Bat asked, with a big chuckle, thinking of how Dubbs must have been dodging those bullets.

"Lucky I guess, 'scared the daylights out of me, felt the lead zinging by my ears, but didn't get a scratch. Collinson managed to dodge the bullets, too, but Decker was plugged. But 'guess you could say he was lucky, too. He was shot in the belly and the bullet went around and come out at his back-bone. He went down and the next shot got him above the knee and that bullet come out at his hip. He had severe flesh wounds but not dangerous. Me and another guy got him on his feet and helped him inside. No law, no doctor in two hundred miles, but he

160

figured he had to take care of his customers, anyway. Soon he was back serving drinks, mixing booze along with a little blood, and consarn if every once in a while he wasn't pouring good whiskey on bullet holes.

Laughing, Bat said, "Yup, 'don't know about the mix but straight stuff is good medicine; sorta wasteful. 'Guess your family was ready to leave town?"

"Well," Dubbs replied, "they've seen a little stuff like it in Dodge and my wife thinks it'd be safer back there than it is in this wild place. But we're thinking now that sometime in the future we'll set-down on a place I've got in mind about eight miles down the creek—east."

Bat and Dubb's visit was soon cut short when a stray bullet hit the Lady Gay's front door. Dubbs dodged, smiled and asked, "Reckon it's that gunslick that rides the strawberry roan?"

"If it is I'll leave town with the rest of 'em," Bat said, chuckling.

28 *Mopping Naked*

Bat and Dubbs glanced out. A cowboy puffed away the curling smoke from his six-gun. Back at the Barton ranch, Dixon's old friends told the scouts, "We'll be in town before long...got some squarin' up to do with a feller—sold us some hosses he stole from a buffalo hunter; 'down east, on Sweetwater Creek."

Things were going from bad to worse in Mobeetie. Henry Fleming had poured the last drop of whiskey in town. The Canadian River's high-rise of late had slowed all freight shipments from Dodge City. Teamsters trying to cross the river gambled heavy. However, Johnny Long's six-mule-team wagon was lucky; they made it. The Lady Gay had supplies, plenty supplies, whiskey for the Saturday night dance.

Dubbs walked out. Henry Fleming came up from the back. "Bat Masterson!" Henry exclaimed. "Seem's a coon's age since I've seen you! How's it going?"

Bat replied, "Well, I've got saddle sores, hungry as a bear, otherwise can't kick. Just got in from doing a little scoutin' for the Army. Looks you're raking it in."

"Tell you Bat, I've never seen so much money in my whole life. I'm putting in another saloon and Bill Thompson's putting in another dance hall. She's booming but short on supplies; even short on girls. There's a rumor going around about lonely women. The Army officers out chasing Redskins and gone for weeks, their wives get lonely; same with buffalo hunters' wives. No big deal in this town, just neighborly. Been west?"

"Rode southwest and swung back northwest. Redskins are still raising hell out there...killed a family, burned the wagon and run off with the horses. Anything going on around here?"

"Been pretty quiet," Henry said. "Oh, some horse thieves got in a squabble up north on the Washita. Three of 'em come down with a fatal dose of lead poison. That's about it—well, there was a little mixup down here at the Bullhorn Tavern. Digger Dugan hauled off a guy, Yankee, new in town, watching his first gunfight—and last; caught a stray bullet. Like I say, that's about it, not much going on in the last few days. Guess Molly gave you the latest news?"

"No, my first stop, what's up?" Bat asked.

"Bob and Bessie are talking about moving to Arizona. They're sort of up in the air. Seem's she's got a health problem. Doctor out here at the Post thinks she's got consumption. Light case, says she ought to be in a drier climate. Don't know how it could be much drier than it is here but that's what the Doc said. Bob and her left half-hour ago for the Fort and Molly's at the house. By the way Bat, I told them if they thought Molly ought to stay in Mobeetie she had a home at our house. The Johnny Long's made the same offer. A sad situation leaving their only kid behind, but chances are slim going west. You can ease the pain; bet she's waiting for you now."

"Well," Bat replied, "never thought about it, but Bessie always seems to be feeling 'porely.' Henry, I'll get on over there and see what's going on."

"Of course Bat, but as you know old Doc out there at the Post does more horses than people. He's the only one in two hundred miles and a week or two away. You can help settle her mind."

Bat rode up at the Brennan's little three room clapboard house. Neat, not a big house but one of the best in the new settlement. Gazing around, he noticed a log smoldering around a three-legged cast-iron pot. The Brennan cat, at the door, dashed around the house, but the Collie dog, asleep in the house shade only raised his head when Bat got off his horse; laid back down—couldn't be bothered by the visitor.

A pot of hot water usually meant one of two things at any pioneer's house...the week's washing or the Saturday night bath. It wasn't night but Molly loved her bathing anytime of day. Her dad dipped/poured the hot water into the washtub setting in the kitchen then they left for the Post. Molly shucked her clothes and was soon ready to get in the tub for her Saturday ritual. The washtub was a tight fit for bathing the adult body but she never thought of it; her mind was on her lover. She backed up to the tub and plopped down. "Oh-oo- wee!" she squealed, and jumped straight up.

Coming out of the hot water she swamped the kitchen floor. She grabbed the mop, she'd have the floor dried up in no time. It was fun, she'd never thought about doing anything like that—mopping naked. Oh, but how shocking it would be to her Mother; unthinkable! She finished her bath and was ready to crawl out. But soon she heard a banging on the door.

"Oh, my goodness, who could it be—was Dogface King back in town—had he seen the folks leave?"

The pink silk housecoat her grandmother gave her years before was hanging on a chair-back. Dripping wet, she grabbed the towel, slung on the robe, rushed to the door and peeped around the curtain. "It's him, it's him, oh it's Bat!"

She ran to the dresser, dashed on some sweet smelling stuff, then went for the door. Another knock rattled the pane. But she couldn't go to the door practically naked. She grabbed a hat then opened the door.

"Uh, Sweetheart, I've never seen you look so, ah-uh, lovely." Bat stammered, grinning broadly. "What a get-up, the big hat, shaped and draped housecoat and all!"

He grabbed and kissed her, then backed off for a closer look. She wasn't dressed for company but she looked good enough to Bat Masterson!

He pulled her close. She slung her hat, and sank deep in his arms. He held her tight and kissed her passionately. They eased up, suddenly it crossed her mind...her Dad and Mother was leaving Mobeetie. Tears filled her eyes. "Darling," she softly lamented, "you'll never know how much I've missed you. The folks are moving to Arizona. It's like another bad dream."

Molly knew there was little chance of ever seeing her Mother and Dad again. And when it crossed her mind it tore her up. She sobbed but there comes a day....

"An unfortunate situation," Bat replied, always ready to lend a sympathetic ear. "I stopped by the Lady Gay to quench my thirst and had a talk with Henry. I know if you decide to stay in Mobeetie you'll be welcome in the Fleming home or at the Johnny Long's, either."

Of course Molly was grateful. It was the agony of breaking up the little family, but she loved her Bat Masterson. Hunting buffaloes was out of his mind and he was ready to quit chasing Redskins. "Gonna settle down in Mobeetie," he said. Henry had offered him a chance to make some money at the Lady Gay and he had his town surveying job, too.

Caressing her, he said, "Honey, 'haven't figured out yet the answer to your crazy dreams, 'I won a gunfight but lost'. 'Makes no difference, I love you and staying with you till our dying day...dreaming, too, of many moons away."

She tried to forget it, put it out of her mind. Silly,

165

wasn't possible, Bat won a gun fight but he lost; a mystery that haunted her. Now, the sound of his voice was music to her ears. She snuggled in close, he squeezed her tight and kissed her again. The anxiety of her family, of everything, faded away. The lovers drifted into a another world.

"Darling, never let me go," she whispered.

He lifted her, took her soft supple body in his arms and....

29 *Jug's Epitaph*

"Whoa, Brownie!" It happened. Bob and Bessie came in from the Doctor sooner than expected. With no fence around the house and the sound of his voice, Bob parked the buggy right in front of the door. Bat dropped Molly, her feet hit the floor, he rushed to the door, and she grabbed a dress.

Bat opened the door and offered his hand. Bob said, "Well, Bat, you made it back and we're glad to see you."

Bessie, coming in behind Bob, said, "Yes, we've got a problem. Molly's told you I'm sure—I've got a light case of consumption. The Doctor says moving to a drier climate is our only hope. We're going to Arizona. Both the Flemings and Longs have offered to keep our Molly as their own. They know the risk of going west. Chances are slim, but-but-I-I." She broke down. The Brennans would soon be leaving Mobeetie.

Tuberculosis was usually a slow death. Blank expressions told it all...the end of a happy little home. Molly and Bessie sobbed; so did Bob. The family was overcome emotionally.

Bat soon broke the silence, "Nothing's going to happen to Molly, not over my dead body."

Bessie pulled herself together. "Yes, we know she loves you with all her heart and it makes us feel better."

"It's not going to be just 'Miss' Molly one of these days," Bat replied, with a smile.

Bessie gave Bat a hug and Bob shook his hand. Bat turned to leave. "I'll let you get on with your planning.

Molly, see you later."

Mobeetie's Saturday night spenders were hunters, soldiers, cowboys, and gamblers. The girl business on Featherbed Hill was thriving. Down around main street the saloons were raking in big money, money from buffalo hides. The hides brought prosperity, however the hide business would soon be history. Settlers looking for land were moving in. But Uncle Johnny figured that damn Dogface, that pain in the butt, would soon scare them away. The hitching rails in Mobeetie were crowded with horse drawn buggies, wagons, and ox-teams, but somehow saddlehorses squeezed in, too.

Saloons swinging west of town were grabbing off Fort Elliot boys. Weekdays soldiers marched for the Sergeant but Saturday nights they marched for Featherbed Hill. The Fort's five hundred white, and three hundred "buffalo" soldiers had no love for each other, but sloshing whiskey was one thing they had in common. The Lady Gay's dance floor was the first in town, but competition was moving in. More lumber was on the way. And saloons grabbing off business were bringing in girls, maybe shady ladies, but "cousins" to visit relatives—a town joke. Not all those kissing cousins hustled back east were easy on the eyes. But the ol' gals didn't care what people thought, didn't care what they said, not with the town full of lusty hunters, soldiers, gamblers, cowboys, and gunslingers. The money rolled in.

But there were complaints from settlers that wanted county organization. Not all families looking for a home could take Mobeetie's way of life. They drifted on. But with law and order, the town boosters thought newcomers would settle in."

The Brennan situation was still on Bat's mind when he rode off on Coalie. Down the lane his horse suddenly shied. Two old hide hunters were mixing it up in the dusty street. Bat thought nothing of it, such stuff went on all time, but soon one broke loose and staggered into Coalie. He seemed blind as a bat and crazy as a bedbug. Bat noticed tobacco juice running down the guy's face. That explained it. His friend had rolled him in the dirt and squirted burning juice in his eyes. A bunch was gathered around egging them on. The drunks "rasslin'n-hasslin" in the streets usually got little attention, however Bat enjoyed this one. They tangled again, rolled in the dirt, and come up spur raking shins. Wobbling around to stay on their feet, they soon started kicking hell out of each other. The bruisers finally finished it off with bare knuckles then shook hands. The bystanders eat it up, loved it; he-man stuff in the wild, wild, West. Bat rode on, headed for the Lady Gay.

Three or four doors down from the saloon, he saw a horsebacker 'thought he knew, coming down the street. Meeting-up in front of the Shores-Of-Hell saloon, Bat exclaimed, "Wyatt Earp!"

"Bat Masterson, you old hound dog!" Wyatt replied. They come off their horses and shook hands.

Bat said, "Just going to the Lady Gay for refreshments."

"I'm ready, the Lady Gay; let's go!" A booming shot went off in the Shores-of-hell saloon. "What's that—go on everyday?"

Bat kidding, replied, "Every other day; wanta look in?" A drunk was raving when they stepped in the door, "Told'ya'n told ya my hoss is thirsty too-too—dry'n'drier!"

Barney, the bartender, threatening with another shot, exploded, "And I told ya to get that sonovabitch outta here!" He fired in the dirt floor at the horse's feet. Spooked, the danged old horse went crazy. People scattered. The horse snorted, broke into a wild bucking/pitch, gassed up, turned over tables, busted a chair, and fell back on his tail. Then back on his feet, he slammed against the bar, crushed dozens' of booze bottles...pitching, he threw the guy up in the rafters. The bronc-rider came down, hit the floor on his feet behind the horse, next to the bar. The bronc bolted out the door.

Barney's voice was gruff, "Now finish your damn drink!" Bat and Wyatt were still laughing about the thirsty horse when they walked in the Lady Gay. Wyatt said, "Good four gaited horse—start, stumble, fall down and fart." Wyatt continued, "Ridin' in, saw Henry up the street, 'said you'd soon show up. Worth a two hundred mile ride anytime to see my old sidekick, but had to rush this one up to bring in a horse thief; got a knot on his head and rides a strawberry roan."

"Got the big head, I'd say. Was he selling gold bricks?" Bat asked, joshing Wyatt about his dealings in "gold bricks;" painted gold.

They guffawed. Kidding Wyatt about his gold bricks was old stuff for Bat. He continued, "How's the boys—Dodge?"

"Good, me and Jim's got a few things in mind and Morgan's ready to do something. We're still talking Arizona and that 'we' means Bat Masterson; haven't forgot?"

"Oh no, but there's money here and got a sweet thing, too."

"Don't blame you for that, but we Earp boys are hauling out of Dodge. Not the town it used to be. You know I've been 'lawin' there but too many politics now."

"You got anything else in mind, like the whole Earp clan staking out here at Mobeetie?"

Wyatt replied, "Yeah, me and Jim's still thinking about ranching here in Texas—north Panhandle. And I hear this place could use some 'law'n order'. Yeah, might

170

be a good place to hang my hat and do some law'n and ranching, too."

"You can do anything in this town you're big enough too. Dodge City has its laws, had a constable here once but he was run out of town. Now the place is as wide open as the gates of hell. Oh, a Texas Ranger drifts in once in awhile chasing outlaws that's found a haven of rest." Bat chuckled, and went on to say, "They'll steal the gold from under your saddle blanket."

Wyatt guffawed. Simmering down, he got Bat's ear, "Don't let it out. Yeah, if they ever get county organization here then there'll be a Sheriff's job. I know there's some wild'uns down here, the likes of Chummy Jones; he's the guy I'm after."

"You could handle it," Bat said, "but there'll be no county organization in '76 or '77, but it's coming. Here it's hunters, land speculators, whores, horse thieves, gunslicks, and gamblers, along with hide buyers and a few cowboys. The majority don't want this county stuff. I've been thinking about running cattle myself. These millions of acres of grass, a guy can run a hundred thousand head and cost next to nothing...if the State ever gets it staked off. But renegade Indians are giving the survey crews pure hell; wiped out five or six up north a few days back."

"Yeah," Wyatt replied. "Saw something up here on Wolf Creek; must have been it. A wagon was burned out and a piece of scalp hanging on a bush. Couldn't figure it out, Redskins usually hang onto those hairpieces."

"Tell you what happened," Bat said. "Lt. Baldwin and his men rode up when the massacre was going on. Two or three Redskins bit the dust, too. The Army's getting the natives whipped down, but these local gun fights— well, they scare the life out of these new settlers. They come one day and leave the next. By the way Wyatt, 'heard Chummy was swung."

"Swung, that figures. Better come back and ask for a job since I know Uncle Johnny's doing his best to get the town moving."

"I'll say this," Bat reminded, "you whipped out things in Dodge City and some of these poor settlers have headed back that way. They said at least Dodge had a town marshal—some law at least. Things may be simmering down here in town a little, but more arguments now on the prairie over who shot what. Herds going down to nothing. A man can get punched in the back pretty easy."

"Now Bat," Wyatt replied, "you know how it is in Dodge —take a guy like Chummy Jones, plugged or swung, it goes out on that telegraph wire then every newspaper in the country headlines it. Here a dozen men could be laid out on the prairie and who would know it? Or look what happened up here in the north Panhandle, you know, where me and Jim's figuring on buying a spread—the Casner Brothers, murdered. There's going to be a dozen killings before that's over with. Say an ox-drover carried the news out about a killing...why, it'd be a month before the news hit the next town. By then who'd give a damn anyway? Mobeetie's a helluva pl...."

"I said shut up Jug, this is my woman!" A man yelled. Jug's table was over a ways. Someone had stole his girl.

A dance hall gal brought out a drink, plunked down on a boy's lap and threw her arms around his neck. She wasted no time, soon was giving him hot sensual loving and laid on the drooling kisses. Squirming, rubbing, she whispered sweet nothings in his ear. The gleeful drunk lapped it up. His sidekicks around the table started whooping it up and poking fun...that is except one. Jug was burning.

"I said, Liverlip, she's my woman!" Jug yelled, but it

got him nothing. He leaned over the table, slobbering and chewing his words, snatched up a bottle and drew back. He aimed at his sidekick's head but the wet bottle slipped out of his hand. A gambler at the next table caught it on the temple and dropped like he was shot between the eyes. He keeled over, hit the floor, and quivered like a leaf. His gambling buddies glanced down. Jug grabbed another bottle and come down hard on his sidekick and smashed his nose all over his face. Liverlip tumbled over backwards and brought the table and his girlfriend down with him. His spurting nose streaked blood in circles and scattered shattered glass over half the saloon. Her lover was three shades out of it when the girl jumped up and hauled-ass; knew what was coming. Liverlip's pals sloshed whiskey in his face, his eyes floated in space.

Jug stood over his friend threatening, giving him the devil. But ol' Liverlip was coming around, coming off the floor, fumbling his gun, got his finger on the trigger and let'er blow! The walls echoed with a deafening roar!

Bat cupped his hand to his ear, "And what was you saying, Wyatt?"

Wyatt chuckled. "Mobeetie's one helluva place!"

Jug's Epitaph

In Mobeetie, town of lure and lore
The Cowboy's patience was thin and wore.
Could be seen that Jug was sore;
Holding his temper was a chore.
Beat and burned and stung to the core,
All he wanted was his loving whore.
"Let go of my woman!" he screamed and swore.
Fumbling his gun, he said "I'll bore
Fill you with lead plumb to the core."

But surely he knew from 'way before
'Tis a few things a man should ignore,
Swallow his pride and walk out the door.
But his pride with his lover did soar;
Nothing like it, and that's for shore.
But now it was shattered, ripped, and tore.
He had some bullets he wanted to pour,
But a surprise for Jug was in store.
His sidekick let go with his old forty-four;
The echoing walls made a helluva roar.
Jug reeled and rocked and hit the floor,
Kicked a few times with the boots he wore.
Squirming and turning he said no more.
And all he wanted was his loving whore.

30 *Wagon Sheet Bullet Holes*

If there was whiskey in the house the Lady Gay never run dry. But by mule train it came in slow from Dodge City. J. J. Long's wagon made it across the river so there was whiskey in town, whiskey in the house! Toting a supply from the back room, Henry Fleming looked around, fuming. "You damn guys know the rules around here; mess up, clean up. Drag 'im out!"

Bat and Wyatt relived every shot fired in Dodge City... every buffalo knocked down on the prairie.

"Yeah," Wyatt said, "gonna try to make a deal on a ranch here—like I say, in gold."

Bat wasn't too surprised, knew about some of Wyatt's deals in gold bricks. "Gold! Telling you Wyatt, this ain't Dodge City, no law, every man for himself, gold in town, just the mention of gold—it'll get around and there'll be hell to pay. There's plenty of 'em around, them gun toting, throat cuttin' bastards that'll cut your throat for a nickel. The name Earp or Masterson don't mean a damn thing in this town."

Wyatt looked around, leaned over, grinning wryly, and whispered, "Have got a few half-bricks to hold my saddle skirt down in this windy weather...and I'm not worried. If some dude steals 'em...." Wyatt paused, gave a big chuckle, and continued, "He's going to be surprised...tickled to death. Ah, that fresh-out-of-the-mint look—'think he's found a goldmine, then madder than all hell when he finds out them bricks ain't 24 carat!"

Bat said, "Well, figured that, but even for a five cent

brick they'll knock you in the head."

"Good collateral, though, anywhere you go, and I'll have a load next time I'm down; Mather'n me—Mysterious Dave, they call him. 'Don't go to Arizona could be ranching here in the Panhandle before long."

Bat cracked a grin, "Good luck, and remember, it's going to take a 100,000 longhorns to stock it."

Bat was a regular customer of Henry Fleming's Lady Gay, but Henry knew the Earp boys as well as the Mastersons' from his Dodge City days. He stopped by their table. "Good to see you Wyatt. Going to be down for awhile?"

"Leaving in the morning, Henry; be back before long."

Henry knew Wyatt and Bat had a lot to talk about. He had no idea how much ground they had to cover, but figured it would go on 'way in the night. Finally Henry tossed Bat the key. "Lock 'er up."

After his usual breakfast at Ellen O'Loughlin's restaurant Bat went to his usual place to buy smokings. Johnny Long exclaimed, "Bat Masterson, miss you more every time you're gone; seen Wyatt?"

J. J. Long was a quiet unassuming man but he had friends all over the western frontier. Like most of them that came down from Dodge City, Mr. Long knew them.

"Yup, good to see the ol' hoss and trying to get him to move down. The Earps are talking about buying a ranch up north of here a few miles. And they're still talking Arizona, too ....Say, you've got the store looking good with all these new supplies. 'Believe I can buy anything here I can in Dodge City."

Mr. Long said, "Wyatt mentioned him and Jim's looking around for a spread up north, there along the Indian Territory strip. I've been told horse thieves are running wild on both sides of the border, but the Earps' could handle it. I'd like to see them stake-out here." Mr. Long continued, "As for store supplies, not quite what you can buy in Dodge City. Having trouble getting some of that stuff, mostly medicine, like these new purgatives. This hoss doctor at the Post thinks these new Calotabs will cure anything. Beats castor oil, he says." A big grin spread across Mr. Long's face. "I think he means with these new pills you beat it to the outhouse faster. But I'm having trouble getting red liniment, too. Digger Dugan's old gray mare died 'count I only had one quart bottle. Kinda feel I owe him another hoss."

"Colic, huh?" Bat asked.

"That's what the horse doctor at the Post said and we doctored her for that; slick operation." Johnny laughed.

"What do you mean, slick operation?" Bat asked.

"We swung the old mare by the neck at the corral, opened her mouth and poured two quarts of castor oil and a quart of red liniment down her goosle. She belched, drenched Digger and Pancho with castor oil and liniment; died anyway. Digger's borrowing that blue donkey at the livery stable now. That jackass is so slow Digger will have another stiff to put under before he gets to the graveyard with the first one....Bad about Bessie, for the whole Brennan family; the whole town."

"Yeah," Bat replied. "They're tore up, world's fell apart. They're well liked, Bob's business is good, and they really had just got settled in. They won't be taking much of his heavy blacksmith stuff to Arizona. He's loading the wagon light as he can but their chance of outrunning the Redskins are still slim. They're real pioneers but it's their only hope for her; her health's everything. Few water holes out across the plains —that level country. A sea of grass from horizon to horizon, nothing but grass as far as the eye can see. Sometimes people get confused. You know, we've heard of it happening before, they lose their sense of direction, and with no land-marks they go in circles. Then they get hopelessly lost and starve for water."

Uncle Johnny said, "Don't know whether you know it or not, but a guy from back East looked things over and was going to buy Bob out but the deal fell through."

"Didn't talk to Bob about it," Bat replied, "but the man seemed to be a hard worker; had to be 'all them kids. Could've made fifteen dollars a week right off; couldn't beat it. What happened?"

"Yeah, the guy beat it, beat it out of town with his family—wife and six kids—about daylight. He had his two plug hosses hooked to his old butcher-knife wagon, and a kid's head poked out under the wagon sheet between every bow. 'Going back to Dodge City where it's half-way civilized,' he said."

"Nothing unusual. I reckon that little shooting scrape at the Buffalo Chip woke up the kids."

Mr. Long said, "I'd like to see the day when the town settles down, permanent growth, that's all we need. I hate to see anyone leave. It's usually that damn Dogface King, but he ain't the only one raising hell when they come to town. This time the covered wagon caught a few stray bullets and got the whole family stirred up. The woman was up in the air!" J. J. chuckled. "She told me, 'We're afraid them all-fired outlaws' bullets are going to ruin the wagon sheet before we can get out of town.' Bat I can't blame 'em. Now, this is no place to raise a kid. But you know one of these days, get some law, get rid of these gunslingers, then we'll have people in here from everywhere to settle; good people like the Brennans. Ranching and cattle, cattle by the thousands that cover this prairie like the buffaloes did in the past. We've got acres and acres of land suitable for agriculture, too."

"Yup," Bat said, "Bob gets along with decent people and I hate to see them leave."

"Well, you know Bat, Bob sees them all at the shop....All kinds, outlaws and good people alike. What would they do if he wasn't around to repair their boots, patch-up their saddles and harness; fix their broken down wagons and buggies? But old Dogface is about the only one that gets on his nerves and that's on account of Molly. He wants him to leave her alone. Bob has no use for him and Bessie hates him; the whole family does. He dodges you, afraid of you, but the boys in town have to kiss his tail; got 'em shaking in their boots. Like I say, the man treats me O K, but he's one more jealous over-bearing bully. He brags, still shooting off his mouth, he laid a brand on Molly in Dodge City. When he's around there's not a man or woman in this town that will be seen talking to her. Hate to say it, but even Mary, my own wife, and Ellen O'Loughlin shy around her, too. People are talking and warning new settlers to watch out for him, and don't be seen talking to that Brennan girl.' The sonovabitch has got to be stopped."

Mr. Long went on to say, "Prospectors are thinking twice before settling here. When you're here he stays hid-out, but when you're gone he comes in and blows around, 'get rid of Masterson I'll run this damn town.' But he's frying now and has been ever since you staked out here. I do have to say this: he gets along with the renegade Indians, deals with them in stolen horses, however he's nothing but a coward; you're his problem."

"Uncle Johnny you know and I know—well, every-body knows the Indians like his orange looking hair; strange to 'em. And I'll say this, everybody knows how hard J. J. Long, Tom O'Loughlin, Henry Fleming, and others have worked to get some kind of law and order for his kind; county organization, pushing, pushing hard,

179

seems hopeless I guess, but you guys just don't give up."

"Well, reckon so," Mr. Long said, going for his Prince Albert, "but about old Dogface. His hair is strange to 'em. I think he's still officially in the Army and they're looking for him now. He gets in trouble and hides out with the Redskin renegades; 'bet that's where he is now. But the whole town is talking, watching, waiting, holding their breath, and they know it's coming. But there's one man he can't bluff, one man that stands in his way, and for Molly Brennan's love, the cold-blooded killer is hell-bent on getting Bat Masterson!"

31 *Trailing Cattle*

Charles Goodnight held 10,000 Longhorn steers on Sweetwater Creek a mile southwest of Mobeetie. They were headed for Dodge City, Kansas. The crew hoped for better luck ahead. Trouble dogged them all the way from South Texas...the weather scorching hot, and everytime the cowboys looked up Indians were cutting steers out of the herd. Dancing heat thermals and blue mirages across the dry country was enough to drive thirsty cowboys raving mad. Wild charging buffalo herds broke the trail-herd time after time, stampedeing cattle over country for miles around. Roaring thuderstorms sparked electricity from steer horn to steer horn. Uneasy cowboys watched in awe, in fear, hell for night herding cowboys on wrung out horses...chasing, yelling in rain and hail...the cyclone wind blowing and twisting, raising the saddles tight on the saddle girths. But come hell or high water they would hold the herd. However, fate played a deathly hand when a saddlehorse stepped in a badger hole; it rolled him, and punched the saddlehorn in the cowboy's heart. The trail herd left enough trouble behind to last until they got to Kansas. Only a cattleman like Col. Charles Goodnight could hold a string together when everything seemed to be going wrong. Cattle drives and buffalo herds would soon be a thing of the past but the drouthy/dry weather would always be around.

Soon the cattle smelled water before Sweetwater Creek came in sight. They ran to quench their thirst and drank until their sides swelled to a strut. The steers were in water up to their bellies tanking up but the thirsty cowboys paid them no mind. Coming out of the saddles they soon flopped down at the waters' edge and filled up, too.

The cowboys quenched their thirst but they had other things on their mind—women and whiskey. Months had passed since they had seen a woman. Imaginations ran wild, they were raring to make the town they'd heard so much about. Col. Goodnight had them draw straws to see who would hold the herd. The losers grumbled but the lucky ones wasted no time—went for a swim to wash off the dirt and odor then headed for town. And the word soon spread on Featherbed Hill about those "poor cowboys" left behind to hold the herd. The boys had just dived in the creek for a refreshing swim when wagon-loads' of gals showed up to enjoy a swim, too.

Mobeetie was jubilant. The Panhandle land and cattle business was on the way. The first big trail herd was moving through. From the Pink Pussycat's Paradise to the Shores-Of-Hell every saloon in town threw a party for the lonely homesick cowboys. They were welcomed with open arms and beds. But first the cowpokes celebrated. They ran their horses up and down the street, a bottle in one hand, six-shooter in the other, yelling, reeling in the saddle, shooting at anything that moved. Squealing pigs, stray dogs and cats ran for cover to soon disappear under the houses. Chickens and guineas jumped straight up when bullets peppered the ground around their feet; cowboy fun. The cowpunchers were making up for lost time but the ducking dudes and dodging drifters thought a bunch of damn fools had rode in.

He was the trail-herd comic, Ol' Shorty they called him. His weather beaten face went into a mild contortion with every big ear to ear grin. His hawk bill nose hung over an expertly curled out longhorn mustache. But his chopped off beard showed signs a cowboy barber had been practicing with a pair of mule shears. The friendly grin on his unusual face always drew a kindly chuckle from strangers. At the Lady Gay, everybody loved it when he danced with Frogmouth Annie. Giggling teenage cowboys stood around poking fun at the "old man." He was twenty-seven.

Ol' Shorty's leather-like, sun beaten face, wrinkled and tanned, was messed up by nature; helped too by the business end of a long horn. A scar across his cheek and a few front teeth knocked out made no difference to Ol' Shorty; he was a dancing fool.

Shorty's big well worn hat never came off. The high crown put him as tall as his over sized jolly partner. He held her tight, shoved their arms out and jerked them back. Reeling and rocking, they danced to the music of Slat Slattery. He kicked his heels, and stomped his feet to jingling his spurs-rowels. Old Froggie pulled her little soused up, shriveled up, fired up cowboy's head hard against her hung out, hung over, hung down breast.

Ol' Shorty, in hog-heaven, grinned like a possum eating green persimmons. She swung him out, pulled him in, picked him up, and whirled him around. The crowd whooped and hollered.

Froggie plopped down at a table and pulled Shorty down on her lap. In fun, she reached up and jerked his hat off. And in a wild state of excitement, she broke out with uncontrolled laughter; found a scalp as slick as a peeled onion. She pulled his head down in her deep valley of cleavage and smothered him with "affectionate" love, winding his stem. He soon came up for air with a sheepish sinful grin. Now this ol' cowboy that hadn't see a woman in many moons was hot as a three dollar stove. She was tearing him up. Ol' Froggie buried his bald head

183

in her oversize bosom again. The cowboys yelled, "A three bagger!" Suddenly Froggie jerked his pants down, and the Lady Gay drunks went wild. It made no difference to Ol' Shorty; he had passed out on rotgut whiskey.

In the 1870's Mobeetie had money, whiskey, and women. Gals like Frogmouth Annie and Silver Belly Sue were all part of the Western scene. Salty, but in a country the hunters called no man's land, where nobody give a damn who shot out the lights, the girls had to be.

Bat was still thinking of the Brennan's, their unfortunate situation, when Charles Goodnight asked him to take over the herd, and "move 'em north." The Colonel had some "puttin' away to do." His wife's brother, Granger Dyer, got mixed up in a Mobeetie gunfight. He lost. Mr. Goodnight wanted to give him a decent burial, even put him in a wooden box; a rare privilege in these parts. His was one of the few recorded deaths in Mobeetie during this time. Many died with their boots on without a prayer, even a pebble for a headstone.

Bat would take the job, help anyone, but everything come together at the same time...the Brennans moving, new job, and King sneaking around, raising hell, keeping Molly and the settlement stirred up. People in town had heard King blow, "Get rid of Masterson and take Molly— run this damn town!" Dogface's threats were of little concern to Bat, but he figured the Brennans would as soon have their last few days in Mobeetie alone. His surveying and Lady Gay job could wait. And for King, he'd take care of him later; face him any day of the week. Uncle Johnny knew Goodnight, told him if anyone could handle the herd Bat Masterson could. No greenhorn, he knew cattle, the Canadian River, and had an easy way with Cowboys.

At twenty-one Bat was older than many on the trail,

but not Ol' Shorty. Shorty was shriveled and wrung out, but an all-Texas cowboy. He loved and laughed with Frogmouth Annie but he was ready to hit the trail.

Along about daylight, Bat yelled, "Let's head 'em up and move 'em out, whippin'n spurrin'!"

Cowboys went after the cattle, yelling, chasing and bringing them out of the creek bottom. On the trail, the chuckwagon led the way, usually pulled by four big mules. Then come Johnny Jones, a cowboy known for his big brown hat, wrangling a remuda of saddlehorses and two extra mules. Then the herd. The point men soon had the lead steers headed for Dodge City. Grazing cattle were brought out of trees and brush then lined in with the moving herd. The long string of cattle was soon passing between Fort Elliot and Mobeetie. The Post and settlement were less than a mile apart and the cowboys liked that. The herd trailed in close to Featherbed Hill at the northwest edge of town. The swing and flank men held the middle string, but the drags, the dust eaters, trailed the mile-long herd, still bringing them out of the creek bottom. People in droves rode out in wagons, buggies, horseback, and even walked to see the trail drive. Visiting city dudes from back east had never seen such a spectacle. European land buyers and their wives stood in awe. How could so few cowboys handle so many animals? But this was his glory, where the cowboy's reputation was born, where he earned his sourdough biscuits.

Bat rode whipping and spurring from one end of the string to the other lining in steers. The winding string stretched longer and longer. The chuckwagon, headed north, passing by town while the tail-end string was still coming out of the creek. Drags riding and yelling, dodging trees and brush, splashing through water, were hard on the tail of the last onery steers. Soon tunes like,

"Come-a-ty-ya-yippy-ah-ay," rolled out.

The watchers choked on dust but they paid it no mind. Bug-eyed people watched bellowing calico steers of every color and description under the sun; they loved it. Steers with art formed horns as long as a rail, twisted and bowed from tip to tip, passed by. Horns clashing, popping, cracking, an unusual sound to the crowd, but thrilled at the sight of the growing mile and a half long string...winding, bending like a snake in the grass, one steer on the heels of another.

The lead steers passed by the excited town watchers and on past Featherbed Hill. The gals in front of the shacks were yelling, waving, and flaunting their wares when Bat rode up. The trail herd was on the move, but a point man was missing; Ol' Shorty, the right point. Bat would've swore he saw Shorty leading the drive a few minutes before, but the dust was fogging.

A wrung out Buckskin horse stood out in front of a shack on Featherbed Hill, a shack called, "The Hen House." Didn't Shorty throw his saddle on a Buckskin back at the remuda? Bat was thinking he did. Trailing cattle was dead serious business, and this string would follow Old Blue, the leader, like a hound dog after a coon, but Bat Masterson could never pass up a joke, either. He knew old sex crazed Shorty was trying to finish off in two minutes what he'd missed the last two years. Bat felt for him, all the boys on the range, but he wanted Shorty with the herd. He eased up to the Buckskin, grabbed the reins and spurred out. Bursting out of the shack, Shorty yelled, "Hey, bring my hoss back!"

Bat rode a short ways, dropped the reins over a sagebrush and loped on. Shorty's crazy action gave Bat belly laughs that almost knocked him out of the saddle. The girls were yelling, jumping up and down, boiled over with hilarious laughter, too. They watched Shorty run

186

for his horse, darting and dodging between shacks, trying to hold his hat on and pants up…his pants slipping down, down to his old knee high boots—boots trying to outrun the rest of him. His chin stuck out like the neck of a sandhill crane. Mobeetie had never seen such crazy action. Shorty had Hen House ways but his Hen House visit was cut short; his sidekicks hardly missed him.

Bat soon caught up with Johnny Jones, not far behind the chuckwagon. When Bat reined-up, Jones asked, "What to hell was going on down there at the Hen House—'saw a guy running like his tail was on fire?"

Bat said, "Hot crew…like this, Shorty was trying to catch up; fastest love making ever!" They burst out with laughter.

The trail herd was moving north and Mobeetie was away back in the distance. All sorts of trail driving tunes rolled across the prairie: "I'm Riding Old Paint And Leading Old Sam," and "Get Along Little Dogies." There were the sad homey songs, too, "Tell Mother I'll Be There," followed by a burst of, "Fall in there, ya ornery sonovbitch!"

The long string of cattle winding around the hills north of Mobeetie would make any cattleman proud. The trail herd went over the hills, out of sight, and the cowboys soon faded away in a world of their own. The sightseeing dudes soon headed back to town with enough memories to last a lifetime. Now the pioneers looked for big things to happen in ranching.

The herd made it to Jim Springer's ranch-saloon on the Washita River the first day, and here they bedded down. Jim's ranch headquarters was on the Canadian River, but in 1874 he opened his outpost ranch-saloon on the Washita fifteen miles north of Mobeetie. However, Bat had friends, buffalo hunters Jim and Bob Cator, that set down a year sooner 60 miles west of Mobeetie in 1873. They came from England in 1871 and onto the Panhandle two years later. And eventually they opened up the Zulu trading post at their dugout living quarters in the North Panhandle. They were located in hostile Indian country 20 miles north of Adobe Walls; it's still a mystery how they survived. Twenty seven Whites and five or six hundred Indian warriors fiercely fought the Battle of Adobe Walls and the Cator boys had no idea what happened until they went in for supplies the next day....Then, they fell into the job of helping bury white people, Indians, and dead horses.

Jim Springer welcomed anyone to his saloon, including Fort Elliot's buffalo soldiers. Mobeetie didn't go after the buffalo boys' money like Jim did. And camping at Springer's the Goodnight cowboys soon found out gambling went over big at Springer's Ranch Saloon.

Bat rolled out the next morning with Molly on his mind. But the point men were thinking of Old Blue, the leader of the herd. The cowboys loved the big steer, his trailing instinct. Always at sunup he was at the head of the line ready to go.

Early of a morning the devious wolves and coyotes sneaked around the herd, making the steers nervous. The wolves were bold, bold enough to come in and rip a steer's flank. Cowboys thought they did it just for the hell of it. The wolfpacks' insatiable appetite never went begging with buffaloes around. The big lobo wolves could drag a cow carcass, and if cornered they could whip a pack of dogs. Pioneers knew the wolf had his place in the balance of nature, however they had no love for him. The wolf would soon go the way of the buffalo and only the coyote would be around to live on rabbits, rodents, and the farmers' chickens.

The trail herd moved on. Old Blue led the cattle off the gentle rolling country, straight for the Canadian

River. A mangy coyote flanked the blue steer. But that coyote picked on the wrong critter. Old Blue gave him the business end of a horn, tossed him in the air, and kept moving on. A riled up Longhorn will take on anything that offers trouble; mountain lions, wolves, or even the lowly coyote.

The sloping country soon dropped off to steep hills and deep canyons. Bat knew there could be big trouble for the chuckwagon. Should the teamster/cook lose the chuckwagon it would be a disaster. Cowboys had to have their vittles. Bat and the teamster chained all four wheels hoping to make the wagon safe; slide it all the way downhill. But the idea of riding that thing scared the daylights out of the teamster; he walked. Soon the downhill-wagon was banging the mules in the butt. The mules hated it, tried to outrun the wagon, but the teamster brought them down safe.

Bat left the herd and rode to a vantage point high on a bluff. There he could see the string from one end to the other. The memory of cattle coming off the rolling plains, down the steep slope, stuck with Bat. The chuckwagon had made it down, then Johnny Jones with the remuda of saddlehorses, and finally the thousands of motley steers pouring off the caprock like a dirty stream of water with whooping and hollering cowboys to keep them lined in. The lead steers were soon brushing through the river bottom salt cedar, over a mile ahead of the drags just starting downhill. Not an animal or man was lost; not even the chuckwagon cook.

Bat heard a swing man yell. "Whoa-ho-now-whoa, you old sonovabitch, whoa!" Bat quickly looked around. A skunk had spooked the cowboy's horse, but with luck, the line held and the steers kept moving on. The horse snorted, gassed up, and went wild...pitched, sun-fished, reared up, pawed the air, come down, and broke into again. The cowboy, his spurs hard against the horse's belly, hung on for dear life. He "pulled leather," but the bronc finally bucked him off. The cowboy had been thrown off horses' before but never at a time like this. It needled him, needled him to tears when he landed in a five-foot cactus! The cowpoke wouldn't let that kind of pricking bother but only long enough to pull out the thorns; all in a day's work.

The cowboy had his britches down when Bat rode up. The boy's naked butt looked like a porcupine. They pulled thorns and mounted up. But soon the Drags were in trouble, too. The cowboys heard a mountain lion scream. Bat looked around, then raced for the tail-end string. The mountain lion boogered the steers and a half dozen broke from the trail-herd; they took off in a dead run. Bat dug in his spurs, the bunch split up. Going after the wild-eyed critters, one of the Drag's rode in close. Bat yelled, "You get them and I'll get these!"

The cowboys were soon racing with the steers, and with their quirts, whipping and kicking them in the tail to bring them back in line. But soon they hit a grassy bog and sunk in deep. Coalie did too, hit the soft ground and sunk to his knees before Bat could leave the saddle. Coming off, Bat landed on a water moccasin. The snake struck his boot-top, but no damage was done. Bat quickly loosened the tight saddle girth to give the horse more freedom, then scrambled to get on solid ground. Coalie fought it with everything he had, struggling, heaving, crow hopping, until he finally hit solid ground, too. The steers struggled, floundered around going deeper and deeper. The cowboys had seen it all, drouthy/dry country, and now this.

32 *Raging Canadian River*

The bog shook like jelly. The steers running hog wild and crazy hit the mud and sunk in deep. Head and horns was all that could be seen. The cowboys kept their horses at a safe distance and went for steer horns with their looping lariats. Roping, tugging, yelling, they soon snaked them out one at a time. The mud covered animals were lined back in the string and the herd moved on. The chuckwagon and remuda waited at the river for the tail-end cattle to move up. The herd was brought in a tight circle and held. The cowboys were talking river crossing when Charles Goodnight rode up. He come off his horse where the cowboys stood waiting. "Well, you boys got 'em here."

"Evening, Sir," Bat replied. "Yup, we did. The river's running high and the steers gaining weight on this grass. Did you get your brother-in-law put away?"

"Yeah, did, and I'll tell you boys, 'never had such confounded luck since I was on a trail drive to a Wyoming Indian Agency. Back then my partner caught a deadly arrow in the leg. Dying, I promised Ollie (Oliver Loving) I'd carry him back home to be buried—promised Granger the same thing. 'Wanted to put him away with dignity, like in a wooden box; 'could find no lumber. Even I did, couldn't find a solitary soul in Mobeetie to do the job...I mean build a box for the dead, so wrapped him in a sheet. But that's not all. Digger Dugan's damned old donkey wouldn't go near the dead, so hauled the body off laying on the back seat of a hack. We put him under and now, rest the dead's soul, he's walking the streets of gold. The way things are in that town 'done all I could; wild wicked place. That fool on that old red roan horse has got the town all tore up."

The river's high-rise was fearsome. Col. Goodnight talked it over with the cowboys. Heavy winter snows in the mountains and warm days had it running bank to bank. People on the north bank were trying to get to Mobeetie. Some had waited for days to cross the raging water. The grass was good, and the cattle gaining weight, but Goodnight was anxious to move the herd to market. The high water looked impossible but the next day Goodnight's patience ran out. He was ready to go. "Bat, she's rolling and dangerous—what do you think, can we make it?"

The Colonel's mention of the red roan rider got Bat's attention, but crossing the treacherous river was on his mind. "Horses' can but don't know about the herd and chuckwagon. Chuckwagon's going to be our biggest problem."

The cowboys watched whirlpools grab chunks of driftwood and suck it under. That was a good sign the horses and steers would have to fight it all the way. The cowboys were apprehensive; had doubts, maybe suicide, but they would try it anyway.

Goodnight took a couple of cowboys and rode up and down the river looking for the best crossing. They finally settled on the place where they held the herd. "Fifty yards across the swiftest part; five or six ropes?" Goodnight asked.

Bat knew Goodnight was warning his men about the dangerous channel, and the ropes they'd need to pull the chuckwagon across.

Mr. Goodnight faced the uneasy cowboys. "Any volunteers?"

192

Charles Goodnight would never ask a man to do something he wouldn't do himself. He had lost two cowboys in the raging Arkansas River on a trail-drive to a Wyoming Indian Agency and didn't want it to happen here.

"I can make it," Bat insisted. "Coalie's a good swimmer, knows the river. I'll tie my hat, boots, and guns to the saddlehorn 'case I have to swim."

Bat rode naked in dangerous water sometimes, but a hundred people were stranded on the north bank; might take him for a bleached out Redskin. Women were in the bunch. The cowboys could handle the tow ropes, but there was the usual problem of swift water. The ropes were tied end to end with one end tied to the wagon tongue. Bat took the other end and urged Coalie in the raging river. The horse hit the deep water and went out of sight; seemed an eternity but he came up. Bat was still in the saddle hanging to the rope, fighting drift, riding the waves, up and down. The rolling water, surfing with a roaring back splash, drenched Bat with silt. Soon he went out of sight, in sight, out of sight and didn't come up.

"Where is he?" Goodnight's voice was rough with worry. "Head out down—where did he go—his horse, did he come up—where's Bat? Quick! Head out down...."

A cowboy yell went up. "He made it at that tree!"

The cowboys yelled, and Bat heard stranded people on the north bank cheering, too. A couple of cowboys crossed to the north bank to handle the chuckwagon tow line, and Bat crossed back to give a hand on the wagon.

Waving and signaling across the river soon everybody was ready. The cowboys on the north bank tightened on the tow line. The nervous teamster/cook urged the team-mules in the water. Chances were slim the trail-herd bunch would have a cook if the rope broke.

193

The north bank boys kept the tow line tight, the chuckwagon team had to follow. A horseback cowboy on each side of the wagon held a steadying rope. The danger was there, the ropes jerking, slacking off, tightening and the cowboys edgy.

The team hit the deep channel and went under. The frantic teamster lost his hat, grabbed for it, but kept urging his mules on. The wagonbed, cradled between the chasis standards, floated up on the standards then settled back on the chasis. Swinging around downstream in the churning water, the wagon soon flooded. The teamster, standing knee deep in water yelled at his team, whipping and coaxing. Soon a tow line knot slipped, jerked, tightened up, but held. And suddenly the upstream cowboy on the steadying rope slammed against the back wheel and swung the wagon around further. The team went under, come up, and the teamster screamed frantically, "The whole damn thing is going!"

The cowboys on the north bank urged their saddlehorses on and kept a hard pull on the tow rope. The wooden bed floated up, up, down, up again dangerously teetering at the standards' top edge. Separated from the chasis, the wagon, the mules and the delirious teamster/cook were gone!

The upstream cowboy yelled at the teamster/cook, "The pots and pans, save the pots and pans, they're floatin' off!"

The swearing teamster screamed back, "To hell with the pots and pans, save the cook!"

Pans and other stuff floated off but there was that steady pull on the tow line. Everybody prayed it didn't break. The team-mules, up and down, fighting the current, washing sideways and crazy, finally held their footing and brought the wagon out on solid ground.

Stranded people on the north bank yelled for the

happy teamster/cook. Waiting to cross, there was people in wagons, buggies, some on horseback, and one was riding a donkey. A few walked, and one old man was leading a goat. Old men, young men, women and kids. And two pretty girls that looked too innocent to be dance-hall gals.

"Good job there, men," Mr. Goodnight said, when the dripping men crossed back to the south side. "Now the remuda?"

"Horses be no problem," Bat replied.

"The herd?"

Bat warned, "Keep 'em out of the whirlpools, but in that swift water...a break in the string and we could lose a bunch in no time. I'll be riding the right swing in case the string bends."

Johnny Jones and two more cowboys soon had the remuda of horses and extra team mules crossing the river, too. Long legged rein free horses had a better chance than cows. Jones held the horses' and mules on the north bank and the other cowboys crossed back. It'd take all hands and the cook to get the herd across, but the cook had all he wanted. Anyway, he had to dry out the vittle makings.

The cattle was ready, the cowboys were ready, and Charles Goodnight was ready, too. He'd try it. He was tough as rawhide, stern with his men, but fair. The ex-Texas Ranger had fought the Indians but had Indian friends. Cowmen sometimes asked cowboys to run a risk they wouldn't do themselves, but not Goodnight. "Never lose your life over a ornery steer," he said once. Horse thieves and cattle rustlers dealt most ranchers misery, but Goodnight would challenge any outlaw that crossed him. His men respected him. The cowboys tip-toed through meadow muffins and mounted up; ready to go.

Goodnight yelled, "Head 'em up and mov'em out

boys, whippin'n spurrin'! You point men jump Old Blue in and the rest will follow. We're at the mercy of God and the river; be careful!"

Prodding and crowding the steers, the cowboys yelled and flailed their quirts. Cursing and coaxing they brought the cattle to the river's edge. Old Blue jumped in and soon others hit the water too. Men and animals bobbing up and down fought the dangerous current. Nothing but head and horns could be seen of the floundering cattle.

As Bat had feared, the swift channel bowed the string in the middle. The line suddenly broke and struggling steers slammed against Bat. Fighting for their life, a steer horn swung around and knocked Bat out of the saddle. Another swing man came in to close the gap. Bat didn't come up, not a chance under the kicking feet of the wallowing steers. He fought the river, gulping dirty water, sand and silt. Coalie headed for the north bank—an empty saddle!

Mr. Goodnight and his point men, bringing lead steers out on dry ground, soon got the word that Bat was missing. Goodnight dropped everything and whipped out on a wild ride down the river. He soon spotted Coalie but no Bat. The floating drift had fooled the cowboys time and again but the Colonel wouldn't give up. He watched whirlpools spin driftwood and drag it under. He knew it would do the same thing with a cowboy that had been knocked out of the saddle; he'd soon wind up in Indian Territory. And there was always the real danger of disappearing in quicksand. The boss took a cowboy and rode farther down the river. He shaded his eyes, looked up the river, down the river for a bobbing head. No Bat, only a dozen steers covered with sand and silt that had been rolled and tumbled.

No sign of Bat so Goodnight sent the cowboy back for more help. The river's muddy back-water, over a mile wide, swamped weeds and brush far from the main stream. The men thought of everything. Had Bat come out on the south bank? A couple of cowboys volunteered to cross back and look for Bat, but Goodnight figured there'd be no use. Steer tracks showed up in the mud where Coalie come out but no sign of Bat. The look on their worried faces showed doubt that he made it; deep concern! On down the river they found a big motley faced steer that had been rolled and tumbled; he stood his ground. Cowboys respect those horns. One swipe and he can rip a horse's belly open.

The men kept riding, hollering and loping up the river, down the river, and fooled by "drift" many times for a bobbing head. Sadly they gave it up and were riding off. But Suddenly they reined up and listened, looked at each other. Where did the yelling come from? The only place it could be was at that lone tree away out there in waist deep water. They whirled their horses around and splashed toward the tree.

A familiar chuckle. "You guys leave a man up a tree without a horse?"

Bat dropped out of the tree, onto a cowboy's horse and rode to dry land naked from the waist down. But since cowboys don't wear shorts except on Sunday he lost nothing but his britches. The Canadian River had done it to a circuit Judge, too, but Bat wouldn't give a hoot'n holler if he'd been stark naked; just too glad to be alive.

Goodnight, bent over with laughter, slapped his thighs, and said, "Well, can't go for that short skirt style, but you done it; don't know how."

Bat stood bottom naked to the world and laughing cowboys. "Like this," he said, "got knocked out of the saddle, had to do something in a hurry. I come up but my sand-logged britches kept dragging me under—

kicked 'em off, but that damn steer rolled on top of me and kicked me to the bottom." Bat nodded toward the motely faced steer. "Fightin' and flounderin' around 'grabbed anything I could. Happened that old sucker's tail brushed my face, grabbed it and hung on for dear life. That big bastard's one helluva good swimmer but the ornery cuss drug me over underwater brush and nearly dehorned me."

"A two-legged bull and no horn!" Goodnight remarked, still laughing.

"Reckon you could say that. Old critter didn't like me tailing him; got in shallow water and turned on me. Never skint up a tree so fast in my life with a naked ass at that."

Bat laughed with the boss and rest of the cowboys. "He wouldn't let me come down. Tell you something else, the seat on that saddle is smoother than the bark on that tree."

The trail boss had sent Shorty to the wagon for a pair of britches. The wagon carried bedrolls and extra stuff in case of an emergency...ropes, saddles, girths, birdles, shirts, britches, odds and ends. Shorty soon came back leading Coalie.

"Mr. Goodnight, don't know what to tell ya, but everything's done floated outta the wagon 'ceptin' what was in the top box and tied down. No britches, no shirt, no nothin' like that. Oh, I got this here towsack that was tied on the sideboard."

Mr. Goodnight stared at Bat. "Now I've seen a lot of crazy things in Mobeetie, but never a cowboy riding down main street in gunnysack rompers!"

His remark sent the cowboys into another uncontrolled fit of laughter. Bat was heading back to Mobeetie. Shoot-outs and drunken brawls in Mobeetie didn't bother Bat Masterson, but towsack rompers scared the life out of him. Some old buffalo hunter with too much to drink might take a shot at "one'o them thar white Injuns."

Bat's sense of humor took over. He glanced down at his bare legs and grinned. "Well, baggy britches, if I gotta, I gotta!"

The cowboys were anxious to help out. They took their pocket knives and cut leg holes in the sack. Mr. Goodnight, with a big grin, remarked, "Boys maybe you better make a small hole there in front."

"Darn small!" come a chrous from the laughing cowboys as Bat stood cracking a big grin, his gunnysack britches pulled on. Fun time, the joshing cowboys whooped and hollered.

Soon Col. Goodnight, a good man, said, "Now you boys gather 'round, got something to say." He looked up, and said, "Now Lord and Master that made this old world and all these cows and some good hosses' too, we give praise and thanks for bringing us across the river safe. Didn't lose a steer or man, and now get Bat and his hoss back across 'cause if he's sinning he's just half sinning; he's just half naked. We thank you, Amen."

Before they rode off the cowpokes had to get in a few more punches, swore they'd never seen a cowboy, buffalo hunter, or even a drunken gunslinger riding across the prairie in burlap britches wearing a brace-of-sixes. They could see the old West changing but not that fast. The potato sack pants were ridiculous but who cared? Bat pulled at his britches and swung up in the saddle.

33 *Potato Sack Rompers*

Bat thought crossing the river where the people waited would be safe as any place. But he had to be sure his rigging —hat, boots, spurs, and guns were tied tight on the saddle before he coaxed Coalie in the water. Coming loose, losing his stuff, would be disastrous. He secured everything with the leather saddle strings.

He got off his horse, looked around—hesitated. If the stranded people happened to see him wandering around on the river bank in tow-sack rompers they'd think he was out of his mind; he wasted no time. But before he swung up in the saddle ...well, nature was calling. He had to get rid of a belly full of gulped down river water. Behind a stand of Jimson weeds, there was nobody in sight, nobody to see him, so he cleared his potato sack britches and let'er rip. Suddenly he cut'er off. A burst of snickering/giggles come from a plum thicket not far from where he was standing; wasn't a man.

Turning, Bat didn't see anyone, but the giggling kept up. He couldn't figure it out, what was going on? He jerked at his sack britches.

On the opposite side of a knoll the bushes rustled and soon a young girl stalked out. She walked toward him. Laughing, she said, "That's about the funniest looking thing I've ever seen!"

He mumbled, "Maybe it is funny looking. I did get everything back in the sack?" Sheepishly, he asked, "Are you lost?"

"Them tow-sack britches! Oh no, I'm not lost, just

want to go to Mobeetie, but it looks hopeless. I'm Susie Shores."

"I'm Bat Masterson. Tell you what, uh-Susie, not safe for wagons, buggies, or even horses, and the river may be higher in the morning; don't rightly know how I can help you."

"I'm just trying to get to Mobeetie to see my poor old aunt—my poor old dying aunt."

Ol' soft hearted Bat could never turn down a plea like that, especially from a pretty girl, her blouse unbuttoned to her belly button. The heat was dreadful, and those beautiful begging dark eyes; he couldn't be so unneighborly. This was an emergency, going to see her poor old dying aunt. He had already risked everything on those old wild-eyed steers, and really, it hadn't crossed his mind not to help this poor girl.

"Tell you what Susie, it's going be risky at best, but if you wanta take a chance, ride back'o the saddle, and hold to the leather tie-down strings...."

"Oh, I can do that," she broke in.

"But here's the catch, we get in deep water and you holding to the leather strings, you'll have to sort of float or Coalie's going under with the weight. It's dangerous, but I've done it before with a friend, and you'll have to watch your heels. This horse hates flopping feet in his flanks."

Bat looked around, nobody in sight. He already had enough of that burlap britches exposure. He swung up in the saddle and pulled Susie up behind. People on the river bank was out of sight and the herd had moved on.

"Now Susie wrap the leather strings, there on each side of the saddle, one around each hand but don't tie 'em. Might want to get loose in a hurry. Grip 'em—you a good swimmer?"

"Yes, but what if I lose my grip the way this water's

rolling; don't want to swim in this."

"Rolling, but not like it was. Give me your shoes, I'll tie 'em on, but first you better pull off your-your skirt...ah, oh well, reckon we're ready; hold on!"

Bat laid his big hand on Susie's and held it when he urged Coalie in the water. She was scared, shaking, but with his hand on hers it sort of relaxed her. She was game enough to risk it, but didn't realize that sand and silt in her clothes would be like lead. Coalie picked his way, walked the bottom until they hit the deep channel; extremely dangerous.

Hold tight, we're going in!" He gave her a quick hand squeeze; no panic now. The horse fought the raging water, went under, hit the bottom, come up pawing, snorted and shook his head. Water splashing his face, he sneezed, snorted again, but in the deep water he kept swimming, going for the other side.

"Oh-oh-oo, Bat!" Susie screamed, holding to the leather strings, drag-floating, she pulled in close to Bat. The raging water was deadly, swift, back-splashing and roaring.

"Hold on!" Bat warned. "We're going to make it! At the mercy of God and this good horse, we'll make it. It's dangerous as hell but we'll make it, just hold on!" Sandy water drenched their eyes. They rolled and bobbed up and down, strangling, bumping driftwood, and swept a mile down stream from where they come in. Close to the south bank, a whirlpool suddenly grabbed them, spinning them around...out of control, out of sight, horse and riders soon come up.

Susie screamed, "It's hopeless! Oh Lordy, help us, help us, we're gone!"

"Hold on! I've got you!" Bat's voice gave her hope.

The awesome river whirled them around like a chunk of driftwood. Swirling out of sight and coming up the

202

horse was soon slung out on a firm sandy bottom. Bat had been through this sort of thing before and thought things were going well. But Susie, croaking muddy water, exclaimed, "Oh-oh, Bat, I-I've lost my clothes!" She scooted close to him trying to shield herself, but Bat was looking straight ahead.

"If we can keep this hoss out of quicksand we'll make it," he said. "I'm thinking that's a quickie spot up there," he said, pointing, and circled the death trap. He twisted in the saddle. "Ah, yeah, what did you say; huh-ho! Now, who's laughing at my potato sack rompers?"

From her waist down, Susie was naked except for some kind of under britches that was ripped from top to bottom; lots of pretty Susie showing.

"Sort of looks like you lost 'em," Bat said, chuckling, "things are looking good."

"Ain't funny," she replied, with a slight grin, revealing the humor in it, too. "Maybe we could find 'em down the river a ways washed up on the bank. I've just got to have something."

She had poked fun at his gunnysack rompers, but Bat Masterson loved to kid, too. "Would give you a fig leaf but no fig trees around; how about cottonwood? Wouldn't surprise me if your clothes are not already in Indian Territory."

She frowned a little and wrinkled her nose, knew she was trapped. But she was brave, had guts, likable, and took a big chance.

"Susie, I'd give you the shirt off my back but not my pants," he said, chuckling.

"Ah-ha," she snickered, "me wear that old potato sack-your raveling rompers; never!"

If cowboys have to shed their clothes to stay alive in a raging river they'll do it. A Judge did it. It's not all that unusual. Embarrassed maybe to come out on a river bank without a stitch on where people waited, but when it gets down to sink or swim, survive or perish, who cared about their clothes? Buffalo hunters had been swept away in the raging Canadian River but showed up later in Indian Territory safe but naked as a jaybird. Trail bosses dreaded the river, had lost cattle, wagons and teams any number of times. Johnny Long had lost three wagons with six-mule hitches. A big Missouri mule in a three span hitch had been rolled and tumbled until there wasn't a hair left on him. The mule drowned but no one ever figured out how he got out of his buckled-on harness.

The Canadian was behind. Riding along, Bat untied the saddle strings on his boots and emptied out the water. But he soon reined up, slid off, and helped Susie off. An unbelievable sight on the prairie, two nearly naked Whites, one in potato sack britches and the other in split lace drawers. It would scare the Indians away. Bat Masterson would never live it down in Mobeetie seen in tow-sack britches. People would swear he'd fell in with the double riding drunken dudes and dance hall nudes. Such carryins' on wasn't unusual in the settlement but rompers wasn't his style.

"Giving you the shirt off my back," he said, cracking a grin, coming off his horse. "Make you a skirt—be a little tight in the waist but beats nothing."

"Thanks, but-but, I-I," she stammered.

"Go ahead. If it's too tight around the waist leave the top buttons open."

She had a small waist and with the top buttons open it'd work. To his surprise she grabbed it and started walking toward Mobeetie.

"Hey! Where ya going?"

"I gotta go-go to the outhouse but there's not any."

Bat couldn't see anything wrong with that; happens.

She walked a ways and soon hid behind a big sagebrush.

While she was gone he squeezed in his wet boots and buckled on his guns and spurs—ready to go. She soon came back wearing her short shirt skirt. Walking up, she laughed, "Never seen anything like that, a cowboy in boots and spurs, big hat, brace-o-sixes, and wearing nothing but rompers...and a smile! Grandma'll never believe it."

"Reckon you're right," he replied, spreading his big grin. "We'll both ride in the saddle; you in front. It's like this, like I've said before, Coalie is no different than most horses; they hate flopping feet in their flanks."

He set her in the saddle and a shirt button popped off. Now there was only one button left, and the tight shirt-tail wrapped around her butt was going to pull it off.

"Better pull it up," he said, "settin' on it—gonna rip it, still wet."

She pulled and tugged, stuck to the bare skin, she couldn't do much with it. And very little coverage but who cared? He swung up behind her and gave a trail herd yell, "Let's head 'em up and move 'em out!"

Bat had figured he'd take the trail-herd as far as the Canadian River then hurry back to Mobeetie. Dogface was still spreading it around town he'd get Masterson and take Molly. Shooting his mouth off, there'd come a day Dogface would have to prove a few things. Maybe he was in town. Insanely jealous, King had followed her from Dodge City and was making her life miserable. But now Bat had a problem, how could he get his mind on his loving Molly in Mobeetie when he was squeezed in the saddle with pretty Susie on the prairie? After all, he was just a neighborly guy, only trying to get the girl to Mobeetie to see her poor old dying aunt.

They jogged along up one hill and down the next.

The sun had dropped behind the hills and it was beginning to cool off. Darkness had caught up with them by the time they reached Jim Springer's ranch/saloon, on the Washita, fifteen miles north of Mobeetie; halfway home. The full moon was bright. Bat could see Army horses crowded around the hitching rail. No doubt, the place was full of military men. Buffalo soldiers lived it up at Springer's booze and gambling joint. Jim was always ready to take their money. And by the sound of things, he had plenty business. Hell raising was going on inside. Loud talk and screaming curses shook the walls. Bat urged Coalie on, hoping they hadn't been seen in what they had on—or didn't have on.

Coalie was tired, had a swaying-foxtrot, but Bat's mind wasn't on the horse. Susie was resting in his arms. He thought she'd forgot how death had stared them in the face only a few miles back. Riding across the hills, after they passed Springer's, she twisted in the saddle and said, "You know something, Bat, I had never been out of my Mama's house before I come to Texas."

He couldn't imagine why pretty Susie Shores would come to a rip-snorting place like Mobeetie, Texas; so innocent. And what about her poor old dying aunt, who was she....and who was "Susie Shores" coming to this wild country alone. Bat was beginning to wonder about that. She rode relaxed. She felt safe with her hands resting on his thighs. If the horse shyied at night varmints there would be no danger of falling out of the saddle.

"Whoa, Coalie, Whoa!" The horse stepped in a badger hole and went down. Bat and Susie tumbled off over his head. Bat held a firm grip on Coalie's reins. He had no hankering to walk home. Susie flailed her arms and grabbed, grabbed for anything to stay in the saddle. Riding in front, she went off first and Bat landed on top of her.

Going off, reaching desperately she latched onto his potato sack britches and held tight. An embarrassing situation, how could he tell her that was no potato she was squeezing? Chuckling breathlessly, mumbling to himself, "This has gotta be a joke. That poor little innocent thing don't even know that's no potato." Bat loved a joke but this was killing him.

"Are you hurt Susie?" he asked, deeply concerned.

"Just wondering about that potato," she said, lying back in the grass, muffling a snicker.

Bat, still mumbling, "Potato? That poor girl is knocked out!"

A pretty moonlight night, and miles from nowhere, she never dreamed of this kind of luck when she left Missouri to seek her fortune in Texas.

She pulled to him and kissed him. Huh, never been out of her Mama's house before she came to Texas? She seemed innocent enough but for some reason ol' Bat was beginning to doubt that innocent stuff. She was having fun, and too, she had ol' fun loving Bat laughing all the way up his potato sack rompers.

"Bat did you ever hear of, 'roastin' ya tater'—an old back-home Missouri joke?"

34 *Susie's Revelation*

Rumbling hoofbeats, gunfire, screams, yells! Bat and Susie listened.

"Let's git them sunsabitches! Didja see that sign? No buffalo soldiers 'llowed in town! Let's git 'em! Mobeetie here we come!"

"Bat, who's that—somebody shooting at us?" Susie asked, very uneasy.

He put his hand to her mouth, jerked at his potato sack britches, jumped up, and pulled her up. "Let's get out of here!" Bat exclaimed. Coalie threw a fit but Bat hung onto the reins. Gunfire and zinging bullets spooked the horse. Pulling hard against the reins, he circled around and around trying to breakaway. Half dragging Susie, Bat got close enough to boost her in the saddle; swung in behind her, and whipped out. "Buffalo soldiers on the way to Fort Elliot," he said. "They've been in some kind of fracas at Jim Springer's ranch saloon."

Coalie was a fast horse and Bat "let him out" in a dead run. The soldiers were firing wild and reckless...shooting at the moon, up in the air; anything. Bullets whizzed around Bat and Susie, he dug in his spurs. The big horse soon left the Army plugs behind, but the shooting kept up. The soldiers were coming. Susie showed her grit, but didn't like to be shot at like they were jackrabbits; a Western welcome she'd never forget. "Why are they shooting at us, Bat?" she asked.

"There's been some kind of trouble at Springer's. I doubt they even saw us, letting off a little steam; shooting off their mouth like their guns. Dang the Army any-way, 'know how to hurt two innocent people, but you're O K."

The soldiers had slowed down but still within ear-shot. Finally Bat reined Coalie to a easy walk. Soon the shifting back and forth in the saddle had Bat thinking about Susie's back-home Missouri joke. But those crazy soldiers were still coming so Bat urged Coalie on.

"Susie, about this poor old aunt of yours...is she dy-ing with the fever; who is she?"

She giggled, elbowed him in the ribs, and said, "Just kidding, really, I heard that money growed on trees in Mobeetie."

Back home, in Missouri, maybe Susie was an angel, but was she coming to Mobeetie for some of that easy money? An old cowboy once said, "Bet thar's over five hundred gurls in Mobeetie," and it was probably true. Bat liked Susie's company, but she had pulled a fast one on the ol' Hoss. He didn't mind. No one loved to pull a joke or tell tall tales more than fun loving Bat Masterson.

Midnight almost. Bat and Susie topped the hill and looked south to the twinkling lights of Mobeetie. To their right, a mile northwest of town, were the lights of Fort Elliot.

"So that's it," Susie said. "All the way back to St. Louis, to Mississippi, even to Louisiana, I've heard and read about, 'Hidetown, Sweetwater—Mobeetie, the wild-est and toughest of them all, where money grows, whis-key flows, and wild women glow...the wild, wild West, and the fast gun is the law.' Is that really the way it is, Bat?"

"Reckon you could say that. Lots of money around, all kinds of people come to gamble. Doc Holiday rides up from Fort Griffin, and Big Nose Kate shows up too, and so does Luke Short. Don't know how many times, but

Billy the kid's been registered at O'Loughlin's cafe/ boarding place. And it's been said the James's rode through a time or two, and there's Mysterious Dave Mather, a gambler, he rides in once in awhile. Clay Allison drifts in sometimes, too. He likes to ride his horse down main street with nothing on but his hat, boots, and gun-belt, firing off his 'sixes', shooting out window lights, and giving off the rebel yell, imitating Chief Mogul."

"You mean nothing on—plumb na-ked?"

"That's what they say, didn't see it, I've been gone a great deal, scouting for the army. They call him, the 'Wild Wolf of the Washita'...don't know much about him, but they say he come out of Tennessee to get some of this cheap Texas land. He 'set-down' close to where Gageby Creek and the Washita run together—few miles back, where we crossed. Strange guy, pulls crazy stunts, even said he'd be buried there some day on the land he had staked out."

Susie said, "All these outlaws, this Mysterious Dave Whats-his-name, and this guy Clay riding na-ked, shootin' out lights—scary to me!"

"That ain't the half of it. 'Don't know if there's any-thing to it, but it's been talked around Mobeetie that Clay Allison and another rancher by name of Johnson had some trouble—hot argument over a water hole on the Washita. The story is they agreed to dig a hole and get in it with Bowie knives. The winner bury the loser but there's never been a witness showed up... 'never run into him in these parts. They say he's a good rancher, knows his horses and cattle. Anyway, 'heard he's in New Mexico now."

"Fighting with knives, down in a hole—deep hole?"

"Reckon so."

"Oo-ooh, that is really scary!"

"Yup Susie, I'll tell you about this place called

Mobeetie: I guess you could say these old buffalo hunters and cowboys sort of keep the peace what there is. Something going on all time. There's another guy that slips around here that's crazy as a loon...cut a man's throat even for glancing at his girl friends; keeps the whole town stirred up. But, good country, the climate's good here, and who knows, you might live to be a hundred."

"I don't know about this place. My Mama used to tell me there's hell on earth. This may be it—scary, but it does make me feel good to hear you talk about back-home people; the preacher's boys. Everybody in the hills know about the James' Boys; some like 'em and some don't."

If Bat was seen sneaking into town in burlap rompers   he'd never live it down. Gamblers had lost their shirts in poker games, pants in whore houses, and left town in tow-sacks, but Bat Masterson had pride; his pants' didn't fit. But he thought Susie was cute in her one button, nearly nothing, short-shirtskirt.

Approaching town, Bat said, "This gunnysack on, going to get out here quick—any idea where this friend of yours lives?"

"Don't know for sure. Been awhile since I heard from her. We were kids together from the time we moved from Louisiana, up the Mississippi, clear to St. Louis. The letter I got from her had been stamped in Dodge City. She was hoping Mobeetie would get a post office before long. Said too, a high ranking soldier was trying to spark her; guess he did. She said she was lonesome, liked his uniform, and thought his strawberry roan was pretty, too; name's Molly Brennan."

Shocked! Ol' Masterson was knocked out of the saddle... almost. Dark, and expecting no lights at the Brennan house, the kitchen lamp was still burning. "Sh-

211

sh Susie, quiet. If Molly sees me in this rig she'll swear I'm out of my ever-loving mind. Now slip off and I'll see you tomorrow."

Reining his horse around, Bat heard Molly yell, "Frenchy McGraw!"

"Frenchy McGraw! What, Frenchy McGraw? That darn gal—Susie? Or Frenchy, has pulled another one on me! Can't believe it," Bat mumbled, looking back, grinning, almost breaking into laughter, "Can't believe it— Frenchy McGraw!" In the lamp light Bat saw the girls hugging, jumping up and down, laughing and giggling. And riding off, he noticed the Brennan's red-wheeled wagon wasn't in it's usual place. Strange?

The next morning he walked in the General Store and sort of eased up behind Johnny Long. With his favorite early morning request, Bat asked, "Got a cup of coffee for a poor boy?"

"Bat Masterson!" Mr. Long exclaimed. "Dogged if I ain't glad to see you back. Get the herd across the river?"

"Yup, did. Don't think we lost a steer. What's going on in the settlement, anything new?"

"You bet, families pouring in, coming to stay 'keep that murdering sonovabitch they call Dogface out of town. 'Got a bunch of lots to stake off, too—well, there's three, just a start. She's booming, hide money pouring in, gamblers stuffing their pockets, the girls are raking it in, and boozc joints bursting at the seams. Couldn't be better. Seen Molly?"

"Not this morning. Figure she's still asleep. Going to the barber shop, clean up, and be on my way to see her. You?"

"Yesterday," Mr. Long replied. "Bessie's been running fever and having coughing spells. Bob figured he'd better get her to a drier climate soon as he could. They left yesterday for Arizona. Molly will be staying with the

Flemings'. Henry's helping move what stuff she's got, now."

"Too bad," Bat shook his head sorrowfully. "Consumption's got her."

"Reckon so. By the way, a guy rode in early this morning— before sun-up—and said Jim Springer....Did you rein in at Jim's whiskey joint on the Washita last night?"

"Nope. Had this girl in the saddle with me, friend to the Brennans—needed help crossing the river; didn't stop. About the time we got to Jim's place 'sounded like all hell had broke loose. We kept riding and soon a bunch of buffalo soldiers got on our tail yelling and shooting. What about Jim, putting in a bigger whiskey joint or bringing in more cattle?"

"Don't know what happened. A bunch of drunk soldiers got in a gambling hassle and Jim tried to settle 'em down...wound up with his throat cut ear-to-ear. Digger's putting him under this evening, somebody said."

"Anything else going on?"

"Pretty quiet but hides are pouring in. Did have something funny happen out here on Featherbed Hill; little shooting scrape. A drifter got mixed up with one of the girls but the old gal didn't take nothing off him." Pausing, with a broad grin, Mr. Long continued, "Seems he wouldn't pay up for professinal services rendered, but the thing that really got the ol' gal's dander up— madder'n all hell—his spurs ripped her featherbed. And you know how it is in this hot weather—everybody has their windows open. Well, a stiff breeze was blowing and goose feathers fogged out of that shack like a snow storm in Janurary."

"Featherbed Hill, living up to it's name," Bat replied with a loud chuckle.

"Well, she tried to pepper his private parts with pellets when he ran for his horse. Best she could do was blast his butt with bird-shot from a .12 gage blunder buster." Uncle Johnny slapped his thighs and with a hearty laugh, said, "About the funniest thing I ever saw, but it got funnier when he jumped on his horse; he couldn't set in the saddle. Whipping out down main street, he stood high in the stirrups, his shirt tail flapping a cherry red butt that looked like a case of the measles—can't figure out what happened to his britches."

Chuckling, enjoying the tale too, Bat joined in. "Give a lot to seen it. The old gals out there can get pretty salty."

"Did have a bad thing happen down east on Sweetwater. A family loading out to come to town was nearly wiped out. The Dad and Mother and two or three kids were in the wagon waiting for the oldest girl, in the house, to bring the baby. A bunch of Indians slipped out of the Territory to do some raiding around, and swarmed in on the family. The ring leader was an old squaw. The twelve year old, with the baby, heard screaming and looked out the window. Horrified, she saw the Indians tomahawking them in the wagon and stealing the horses. The girl ran with the baby and hid under the creek bank until the renegades were gone."

"That won't be happening much longer," Bat replied. "Another year and the Government mopping up will be over with, but there will still be a few friendly Indians around. Not good news, but guess 'better get over to the barber shop and get slicked up."

"Yeah, she's missed you," J. J. said, with an affable grin. Bat walked in Robert Baley's barber shop. "Bat, how's it going?" Robert asked, "Missed you here of late—haircut?"

"Haircut and shave," Bat replied, "trim my mustache, too. I'm doing alright, Robert—you?"

"For myself, yeah, but of course the town gets stirred

214

up when this guy on the red roan rides in. Get the herd across the river?" Grinning, Robert added, "Mustache fuzz getting a little heavy, coming on; have one yet, looking good, sideburns too."

"Yup, didn't lose a steer." Bat, chuckling, said, "That lip fuzz has turned to hair, eh? Thought I'd slick up a little, going over to see Molly. J. J. said her folks left for Arizona."

"Yeah, they did—going to see Molly? Got some new stuff here she'll like; smell of that, look at that bottle too; fancy!"

"Um-um, Lilac Lotion, rub on a little. Here's the quarter, better hurry on over there; see you later, Robert."

Bat left the barber shop and rode to the Bob Brennan house. The place looked deserted. The jovial cobbler/blacksmith would be missed. People in town trusted him. He knew more about what was going on in the settlement than anyone else; even the bartenders. Bat tied up at the hitching post. He doubted anyone was there. Anyway, he would close the front door. He reached in; a hand grabbed him.

"Molly you scared me, might've made me hurt myself" he said, joking.

"Bat, Honey, I've missed you!" She was all over him. "The folks left for Arizona yesterday and I'm already homesick for Mom and Dad, too."

"I heard—stopped at the store," he replied, embraced and kissed her.

They relaxed. "Um," she said, "love that new lilac lotion. I'm moving in with the Flemings. Henry's doing my moving and Frenchy, my friend from Missouri, is helping. I'm waiting for them now, but really Mama didn't have much to leave me. They've already took over a little stuff, but that's about it except for this chair, and quilts, and things piled here in the floor."

215

Naturally Molly was tore up, her folks leaving. Bat tried to settle her down. "Poor Darling," he said, pulling her close, "don't worry, Bat's going to take care of the Brennan 'Baby."

Squeezing her tight, he kissed her again. The lovers soon got lost in another world. Her Mother and Dad was gone and Bat's ride from the river with Susie—or Frenchy—a thing of the past.

Loving Molly, a few kisses now and then, embracing and squeezing her, forgetting everything else, he got his boots tangled in the quilts. But that was nothing for Bat Masterson, he would never let a little thing like that stop him; even if he was hobbled. Carried away, he fell over backwards, knocked the chair over, landed in the bedding and brought her down with him. Like a couple of fun loving kids, they wrestled around scooting and scrunching in, and soon ooched off the quilts. He had a deep longing for her on the trail. Now, he was ready to make up for lost time...and oh, how she loved his romantic ways. In his jovial, humorous way, he said, "Honey, I've said it before, say it again, nothing like it, this beats shooting buffaloes anytime."

Chuckling, she added, "Or kissing horses?"

"Whoa, whoa!" When the rattling wagon stopped Bat and Molly froze; listened. Ol' Henry had brought his wagon and team right up to the front door. Frenchy jumped out before the thing stopped rolling. There had been times when Bat Masterson got in a hurry but never at a time like this. He barely jumped out of the quilt-pile before Frenchy burst in. She was grinning like a cat eating cream. But the half grinning Bat and Molly looked guilty as sin.

Frenchy's big smile told it all. She figured her friend was having fun like she did on the trail. She said, "I'm sorry, you-er-ya'll got things ready to go?"

Bat, shaking off a little embarrassment, said, "Well-er, yup, just going through the house—yup, just going through the house, looking to see if there's anything left."

Frenchy's big grin spread over her face; didn't believe a word he said. Henry soon came in grinning from ear to ear. He had things figured out, too.

35 *Wildfire*

Only two to the room, two to the bed, so Molly and Frenchy were set-up in the Fleming home. Others were not so lucky. Mobeetie was running over. Buffalo hunters and cowboys crawled out of the old iron-stead beds early of a morning...up-all-night drunks and gamblers fell right in behind them. Hot summertime, rooms were scarce. Many a man rested his weary bones in the grass. Gamblers and hide hunters, men with money jingling in their pockets, had a warm bed in the winter until their money ran out, but when their money was gone their buxom bedmates booted their butts out in the blizzards. Mobeetie had her share of beautiful women and there were "mooses'," too. Beth Barton and Frenchy McGraw could draw a man's attention anytime. But "The Rose Of The Canadian," Molly Brennan, shy and beautiful, was loved and respected by everybody.

Trailing cattle, Bat's town surveying job went begging. Even his little Indian helper, Tah, had gone back to the tribe. Bat spent most of his time at the Lady Gay. That's where he loved it best. Neighborly and friendly, everybody liked him, his surveying...no comnplaints with his generous land measurements. But still he often wondered if people would be scratching their heads over his self-taught civil engineering a hundred years later.

Only eighteen months had passed since Quanah Parker and his Braves were severely humblized at Adobe Walls, and Bat Masterson rode into Hidetown. Around the little settlement, high in the Texas Panhandle, on

Sweetwater Creek, literally millions of buffaloes roamed the prairie. By late 1875 the buffalo slaughter was in full swing, animals dying by the thousands. A couple of years and it'd only be sun-bleached bones to show for the vanishing herds. The changing West almost blew his mind, he watched people fogging in and ranches going together.

Along with the vanishing herds, the free spirited redman's unlimited range was a thing of the past. Fort Elliot was one of the last military Post set-up to keep the Indian "in his place"; the Indian Nation. It was called progress but the natives had no use for the white man's kind of civilization. Indians slipping out of the Territory, back to their old hunting ground, only found disappointment and sadness. After the buffaloes were wiped out what could they do? Their way of life was devastated. They faced starvation, they had to return to Indian Territory.

At the sound of the last buffalo shot there would be a stirring around of Mobeetie's motley bunch. More schemers and dreamers would follow come ranching and cattle. Buffalo hunters, hide buyers, friendly Indians, and Government people would soon vamoose, but gunslingers, gamblers, horse thieves, and whores would hang around to meet the new settlers fogging in...ranchers, European syndicate land buyers, cowboys, and cattle rustlers. The O'Loughlin and Manlin hotels were running over.

Mobeetie news was slow getting to the outside world. Gunslicks ready to show off might get a little attention, however Digger Dugan and his Mexican helper would rather they settled their differences on the prairie. Local news was usually buried and forgot about before it reached Dodge City, but still scores were to be settled.

County organization had been talked for sometime but Uncle Johnny, Henry Fleming, and Tom O'Loughlin hadn't been able to get 150 permanent citizens to sign-up. But with the last Indian settled in the promised land, ranchers coming in would soon force legal law and order. New settlers willing to endure the environment were already putting big spreads together.

The investors in England, Ireland, and Scotland, "snakebit" on American land deals, were a little shy of Panhandle ranch bargains. But fast talking land tooters soothed their nerves, promising there would be no scalping parties. Convinced the Rangers would take care of the outlaws, cattle rustlers, and clean up the renegade Indians, millions was soon laid down for Texas prairie.

The "proper" Europeans had the buffalo hunters and cowboys chuckling. The Englishmen had never seen the Western saddle or the mustang saddled with it. They stared at cowboy boots and thought ropes were only for hangings. The big guns on the cowboys' hips were frightening. But Texas honored European nobility. Towns were named after Kings, Queens, Dukes and Earls.

Bat, Rip Nesbit, and John Corcoran were saddling up at the livery stable when a couple of English syndicate buyers, with their ladies swinging on their arms, came around. The bold one, a man, said to Bat, "Excuse me please, ol' Chap, the meadow muffins we hear about, we don't understand—the rainfall too, only seventeen inches each year—and Laddie we have been informed there can be changes in the weather quite suddenly?"

The boys hid their grins. In his usual way, Bat replied, "Sir, ah'll tell ya about the meadow muffins, they belong to the cows—if we're lucky we'll get seventeen inches of rain a year." Fun loving Bat could see they were all ears. Politely, he added, "Don't know if you could say the weather changes fast or not, but a hunter tells me one of his team-horses keeled over with heat exhaustion and before he hit the ground the other one froze to death."

"Thank you Laddies." Awed, half grinning, they walked off.

Molly was down in the dumps, her folks had left for Arizona, and she knew the risk of trailing through Indian country. She thought of a hundred things that could happen to her Mother and Dad. The wagon, what if it broke down—Indian raid—a horse died? She wondered but would never know. However, Christmas 1875 was coming up and time to be cheerful.

Henry Fleming walked out with a bag of Arbuckles Coffee when Bat walked in the store. "Bat, 'left you a bag," Henry said.

Bat chuckled. "Good, come over and we'll have a cup."

"Morning, Bat, 'get Molly squared around?" J. J. asked.

"Yup," Bat replied, "but she's feeling mighty low."

"About her folks—I can see that, and she said something to Mary and Ellen about some kind of dream she can't shake off—you won a gunfight but lost; sounded like a riddle to me."

"Like you, 'don't know about that; sounds crazy. But one day she's up and next day she's down. Thought I might do a little something special for her, Christmas coming up."

"What've you got in mind?"

"Like to buy her a horse, but...."

"But can't find the horse?"

Bat chuckled. "Found the horse but can't find the money."

"Run dry, huh—no hide money?"

"That's it."

"Kiddin', knew hide-huntin' was over for you. How much?"

"Way up there, mighty good hoss; 'round forty dollars."

"Well, Bat you know the old saying, a forty dollar saddle and a ten dollar hoss...let's make it a forty dollar saddle and a forty dollar hoss; just make it a hundred -- how about an even hundred?"

"More'n enough; 'preciate it."

"The luck of Bat Masterson...it's going be a shame the way he takes the boys money at the Lady Gay's gambling tables."

New Settlers in the Panhandle soon found out the weather does go from hot to cold, or cold to hot, in a very short time. In 1875-76 winter days were like that.

Bat reined up at the Fleming home, knocked and Molly opened the door. "Morning Love, you might take a sweater or light jacket; tie it on the saddle."

"What are you up to, Bat Masterson...a sweater, jacket? Another one of your jokes, bum-shot?" She loved to kid him about his skill with a gun; knew he was the best. To him, her mood was pleasant; sounded good.

Her eyes were on the red horse tied at the hitching post with Coalie. "Never seen that horse before—pretty," she said, walking out with Bat.

"Yup, goodlooking horse, well arched neck, got a star in his forehead, a little bit of snipped nose, and ears that pitch forward easy, just like the dark red horse you've always talked about; your Christmas present."

"I don't believe a word of it, Sweet William," she kidded.

"Yup, yours," Bat replied. She grabbed and kissed him. "This horse has some unusual history." And Bat went on to say, "A couple of guys riding with Dutch Henry come down with lead poison trying to steal him. Gunfire spooked him, but he's simmered down since he was found over here on the Canadian River. He's gentle but full of life—Wildfire. I found the owner and bought him."

222

Bat boosted Molly on Wildfire then swung upon Coalie. They headed east for Sweetwater Creek, down where it meanders on into Indian Territory. Molly's horse was swift as the wind. She "let 'im out." She hadn't felt so good since her parents left for Arizona. It was fun, she loved it, riding and loping Wildfire over the hills with the wind in her face, and hair straight back. They reined up at the creek. Redbirds were flitting around and left-over summertime woodpeckers were hammering out their rhythms. Bat jumped off his horse but Molly stayed on her's.

"Bat, I heard noises—water splashing!" she said.

"Think nothing about it, Darling—muskrats," he replied. Coming off her horse he caught her and started for the water.

"Put me down!" She yelled.

He swung her around and around until they were drunk and fell flat in the grass. Bat thought there was nothing like romancing in the soft prairie grass. Relaxing in the warm sunshine, Molly's head rested on his chest. He tickled her nose with a blade of grass. She snorted, and with reflexes, she gave him a big whop on the face. But soon she was sorry.

"Sweetheart, did I hurt you?" She asked, scrunching up to him in a loving sort of way. She didn't hurt the ol' tough hide hunter, but neither did Bat Masterson fool around when it come to having girl-fun in the grass.

"You know something, Molly Dear—Christmas coming on, I felt in the spirit when I was looking for your horse. Green Christmas trees and pretty decorations such as red strung up crepe paper everywhere you look; really put me in the mood."

"Red and green—but you did find a beautiful red horse."

"I looked for a green one."

"Bat Masterson, you crazy thing...the red one will do for this Christmas. Maybe a green one next Christmas, ha!"

A sudden rustling in the reeds brought Bat upright. He placed his finger against Molly's lips. "May be Redskins," he whispered, "and may be that old red roan is tied up out there somewhere. Let's get behind them cattails."

Along the Indian Nation border was danger of renegade Indians, but no natives had been seen here of late, not since the twelve year old girl saw her parents tomahawked; killed, while waiting in the wagon for her to bring the baby.

Molly was brave but fearful. Bat eased her over in the brush with his "sixes" ready, parting the reeds and glancing in all directions. "Honey, it's O K," relief in his voice. "Not a band or they'd already have two scalps in the bag."

Indian Territory lay only a few miles east. The Whites knew murdering renegades were roaming the country. But usually it was peaceful Indians that had come back to their old stomping ground. Some often wandered up the creeks and rivers never knowing when they crossed the border.

Molly hung onto Bat but he made sure the guns on his hips were free. A dozen steps from where they stood the tall winter-dead Jimson weeds soon parted.

Pushing through the brush was an old Indian squaw. She set down on the creek-bank. Bat and Molly peered through the reeds and saw the woman watching the fish. A redbird lit on a limb hanging over the water not far from where she sat mumbling, talking to the birds and animals; her friends of nature.

Why all the hatred between the Indians and Whites?" Bat wondered. The Redskins had gone after his scalp, missed a few head skinnings, and hated some of the bastards that ought to be killed—like the old squaw and her bunch that murdered them in the wagon down the creek—but couldn't an honest agreement have been worked out before the Whites kicked them off their native land? The poor old weeping woman was a picture of sadness, of sorrow, a native longing for her long lost way of life.

Bat was ready to move up, he reached for Molly's hand. "Follow me." They came out of hiding and the squaw looked up. Her head was covered with a ragged yellow shawl. Bat gave her some kind of hand-sign language.

"What did you tell her?" Molly asked, low.

"Don't be afraid.' Let's move up."

Moving up a half-dozen steps from the woman, Bat made more sign language. The aged woman answered, but Molly had no idea about the signs or what they were talking about. She tugged on his arm. "What did she say—what did you say—is she lost? Did they kick the poor old thing out of the tribe?"

"Said she came up the creek from where the soldiers drove them—soldiers looking for raiding renegades." Bat was convinced the old woman had nothing to do with the roving bands making it miserable for Whites' along the border. He went onto say, "She's trying to find her grandsons—said their mother is missing, too, but I didn't tell her what happened on the Washita."

"You mean...?"

"Yup, my little Indian helper. I told her they hung out with the Delaware scouts camped on the creek west of Fort Elliot, in the wig-wams. I hardly know what to tell her since Tah's been gone for days."

The awkard conversation continued until the old squaw pulled the dirty shawl over her face.

225

Molly's eyes were questioning. He continued, "Said she longed to see her grandsons—had many lonely nights—cried with the wolves. I told her the boys left Mobeetie and joined a Comanche tribe. She thinks they're with the Great White Spirit in the sky. Mobeetie was her last hope."

The sight of that poor old weeping Indian woman sitting on the creek-bank touched Molly. "I had never thought about the sadness and suffering the native people are going through. I don't see them all being bad; not right!"

When Bat and Molly rode off the woman was still talking to her friends of nature. They rode slowly, thinking about the plight of the Indians, but enjoying the summer like weather, too. Bat took a deep breath. It was almost a perfect day, but he wondered who put the jinx on his courtship.

"Oh, Bat, we're in trouble—Indians!" Molly exclaimed, pointing ahead."

"Nope, not Indians," Bat replied, shading his eyes, chuckled, "soldiers, but don't believe those guys can walk a straight line."

They soon caught-up with two men walking toward Mobeetie. One was toting two big red-headed birds and the other one carried two shotguns. "Hi," Bat said, "looks like you've got your dinner there."

"Hello," one slurred voice replied, "we're officers at the Fort. Yeah, fine prairie chickens—practicing up a little, doing some shooting at an empty bottle, shot too close to the team-horses' feet. Don't know why, but them crazy old horses ran off; so did our guide!"

Not far from town, Bat and Molly rode on, left them wobbling along. "Ran off—smart guide, smart team! Prairie chickens—red-headed buzzards!" Bat said, laughing.

36 *The Long Shadow*

It was a late warm evening when Bat and Molly left the Fleming home and headed for the Lady Gay Christmas special. Wasn't far, they walked down main street worming their way around wagons and buggies parked in the street. They passed saddlehorses and a few buggies tied-up at the hitching rails. To throw a town celebration, it was usually pulled off at the Lady Gay. Bat liked it there, the best place in town, and the only two story building within 200 miles. The high double doors were not unusual, nor were the saloon's swinging bat-wing doors. But for drunk cowboys wanting another drink the swinging bat-wing doors didn't always keep the boys from riding their horse inside. Bat worked there part time; there most of the time. But he spent time, too, at J. J. Long's store where he had his surveying office. A crowd was milling around the White Elephant saloon when they walked up. Loud talk could be heard.

"What's going on, Bat?" Molly asked.

"Think nothing about it, Darling. Another locoed show-off in town."

"But...." Molly got no further. Six-guns started popping off. Bullets whizzing through the air kicked up dust around their feet. The lovers lost no time ducking behind saddlehorses and buggies. Bat looked around...saw nothing unusual. They moved on, but everybody started shoving and pushing back, clearing the way for a strutting bowlegged gunslick. Coming down the street, he walked slow. People gave him plenty room. He stopped, spread-eagled and set, ready on the draw with his brace-of-sixes. He cast a long lean shadow that stood out like a diamond in a goat's butt.

Mumbling, slobbering, chewing his words, he never turned his head. Soon he snarled, "Come and get me!" His dead-set eyes were on a whiskey barrel down a ways rolled out in the street. Soon a cowboy's hat slowly raised up behind the barrel. The gunslinger's .45s' roared! Women screamed and men ducked.

Bat exclaimed, "What's going on around here...that show off bowlegged gunslick wobbling down the street, and the damn fool on that horse racing through the crowd bumping people?" Chuckling, he added, "Even crazy for Mobeetie."

"Who was he, Bat, the guy on the horse?" Molly asked.

"Don't know but he's hell-bent on something...sorta figure he's a sidekick to the hunkered-down kid behind the barrel-the one the gunslinger's after."

The guy on the horse meant nothing to the gun-fighter; paid him no mind. But suddenly he realized someone at the barrel had tricked him, made a fool of him. The boy raised his hat on a stick but now the kid was in big trouble. The gunman swaggered toward the barrel, "Gonna get that sonovabitch!"

But the boy's sidekick, the fun loving cowboy on the horse, was after that gunfighter. He gouged in his spurs, ran his horse back by, threw a lariat loop, caught the gunslinger by the neck and jerked him around; his guns went off! The cowboy's horse bolted through the crowd, dragging the gunslick on the end of his rope. It was nothing throwing a looping lariat at someone in Mobeetie, but wild shots sent the jeering crowd scurrying for cover.

An old buffalo hunter slurped tobacco juice, rubbed his sleeve across his dirty beard, and said, "Ha, ha, ain't never seen one like that'un—guy hung standin' on the ground."

Two hand-holding lovers hurried on to make the party. But the partying for the 1875 Christmas was too much for some citizens. The booze joints were crowded and the spirits flowing. Ellen O'Loughlin was disgusted when she said, "It seems these wild drunken gunfighters are all trying to out do each other!" Mobeetie's reputation was not of the best.

Bat and Molly walked in the Lady Gay. The musicians were tuning their instruments but the jolly black banjo-picker was missing. It soon got around the buffalo soldier happened onto some bad luck at Springer's ranch/saloon. He was killed in the same barroom brawl the night Jim was murdered. But Slats hustled another musician that was good on the guitar and fiddle. They called him the "fiddlin' fool." The Tennessee plow-boy walked all the way from the Volunteer State to seek his fortune in the West...slept in the grass and lived on wild berries, roasted possums, and cottontail rabbits.

As they made their way to the back Bat nudged Molly, "That guy with Frenchy, is that Temple Houston—Sam's youngest? I saw a drawing of him once; looks like him. Maybe he's looking for a home. I hear he's coming to Mobeetie soon as we get county organization...whenever that is."

"Hadn't told you, 'had his eyes on Frenchy—business man, does look a lot like that Temple Houston drawing, but it's not him. Frenchy said her friend, Mickey...Mickey McCormack, a gambler, might be putting in a livery stable—even a skating rink if you can believe that. He's got money, big money, and wants to get started. He's crazy about her, and she admitted he's getting her 'sugar,' too; got a way with men."

Bat chuckled, thinking back a few days. "Yup, good

gal, fast worker, I'd say...did you say putting in a skating rink?"

"Yeah, swears it, but getting the lumber freighted out of Dodge City is something else."

"Don't know about that. Guess you could find him skating in a herd of buffaloes, too." Bat laughed, "Sounds crazy to me."

"Oh, but Bat, he's smart," Molly come back. "You know they've got 'em at other Army Posts, and he thinks these five hundred Whites and three hundred Buffalo soldiers they're bringing to Fort Elliot will pour in the money."

Bat and Molly always got plenty attention at the Lady Gay. A stranger would never take it the handsome guy was once a buffalo hunter. But if two half-naked people were seen riding across the prairie, a man in towsack britches wearing a brace-of-sixes, and a gal with nothing on but split-lace drawers, then you could believe anything about Mobeetie. It was rumored overseas there was nothing in the Panhandle but head-peeling Redskins, manure-splotched buffalo hunters, and tobacco squirting cowboys that slept with the bears, and lived on rattlesnakes and lizards. But Bat Masterson, the dashing devil, had the visiting dignified English ladies in a tizzy...took notice, loved his dark hair, friendly eyes, and easy smile; not what they expected on the Texas prairie.

After dancing a couple of hours Molly and Frenchy struck out for the "little house on the prairie." The guys just strolled out in the dark. Bat and Dr. Pryor Shelton, the new Doctor in town, and Dr. Evans, from the Army Post, all ambled out together and stopped behind a buggy.

Having their smokes, Dr. Evans said, "Well Bat, haven't seen you since you and Dixon reported to the Post on your last scouting job—had an arrow-nicked arm but you look healthy now."

"Still kicking," Bat replied, "but not too high in these tight boots—sort of got me hobbling along. Got 'em wet on the creek cutting stakes for a settler's town lots." Bat continued, "Dr. Shelton, guess you've got all these home-sick cowboys and buffalo hunters happy—notice you're limping?"

"Well, part of them," the Doctor said, "but not in too good shape myself. This old hoss, first one I bought from Bonney, (Billy the Kid) boogered and piled me—hurt that Civil War hip. (Dr. Shelton carried a ball in his hip from the war.) However, looks like these guys mixed up in gunfights will keep me busy—wrapped up a few already. And even made one ol' cowboy happy that got snakebit. You know Charlie Cummings—call him Charlie Cucum-ber—eats cucumbers like bananas."

"Rattler got 'im, huh—had it rough, I bet," Bat said.

"Did, but saved him. He's squatted a ways from town out here. Few days back his sidekick rushed in wild-eyed and crazy -like and said, 'Doc you gotta do some-thing! My friend Charlie Cucumber got bit by a rattle-snake.' Told him, 'Tell your friend to put his foot in coal-oil and I'd be right out,' then he was gone. I got on my horse and rode out in a hurry...got there and the guy had his foot in a bucket of coal-oil, holding his finger high as he could."

"Why?" Dr. Evans asked.

'Well Doc,' he said, 'that's where the snake bit me."

From a round of belly laughs, Bat still chuckling, said, "Finger's a long ways from his heel. I'd say he's got a well-oiled heel."

Soon the boys heard Molly and Frenchy coming down the path, feeling their way in the dark; dark as a sack of black cats. Leisurely walking, they had no idea Bat and the doctors were pausing behind the buggy. Frenchy was

231

talking about her Mickey, saying, "Molly, he loves my sugar—done made ten dollars; wrote a letter for him."

The girls were soon gone, but then a gun-happy fool emptied his gun at a man running for his life. Dodging bullets, the guy run for cover, run for the dark...around the building, and slammed head-on into Bat; knocked him down. Bat jumped up ready to square off but the guy was gone; so was the doctors.

It rankled Bat but dodging bullets was not unusual here in the 1870s. Groping in the dark, he was re-rankled when he stumbled over two lovers making out in the grass; fell flat on his face. He figured he had enough; only come out for some relief.

Mobeetie was a haven for people not only dodging bullets but the law, too. Names didn't mean a thing. The likes of Earps, Billy the Kid, Clay Allison, Pat Garrett, Luke Short, Mysterious Dave Mather, and others matched gambling skill everyday with the likes of Big Nose Kate, Poker-Face Alice, Velvet-Ass Vickie, Big-Tit Betty, and others. Maybe they didn't hang around long, but they come and soon discovered it was like the newspaper said: "Where money grows, whiskey flows, and wild women glow."

By now the Governor of Texas had heard about the wild stuff going on in the Panhandle. Since there was no law, no county organization, he threatened to send in the Rangers. Nobody paid him any mind. Who give a hoot'n holler what the Governor said? The State Capitol was over five hundred miles away, and he admitted, "That's one helluva long ways by buggy." He didn't have time to mess with a bunch of renegade outlaws practically in another world. The Rangers were kept downstate chasing Indians, outlaws, and Mexican banditios along the border.

37 *Saloon Skunk*

It just wasn't Bat's day. Flattened out near the Lady Gay, but back on his feet, he heard a girl yell, "Hey, stop that slut!" A gal soon whizzed around the corner in the lantern light. Hot on her tail was Mabel who worked at the Shores-of-Hell. "Mabel the navel" was a label hung on her, but now she was hanging one on the other girl...not a label, a mop, grazing the gal's butt every step she took. Molly and Frenchy, waiting at the saloon door, saw the ruckus going on and burst out laughing. Mabel tripped and fell flat on her face in front of Bat. The embarassed girl quickly got on her feet but the other girl was gone.

"Well, looks like you lost the race there," Bat said, struggling to hold in a laugh, too. He soon sniffed the trouble.

"Second time the bitch has done that!" Mabel said, blowing like a race horse. "Just wanta get my hands on her."

"Yup, 'know what you're talking about," Bat said, chuckling.

"Yeah, Old Skunk Juice Jessie, next time she throws a skunk in the Shores-O-Hell 'get more than a mop. She claims we're stealing all the boys. Old Spraddle Shirley throwed in a stink too, once; done the same thing."

"Yup, I've seen it happen before," Bat said. "But a dead skunk in a sack is no problem—grab the sack and throw it out."

233

"Throw it out hell! That damn thing's alive and running all over the place!" Bat was polite but finally he come on with a belly laugh that shook his insides. Molly and Frenchy were still waiting at the door when he walked up. The saloon gals' fracas was not uncommon. A nice way to end a party. Bat took Molly home.

Mobeetie in 1875 was the center of Panhandle activity with over five thousand hunters in the area. It didn't look good. In a couple of years it'd all be over with. It'd be a lucky day to see a buffalo on the high plains in 1878. Ranchers were already flocking in to grab off rangeland with the last red man gone.

The railroad companies had heard of the booming high plains country. They soon came to Mobeetie to look over the prospects of laying a line to the Panhandle settlement. Registering at the O'Loughlin hotel, the word got around that Billy the Kid was staying at the hotel, too. The railroad people soon left town. The citizens hoped for a railroad but there would never be a buffalo hide shipped from Mobeetie Texas by rail.

Fort Elliot was established as a military base to mop up the Indians and contain them in the Indian Nation. The Panhandle Indian situation would soon be over, but still not enough permanent citizens for county organization; this concerned some people. Bat and Hank Dittmos kept working, laying off town lots that would never sell, but they loved those $10 gold pieces. Bat was lucky to have it both ways...his surveying work and his job at the Lady Gay where the big money floated around. Mobeetie would drink to anything and bet on everything.

Day was done, and the sun had gone down when Bat walked down to buy smokings. He run into a couple of old sidekicks, Rip Nesbit and Baldy Beechnut standing in front of the Shores-Of-Hell saloon. "Hi," Bat spoke, "now what are you guys up to?"

"Gonna do some lookin'" Rip replied, chuckling.

Baldy come in, "Yeah, another smoke ring contest."

"A little early ain't it?" Bat asked. "Been in there before but I've never seen one. Don't have much time, gotta have smokin's before the store closes."

Rip replied, "Ah, goes on every night now from sundown to sunup. Let's go, come on Bat, usual stuff, brings 'em in."

They walked in the saloon and made their way through the noisy crowd. Soon Barney, the fat bartender, bellowed, "Gotta have your attention! In this contest the girls are going to blow smoke rings at this handsome gentleman...thousands of miles from home, all the way from England just to have some clean fun. He buys land too, got on clothes just can't see 'em! A family man, lives by the highest moral standards, never gets off the straight and narrow, and done some readin' in the Good Book once!" The Englishman looked around to see who he was talking about. Barney continued, "Give him a big hand! Now ya'll gals line up and get your cigaretes and cigars ready, walk by, blow your three smoke rings at him and move on. And we wanta keep this establishment clean. No pizzin' on the floor are nothing like that...you hafta, kick a little dirt over it."

The girls made their pass, the bartender hollered, "Give me your attention, got an important announcement. The gentleman has picked the winner. Loose Lucy gets the prize!"

"She don't get much!" a voice yelled. The crowd went wild. Barney roared, "Quieten down!" They paid him no mind, so in his rough bass voice, he bellowed again, "Ya'll shut-up or gonna throw ya ass out!"

Someone spoke up, loud, "Barney did anybody ever tell you your bald head looks like the north end of a south bound baboon?"

"That you Buzzard Breath?" Barney grabbed his gun and splintered the door as old Buzzard Breath dashed out the back.

Baldy said, "Ol' Barney's lowered on Buzzard Breath so many times the door looks like a sieve."

Bat replied, "That's enough for now, gotta get my smokings."

The next morning around a half hour after sunup Bat dropped by to see the man who thought he lived in paradise.

Firing up his pipe, Johnny Long said, "Well, my friend, how's it going, give me the latest on Molly, of course."

"Tell you what Uncle Johnny, there's not another one like her. Now, has this town's honorary mayor got Mobeetie to the snubbing post?"

"Bat, you know better than that, even heard griping about the girls dragging men off the streets in broad open daylight; gals like Loose Lucy and Bad Breath Bonnie. Can't believe that's a legitimate gripe, can you?"

Bat replied, "Sounds like some old geezer past redemption; good girls, just need money; not crybabies."

"Some of them will grab them old boys and slam 'em in bed."

"Yup," Bat said, "there's gals here that's been on the buffalo trail for years. You know, like Doc Holiday's partner there around Fort Griffin. Doc in town?"

"Somebody said he was, haven't seen 'im, but did see Luke Short. These guys' riding in are after some of this easy money," Uncle Johnny said.

"Doc's got a health problem—consumption, going west to a drier climate and might meet the Earps here later. Big Nose will be with him and you can bet your bottom dollar on that. And I bet she can blow them smoke rings, too."

"Oh yeah." Uncle Johnny added, "Never seen anything like some of them old gals. They can blow smoke rings around the moon."

"Guess you know about the smoke ring contests at the Shores -O-Hell—a circus? 'Dropped by last night with Baldy and Rip."

"Last night? Don't reckon I did," J. J. replied.

"This Englishman, syndcated land buyer from England, was the winner; got the prize. He thought he'd found some real art."

"Now Bat, you know down there at the Shores-Of-Hell anything goes. I mean anything; hell hole! Oughta be run outta town. Smoke ring contest, been doing it for some time, reason so many killings there. Whores thick as fleas on a dog. Of all the saloons in town the Shores-Of-Hell is the wildest and wickedest. Ssmoke ring contest—got art? Ha!"

Bat replied, "This old Englishman, drunk as a skunk up there on the platform last night thought so. Big joke."

Grinning, Uncle Johnny said, "Not unusual there, the winner gets the prize, but what's the joke?"

Chuckling, Bat said, "Someone on the dance floor yelled, 'Try it Big Snout Stella!' Ol' Rip Nesbit hollered out, 'She would but she can't get the smoke rings past her nose!"

"A crazy bunch," J. J. said. "Well you know some of these new settlers don't go for that kind of stuff; can't blame 'em. But usually it's Dogface they've heard about. They keep moving on. Guess you're going to the big Lady Gay shindig?"

"Yup, try to make 'em all," Bat said. "Molly and Me with bells on. You coming?"

Bat worked for Henry at the Fleming-Thompson Lady Gay and was there most of the time. Where Bat hung out that's where Molly would be. Bat frowned.

Funny, Henry Fleming hadn't mentioned another party to him. It hadn't been long since he throwed the big Christmas party, but Bat thought ol' Henry had been acting a little strange here of late.

Uncle Johnny said, "Love to but as you know, arrows messed up my leg shaking days a long time ago."

"Haven't told Molly about the party but we're talking."

"Like about the future?" A big grin spread across Mr. Long's face. Bat knew J. J. was pleased to hear it.

"Yup, looking ahead," Bat said.

"Good news. Then a little new citizen...come right, throw you a party. King's blowing around you'll never make another one."

"Yeah, still spreading it, eh—been around?"

"Sneaking in and out—no question, dodging Bat Masterson. I heard he's hid out on the creek now. Hunters' wives are staying inside. Something's got to be done. They know if they're seen talking to Molly what will happen; happened before, their husbands' catch hell—throat cut. He's slipping around these saloons cutting girths and bridle reins, runs off saddlehorses', cheats at card games, and pistol whips soldiers. He threatens any man seen friendly with the whores he calls his heifers. He's deadly with either hand, pistol or knife, but he runs from you and I figure it's because you've beat hell out of him couple times. Even in Dodge City he gets by the law by pulling that knife first—shoots the other man when he goes for his gun, then swears the other guy pulled down first. Like the buffalo hunter that opened the front door here for Molly; coldblooded killer!"

"Charmed life?" Bat replied.

"Might say that. He's blowing around: 'Even a dumb-ass like Bat Masterson ought to have sense enough to know who's running this damn town.' He'd like too, but for you Bat...well, you make him quake in his boots. Thinks he's tough, but look at one of them guy's that come down here from Dodge. He'd gunned down three or four men, a tough hombre too, but when he got here a cowboy stretched his neck with a lariat."

"Yup, "Bat said, "I remember that, the boys in Dodge would've got that mad dog if it hadn't been for our old friend Manny Dubbs."

Bat turned to go; he paused. "Looks like someone was practicing when they drilled your door there."

"Heard something, thought nothing about it," Mr. Long said. "Shooting and cussing going on every night 'round here. Yeah, a trigger happy gunslick showing off his writing skill, I guess."

"Looks of them holes could be a 'K'," Bat added.

"Right, 'K' for King, curse on the town. He won't last long...could soon be swinging from the highest tree, but I'm betting it's going be a helluva bang, and he ain't fast enough."

"Yup, a hundred years from now skeletons like his will be found on the prairie plugged by someone that hated his guts."

J. J. said, "Before you go, 'still wondering how you tracked old Dogface along the border—over east, awhile back?"

"Had him like this, only one way he could get away...."

A bullet hit the store front. Johnny and Bat ducked. Two teamsters buying tobacco dropped behind whiskey barrels. Really nothing, just wild shots from across the street knocked out the glass in the wooden door. Uncle Johnny and Bat looked at each other and grinned.

"Hate that," Mr. Long said. "That glass had that fancy writing on it—'J. J. Long Gen. Merchandise.' That old circuit riding preacher did that for me; could use that brush. By the way, the old Indian fighter/preacher is back in town...better wait on these guys getting coffee and stuff."

"Won't see him at the shindig," Bat said as he walked out.

At evening twilight Ellen O'Loughlin rushed over to the Long house in a tizzy. "Mary, Mary, hurry, quick, shut the door and pull the curtains, got something to tell you that's going to blow the lid off!"

"Now Ellen, you got that old gas on your stomach again?"

"No! Town's not going to take this. 'Saw it with my own eyes; happened behind the Shores-O-Hell. That mean old Dogface caught little Mabel, slapped her and knocked her down. He said, 'My boys saw you at the Lady Gay with a mop. The bad part is you was seen talking to that damn Masterson.' She's a shady lady Mary, but it's terrible. Just don't know what to say!"

"Sh-sh, you know the boys are talking a neck-tie party for Dogface at the same tree where they swung and doctored Digger's old gray mare."

"Yeah, Tom mentioned it, said something's got to be done in this town. Oh, I just knew he was going to kill that poor girl; nobody around to help her."

"Now Ellen, keep it quiet, it ain't going on much longer. He could be run out of town, could be a necktie party, could be a gunfight, but as you know every woman in town is setting on pins and needles; the men can't wait. You remember what Molly said, telling us, 'A dream haunts me, got the feeling there's going to be a gunfight. Bat won but he lost.' You know Ellen that's a mystery you and I haven't been able to figure out—won but he lost—and she can't either. Knowing Bat Masterson it don't make sense, and that's bothering her. She thinks Dogface will bring his sidekicks in, too. Everybody in town knows what's going to happen the next time him

240

and Bat meet-up."

Tom O'Loughlin walked in Long's store the next morning about nine o'clock. He spoke, "Hi John."

"Yeah, Tom been wanting to see you," Johnny replied.

Zeb soon walked in too. "Hi fellows, now with you two guys 'guess we could have a town meeting of some kind, just had Henry. Baldy will be here pretty soon."

Uncle Johnny said, "Glad you come in. Fixing to tell Tom, we just as well get ready for a necktie party...this guy running around here keeping the town stirred up."

Tom replied, "I think Bat will put an end to it before long, catch the bully right."

Zeb spoke up, "Tell ya 'bout Bat, best guy you ever saw, but he likes to play games—got old Dogface dodging."

"You're right Zeb," Mr. Long said, "treats him like a cat does a mouse; has no fear whatsoever of the guy."

"Yeah," Tom added, "Bat's beat the hell out of the overbearing bastard a couple of times and the darn fool keeps coming back—and he's dangerous."

J. J. replied, "Right Tom, can't figure the guy out. He'll pick a fight with a man just because his wife was talking to the bully's girlfriend."

Zeb spoke up, "It's a wonder somebody hasn't got him before now, but of course we know what King's up to—got it in his head to make it a big show the day he guns down William Barclay Masterson."

Uncle Johnny said, "You're right Zeb, everybody in town knew from the very first day nineteen year old Bat Masterson rode in to this settlement King wanted to get rid of him. Now, me and Henry's throwing a big party for Bat and Molly Saturday night, and Mickey McCormack and Frenchy will be in on it too. I'll talk to Henry about this. He'll want to get in on it, so let's see—

241

why don't we get back together, say Monday."

"Suits me," Tom replied.

"Me too," Zeb and Baldy joined in."

38 *Growing Tension*

On January 24, 1876, the night was cool and windless in Mobeetie, Texas. Uncle Johnny Long and Henry Fleming was throwing a surprise party for Bat Masterson and Molly Brennan. Bill Sty, the Lady Gay's manager, and Red Day the bartender, had a hand in it, too. And so did Henry's partner, Bill Thompson and his brother, Ben. Bat and Molly walked in the Lady Gay and yells led by Mickey McCormack and Frenchy shook the walls. Bat felt good about it, Molly deserved it. Everybody in town loved her, however Bat thought the reception was unusual. Something was going on. They beamed, smiled, and nodded on the way to the bar in the dim lit room.

The big bar length mirror reflected a handsome twenty two year old lover with his sweetheart proudly swinging on his arm. He had spread it on a little but Henry and Uncle Johnny convinced him this was a special night. He didn't know why. His hand faced shirt ordered out by J. J. Long's General Merchandise Store wasn't too unusual in the West where there was money. Just a little something extra for special occasions. His pinstripe gambler's pants come from Dodge City, too. Hung Chung at the local Chinese laundry pressed them to fit like a glove.

The red silk bandana around his neck was to keep out the cold, but the red silk sash he wore around his waist was, he said, "Just for the hell of it." His gold watch fob engraved with a grizzly bear, swung on a chain that stretched from vest pocket to vest pocket. The jewelry sparkled like a winking star.

Bat blow-dusted his big silver belly hat and gave the beady eyed diamond back rattlesnake hatband a little adjustment too. His high heeled, high top, spit polished black boots jingled gold mounted spurs, spurs with an unusual harmonious ring. His sterling silver studded belt matched his holsters, holsters that packed a brace of silver plated "sixes."

His string bow tie as black as his jacket; and his jacket, the Chinese tailor give it a special cut for easy access to the Colt .45s' that bulged on his hips. Bat could get away with it in Mobeetie, even wearing a derby hat, but the old grizzled hide hunters around town would warn a new-comer: "Never take Bat Masterson for a dude. He's fair, but don't cross him. He's quick as a cat and deadly as a rattlesnake; just a good dresser."

Bat and Molly didn't understand all the attention they were getting. Still he thought it was all for his darling Molly. He had never seen her so beautiful. Her eyes glistened, sparkled like diamonds over her cute dimpled cheeks. Her marcelled wavy dark hair touched the voluptuous twin peaks of her hour glass figure...squeezed in her pretty party dress. He liked everything about her, even to his gold locket gift that nestled in her beautiful deep cleavage.

"Quiet now! Everybody listen up!" Henry Fleming boomed. And like always, the good time Joes paid him no mind. As usual, he pulled his old .45 and blowed the rafters. The noise died down. "Before the music starts got something to tell you."

Bat gazed out over the crowd, surprised that some old acquaintances made the party. Beth Barton, stylish and pretty, was hanging onto her Jim, still with a gleam in her eyes. Glowing Frenchy McGraw, soon to be

Frenchy McCormick, was swinging on her Mickey's arm proudly flaunting the glittering bracelet the gambler laid on her.

Soon Bat saw some of the old buffalo hunters' and other friends come in the door...Rip Nesbit, John Corcoran, Johnny Jones, Mark Huselby, Billy Joe Carter, Baldy Beechnut, Zeb Hunter, and Robert Baley, too. And from as far away as Dodge City, Bill Tilghman, Luke Short, amd others had showed up. Zeb "put on the dog" for Bat's big party. His sand washed, high riding britches were faded but clean; best he could do. Just as dignified as any country lawyer at a hog calling contest. Many of the lovers' friends had shown up; scheming going on?

Henry gestured. "Uncle Johnny and me hatched up this little party for our friends, Bat Masterson and his one and only, Molly Brennan!" The crowd yelled, looking toward them.

"Well-er-ah," Bat stammered.

"Hope Molly don't change her mind before ol' bashful Bat gets it out. Drinks are on the house. Get it going, Slats!"

The saloon shook with fun and laughter, but revelry was going on all over town, too. Mobeetie was a beehive of buffalo hunters, cowboys, prospectors, gunslingers, gamblers, and girls, in a changing world....The West, from buffaloes and Indians to cattle and cowboys; a passing era. The Lady Gay bunch, noisy as usual, and the over-tanked guys threatened to get wild, but ol' Henry didn't fool with them; threw them out.

The first drinks were on the house, but the free loaders soon had to shell out. All the saloons in town enjoyed a brisk business for it was as usual, drink to anything and bet on everything. A friendly smile and a loving woman for every lonely man that drifted in off the prairie where money grows, whiskey flows, and wild women

245

glow.

But this party had been whipped-up for a man and lady, a man that had done it all...buffalo hunter, Indian fighter, surveyor, scout, and romantic lover. But more important for the wildest town in the West, he packed a big gun.

The music stopped, the crowd gathered around Bat and Molly. The girls pushed in, they loved the handsome devil. He knocked the women off their feet. Visiting ladies with the land buyers from overseas stared. Ogling men shoved in too to admire Molly's low cut dress. The couple smiled and beamed with pride. They paid no attention to the noisy juiced up men that were already swinging the gals around to Slat's music.

There were braggarts in the crowd, too, proud of their gun handling skill. Bat ignored them. The barroom gals' striptease performance went over big to the hoots'n hollers of, "take it off." This was a night for Bat and Molly to remember....A night for the whole town to remember, and would talk about it for years to come.

The lovers danced the waltzes slow and easy in a dream world. Hanging in close, and with her head on his shoulder, Molly whispered, "Oh Bat, this could go on forever."

"Molly, Darling, why not? You know what the Good Book says: 'Eat, drink, and be merry for tomorrow you may die.'"

"Yes, I've heard it said like that, too, and who knows in this place?" Molly was having fun but deep inside she was troubled, uneasy, haunted by a dream she couldn't shake off. How could it happen, Bat won a gunfight but he lost...yes, how could it happen? He knew she wasn't afraid for herself; brave but worried that a killer was out to get her man. Before Bat come along she watched King cut a man's throat, a buffalo hunter who only smiled and opened the door for her. She felt a party to it, never forgot it. And the friendly mule-skinner that had just rolled into to town...his throat slashed from ear to ear. It had been a month since Bat pistol whipped and beat the hell out of Dogface Melvin King. And he hadn't been seen around town since, but his sidekicks had put out the word: "Masterson won't live to see the light of another day when our 'Boss' comes in. He's gonna show that damn buffalo hunter just who's running this town. He laid a brand on Molly Brennan before Bat Masterson come along, and Dogface ain't putting up with anymore of Masterson's horseshit!"

People in Mobeetie thought the world of Bat, and Molly was "just a doll." They loved the young couple and watched the romance from the very first, but King, the jealous suitor, swore to end it. But Molly's friends, the Long's, O'Loughlin's, and others were concerned, couldn't see Bat Masterson winning a gun fight but losing; a mystery, how could it be? Who'd believe it? Not a soul in Mobeetie. But this love affair, what was going to happen? Anxiety and talk was running wild in town.

King's sidekicks could hardly wait to tell the Sergeant Molly was spending time after closing hours at the Lady Gay with Bat Masterson.

Who's business was it? Maybe Bat did stay longer...wasn't unusual, he locked up the saloon for Henry sometimes. The town was on edge, and no one doubted King would come for Bat in the dark with a sawed-off shotgun; the favorite weapon of a cold blooded killer.

The night before the party King slipped into town but he hadn't been seen. Soon as he rode in his boot lickers let him know Molly was entertaining Bat after hours at the Lady Gay. But he didn't always trust the bunch he hung out with. He wanted to see for himself.

247

The moon had gone down and the night was dark. Slipping around the Lady Gay the night before the party he got his sidekicks to hold him up to a high window at the rear of the saloon. He peered through the broken glass. What he saw in the candle lit room left no doubt. He went into a blind rage, "Masterson will make the party but never live to see 12:00 o'clock midnight!"

Now, by the night of Janurary 26, 1876, everybody in town knew of King's talk, his Midnight threats. The big clock at the Lady Gay was ticking away, moving up close to 9:00 o'clock. Bill Sty watched the front door. He looked at the clock, thought Dogface would burst in anytime to make it a big show. Red Day, a husky man, red curly locks dangling, serving drinks, cut his eyes, rolling them shifting back and forth, glancing toward the door, to Bat, to the clock—9:15. He liked Bat Masterson, but watched for Dogface to burst through the door swinging his Bowie knife with his gun a-blazing. Red made sure things were clear behind the bar. He had ducked out of sight there many times. And on the street, he'd seen a couple guys killed that met-up with King. Hank Dittmos winked at Bat, knew he could handle it any day of the week. Henry Fleming didn't think King would show up. He'd be more sinster, shoot a man in the back, wait for Bat outside the door. Now, come hell or high water, Corporal Melvin King would make it a big "happenings" the day he gunned down William Barclay Masterson! But Bat, gambling at a card table with Panhandle Pete, Dr. Shelton, and a buffalo hunter, seemed to be the most relaxed person in town.

Dr. Shelton, across the table from Bat, raised up out of his chair, and said, "Bat, it's only about 9:30 and you've already cleaned me out."

Suddenly, like a morgue, the saloon got quiet. People knew of the midnight threat, they stared, looked around,

248

looked at the clock—9:45. King and three or four of his buddies burst in the door and headed straight for Bat's table. Bat glanced up. The girls behind the other gamblers shifted over but Molly, holding to Bat's chair, didn't offer to move.

"Masterson, you holding this spot for me?" King blurted.

Bat had gambled with King before; he eyeballed the Corporal severely. "Could be," he calmly replied.

Gambling for $10 gold pieces had gone on for hours. Pete soon dropped out and thirty minutes later, at 10:00 o'clock, the buffalo hunter; now Bat and Dogface. Dogface had two kings and a queen. A sidekick snickered, a dead giveaway on a high draw. His crony whopped him over the head with the butt of his pistol. From his hand, Dogface threw a king, Bat threw a king...Dogface, his last King, his devilish grin cracked his pock-marked face.

But Bat had the last deal; took his time. Beads of sweat popped out on King's face. Would King carry out his threat? 10:30 and coming up to midnight. The silence in the saloon was weird. Patrons froze, others slipped behind tables, the bar, and some beat it for the door. All eyes were on Bat Masterson. His bluish-slate-gray eyes, cold and fearless, drove daggers in the shifty eyes of Dogface Melvin King. King didn't dare make a threatening move. Bat threw down. Ace high! Snarling, King and his sidekicks stomped out.

"A little past 10:30 and it calls for another drink!" Bill Sty yelled.

The Lady Gay was closing down early. Henry done it for Bat and Molly. He came to Bat's table and touched his shoulder. "Ben and Bill Thompson will be around, and you may want to stay a little longer. To top off the party there's a bunch going to sernade you two come midnight. It's your party, your night." Henry paused,

"It's getting close to 11:00 and I'll be leaving pretty soon. When you leave, bar the front door. Be sure she's locked front and back; here's the keys, have fun!"

The Thompson boys went out the door at 11:00 o'clock. They were soon looking for the nearest open saloon and would let the lovers carry on in their own sweet way. But the Thompsons' would be back at midnight with girls and more of the Lovers' friends to finish off the celebration, too. When they went out they left the back door unlocked.

39 *Climax*

The Lady Gay party was over, the crowd cleared out. Henry went through the saloon to see the damage done—wet floor, broken glass, stuff like that. In the back room he kicked things out of sight and straightened up a little, all for his special guest, Bat and Molly. He fixed the couch cover and squared up the throw-carpet...threw a log on the smoldering fire and turned the lights down low.

Molly followed right behind Bat on his way to bar the front door. He had barred that thing for Henry so many times he could do it with his eyes shut. With thanks to Henry and Uncle Johnny, now they had the Lady Gay to themselves. But at 12:00 o'clock midnight the lovers' friends would be back to finish of the big party. Bat locked the door then grabbed Molly up and squeezed her. Of course she squealed a little but that was about it; what she wanted. He pulled her to him and kissed her as he laid her on the couch in the back.

"Ah, Sweetheart," he said, "the bunch will be back at midnight and we don't have time to waste. Honey it seemed we'd never get back together but your're always on my mind."

"I know my love," she replied, "but you're always doing things for other people—on the go—just been a week, seems a month."

Bat thought the best way to relax the body and soul was to shed the "rigging" he had on. And he was willing to help his lady-love get confortable, too.

251

His gun-handling skill could hardly be matched but still he wasn't too good on women's clothing. After all, hunting buffaloes had been his life, but romancing pretty girls was far more fun. He'd never give up on a little old button, but her only party dress couldn't be ripped or raveled. There wasn't a spool of thread this side of Dodge City. Fumbling with the buttoned blouse, the thrill and excitement almost had ol' Masterson besides himself. He shrugged, the feel of her soft warm body would make any old cowboy jump out of his chaps!

Back yonder...Bat knew how young hunters sat around the campfire dreaming about beautiful girls...always bragging about the pretty things they left back home. Naturally in a man's world they do dream about beautiful women—girls they long for, fight for, and die for. He'd tell the world, "Dreams do come true"— and that's about all he could say while tightly squeezing Molly's charms. But suddenly he relaxed, and said, "Honey, 'love you and got something to say—er-ask you."

Molly was shocked, she couldn't figure out what was wrong with the guy—a crazy way to treat a passionate woman; stunned, her anger flashed red-hot. But shy ol' Bat was soon back in the saddle again. "Yup, Sweetheart, got something to ask you, will you ride double with me— always?"

The girls in Mobeetie thought handsome fun loving Bat Masterson would be any lady's dream come true. And there was no doubt about it in Molly's mind from the first day she laid eyes on him. Now she told him so in her own Western way, "Darling, never heard sweeter words. My love, we'll ride double always, my foot's in the stirrup, kiss me again and never let me go!"

With a sensual kiss he slowly worked his hand over her soft warm body. Her luscious kisses were ravag-

252

ing—overpowering. He gently stroked her body over and round, slow and easy...a young buffalo hunter's dream come true. He caressed and kissed her again and again, exploring the secret of her charms. Anticipation was killing the young lovers. A night to remember —the outside noise, they paid it no mind. Soon the old musical couch began to rock and squeak. Creeping off the carpet, the cover hit the floor; the pillow. The squeaking springs grew louder and louder...rocking, squeaking, rocking, the bed banged the wall! Molly shrieked, "Oh my love!" Relaxing, the lovers were roped and tied in a bond of love as strong as death and happy as Heaven, oblivious to the world around them. He kissed her and slowly stroked her body. They lay limp as a loose laced lariat. The old wind-up clock was ticking away at fifteen minutes until 12:00 midnight. The happy sernading bunch of friends would soon be coming.

Bat Masterson had grit, tough as rawhide, wasn't afraid of the devil himself, but deep inside he was soft hearted. He kissed away her salty tears of happiness.

But Bat Masterson wasn't "saddle-broke." Molly Brennan was overwhelming. Again he....Someone was banging on the front door! Heaven only knows how long it had been going on. Bat and Molly lay still, didn't move a muscle—listened. Henry Fleming—the Thompson boys?

"Darling, the sernaders?" Molly whispered.

"No," Bat replied.

40 *Dogface At The Door?*

Past a quarter to midnight and the knocking at the front door never let up. Molly asked again, "Honey, could it be Henry Fleming or the Thompson boys?"

"They wouldn't do it," Bat replied, "but some damn fool is trying to knock the door down."

Molly was livid, and Bat Masterson was in no mood to put up with some son-of-a-bitch hell-bent on bursting in at a time like this. The door-knockers wouldn't go away. The lovers lay still; heard voices? The banging kept up. Furious, Bat exclaimed, "Damn it, they're going to break the door down!"

The big hand hit ten minutes until midnight; dressed, Bat slung on his gun-belt, and said, "Sweetheart, you're ready, let's go." They held on to each other in the dim lit room making their way to the front door. There, he pulled her to him and kissed her passionately; her lips were quivering. A woman's intuition... worried not for herself but for the man she loved. He kissed her again and whispered, "Honey, I love you."

"I love you too, Darling, but don't—please don't open that door; they're going to kill you!"

"Open'er-r-rup, gotta have a drink!"

Who's were the slurred voices? The door rattled and shook...coming off the hinges? Could it be an old scouting partner—buffalo hunter—King to settle a score? Bat knew when the door come open anything could happen. Strangely enough, neither Bat nor Molly was too concerned about their own safety. She knew King would kill her lover just for the hell of it. In the dim light Bat glimpsed at the big clock, ticking away, moving on up close to 12:00 o'clock midnight. King's threat flashed his mind.

"Hurry'rup, gotta have a dr-ri-nk!" The voice was rough.

Molly cringed at the thought King's Bowie knife would slash through the door at Bat's throat; haunting fear gripped her. She whispered, "Is it over the card game? King has been hell-bent and threatened to kill you ever since he laid eyes on you...even boasted today you would never see 12:00 o'clock midnight."

"Card game? Naw, not really, he's jealous—burning, can't get over it." And looking her straight in the eyes he said, "He can't have you."

They stood for a minute. "Honey, the bolt—be ready with your hand on the bolt." She looked at Bat—to the door—back to Bat, her eyes pleading, begging, "Please don't open that door." Soon from her trembling lips she whispered, "Darling, only God knows, 'you won but you lost." Bat would do what he had to do, on his honor, no man, come hell or high water, would come between Bat Masterson and Molly Brennan. He patted her shoulder and kissed her again!

"Sweetheart," he said, low, "pull the bolt and stand back!"

41 *Deadly Encounter*

At five minutes until 12:00 o'clock midnight Molly slipped the bolt and the door flew open. Dogface Melvin King, full of rotgut whiskey bellowing and cursing, burst through the door with a gun in one hand and a Bowie knife in the other. Bat was ready for him when the door swung back....But Molly screamed and jumped between them. Hell-bent on getting Masterson, Dogface ignored her. Blazing guns! A helluva roar! A bullet ripped through her body into Bat's groin. Jolted, he held Molly up, shoved his gun past her, and slammed a slug into King's heart— spun him around—wild-eyed, he blinked...blood gushed, reeling, he staggered, twisting, sinking, he hit the bar-room floor. Molly dropped at Bat's feet, his knees buckled and he lurched forward, falling to the floor, too. King lay spread-eagled in the clearing smoke.

Bat, crumpled on the floor, lay dazed and bleeding, reached for Molly...near, but seemed far away. He took her by the arm to ease her over close. She didn't move, her breathing was short and hard, her eyes closed and opened, her life ebbing away. Her dress was splotched crimson, blood oozed from her stomach, but the hole in her back gushed blood. Her lips moved —trembling.

Bat leaned on his elbow and bent over to listen; she gasped for air. He tried to raise her head but was help-less. With hidden strength he slipped his hand under her blood-soaked hair and eased her head in his lap, rubbed her forehead and stroked her youthful cheeks; tenderly caressed and kissed her. Bat's pain was killing

256

him but Molly's suffering was all but gone. She moved her lips, and struggled, struggling to say something. He kissed her and bent low...lower to listen.

"D-a-r-l-i-n-g," she whispered low, "looks like we're riding out double."

He kissed her again. Her soft affectionate smile aroused tender emotion. A tear here and there, on her cheeks, on his, for the one they loved. She slowly closed her eyes and with a final gasp for breath she lay limp in his arms.

Ben and Bill Thompson, with their girlfriends, along with other midnight sernaders were at the Shores-Of-Hell a couple doors down. They first thought the gunfire was down the street from the Lady Gay. They knew the saloon's front door had been barred but the sound had come from that direction. They ran for the back door, rushed in just in time to see King's sidekicks moving in to finish off Bat. Ben Thompson jumped on a faro table with a gun in each hand, legs spread, and with scathing authority he burst out, "I'll blow the first sonovabitch to hell that lays a hand on Bat Masterson!" He backed them to the wall and took their guns.

Someone ran over to a nearby house and shook young George Curry (14 years old) out of bed, told him to hurry to Fort Elliot with a message for Major Hatch: One of his soldiers had been killed in a gunfight.

A long time friend of Bat Masterson, Ben Thompson realized Bat had a bad injury...he also knew how hard it would be to keep a man like Bat Masterson in bed.

42 *Gone*

For eight weeks Ben Thompson stayed with his friend, stayed until Bat was able to get on his feet.

Johnny Long and Henry Fleming would see that young Molly Brennan was put away with decency, even put in a wooden box. When the sun broke the horizon the next morning, Mr. Long was out looking for him— the old half-scalped Preacher. His mule was saddled and the man was cinching up when Mr. Long walked up and spoke, "Good Morning."

"Yeah, good morning there," replied the friendly fellow.

Preachers were never seen in Mobeetie, the town had no use for them, but this old ex-hide hunter they respected. No one knew much about him, where he come from or where he went, still riding that old gray mule.

Mr. Long asked, "Brother Parson, just wondered if you'd do some reading from the Good Book and do some talking over Molly, Sir—do a prayer?"

"Well, did-didn't know...." The Preacher hesitated. "The cobbler, er-smithy—fixed my boots. Fine little Christian family. His girl?" This wasn't new to the man who had stared death in the face many times.

"That's right—slug slammed her."

"Heard some shooting but paid it no mind. Be glad to help anyway I can. Ain't much on funerals but I've done a lot of praying in my time."

The old self-proclaimed, self-taught preacher was an humble understanding man.

Bat lay in bed helpless and half dead at Fort Elliot's Infirmary. He felt useless but his thoughts were with Molly, and today she was going to be put away. He had to go even if they had to carry him out and set him in a buggy. He owed it to her. His condition was serious. Doctor Evans told him not to do it but he was going anyway. In severe pain, he rode out lying on a buggy seat.

Digger Dugan led the way with his old sorrel mare and blue donkey. Buggies, wagons, and horsebackers all strung out, headed south in the slow moving procession.

Friends gathered around, came in close to show their respect for the "Rose of the Canadian." The Preacher hummed and half sang, "Amazing Grace." The women soon joined in. Somber, with hats off, cowboys and hunters who had heard religious songs years before, reverently joined in, too...off key, picking up a word now and then. The Preacher soon untied the string around his worn Bible and read from a couple of places he had marked, "What does a man have if he gains the whole world and loses his own soul?" The crowd stirred uneasily. The preacher continued driving home the message, "What greater love does one have than to lay down their life for a friend?"

Six men, cowboys and hunters, lowered Molly in the grave, cradled in their lariats, on a ridge overlooking Sweetwater Creek. At this point Bat's red bandana came in handy. From where he rested in the buggy seat, he motioned for Uncle Johnny. "Place this red rose at Molly's head." Other winter time crepe-paper flowers and bouquets spread across the mound of dirt where Molly Brennan lay.

Bat was tough, face any situation, but he was touched like never before. He wondered why, but what could he say? She had loved him with all her heart and laid down her life for him. A sentimental man, he never forgot

Molly, her haunting dream...."A gunfight he won but he lost." He always wore a red rose in his lapel on the anniversary of Molly Brennan's death.

Bat lived to tell of the senseless killing but he lost his taste for Mobeetie, Texas. Talking with his friends one day, Johnny Long, Mark Huselby, and Johnny Jones, he said, "I came to Texas to hunt buffaloes, got caught up in the 'Dobe Walls battle, lived here and worked here, and now it looks like the guy on the strawberry roan ended it all."

Uncle Johnny spoke up, "Talking about the red roan, we've never figured out how you tracked that horse—like an Indian."

A chorus come from Mark and Jones, "Yeah, we've all wondered ...what's the secret?"

Bat said, "Ah'll tell you about that old horse—lost him at the river but he's got an odd hoof. The frog on the right front leaves a 'V" in wet dirt when he lays it down, but the the tracking back hoof usually wipes it out. You have to catch it just right."

"Odd, I'd say," Mr. Long replied.

Johnny Jones said, "Seen odd markings but never like that." Bat said, "Well, I'm pulling out of here, going back to a civilized country—Dodge City. Adios my friends.

After the gunfight Bat was left with a limp and carried a cane the rest of his life. It's been said he soon started handing out justice with his cane in barroom brawls as skillfully as he handled his "sixes."

Johnny Long was always a booster for Mobeetie and the Texas Panhandle; never gave up hope. After the 1890's the town settled down. He died August 8, 1925. Gone too were the millions of buffaloes on a thousand hills...the Indians from the land they loved. And gone was, "The Rose Of The Canadian," the lovable Molly Brennan, and the man she loved...a man that left his mark on Texas, the dashing Bat Masterson. And as the years rolled by memories lingered on. Old friends were convinced Molly's ghost always returned to the windswept prairie on that fateful day. They heard voices, Like Whispers In The Wind, "Bat Masterson won a gunfight but he lost."

About *"Like Whispers in the Wind"*

These excerpts and episodes, true or assumed to be true, may or may not be in chronological order. Names mentioned on these pages are Panhandle pioneers.

Chapter 1. Bat Masterson came to Texas as a teenage buffalo hunter. Before he settled in Mobeetie, (Mobee-tee, Indian for sweet water), he scouted for the Army battling Indians. Ruggedly handsome, a great prankster, and a fun-loving tall-tale teller, once he had the job of counting Government mules. "The dullest job I ever had," he said.

Walter Weed landed in Mobeetie with 100 barrels of whiskey.

"The Shores-Of-Hell," one of the first saloons in Mobeetie with a reputation of, "More girls than any place in town."

The two-story Lady Gay saloon, the bottom floor adobe, had a dance floor, naked gal wall art, and bar-length mirror, was owned by Henry Fleming and Bill Thompson. Bill was a brother to Ben Thompson, the well known gunfighter from Austin, Texas.

Henry Fleming was elected the first Sheriff, of the first county in the Texas Panhandle, by one vote. The county covered an area about the size of Maryland and Massachusetts combined. Henry Fleming's rock-house still stands today and is lived in.

The Tom O'Loughlins' first made their home into a cafe/boarding house. There was the Manlin hotel too, then O'Loughlins' built the Grand Central. Then came the Mark Huselby Hotel.

Molly Brennan beautiful daughter of Bob Brennan, blacksmith/cobbler, called "The Rose Of The Canadian."

Melvin King, a Corporal in the Army, who claimed to

be a Sergeant, a town bully, threatened any man or woman that was friendly with girls he claimed as girl-friends, especially Molly Brennan. The insanely jealous cold-blooded killer boasted he had killed twenty men before he came to Mobeetie. In Mobeetie, he cut a mule skinner's throat that only tipped his hat to Molly on the street. And he slashed a buffalo hunter's throat that opened the door at J. J. Long's store for Molly. Ambi-dextrous, good with his Bowie knife or pistol in either hand. Extremely dangerous, he accused a stranger of stealing his horse and cut his throat in the Lady Gay Saloon.

Chapter 3. Fort Elliot was named for Major Joel Elliot, killed in Custer's massacre of the Cheyenne Indi-ans at "Black Kettle," in Indian Territory, in 1868—35 miles east of Mobeetie. 500 white and 300 buffalo sol-diers were stationed at Ft. Elliot.

Telegraph lines were strung to Fort Elliot, connect-ing with Fort Reno, Fort Sill, and Fort Dodge.

Pioneers in the Panhandle estimated some buffalo herds run as high as 5,000,000 animals.

Chapter 2. A buffalo that fought to the bitter end 35 miles southwest of Mobeetie.

Chapter 5. Doctoring livestock cuts with prairie snuffballs was common practice with early day ranch-ers.

Chapter 6. Bill Sty was the manager and Red Day the bartender at the Lady Gay saloon in Mobeetie.

Chapter 8. A Mexican lost his wagon and team half-mile southwest of Fort Elliot in Sweetwater Creek dur-ing a raging head-rise. Neither the wagon or team was ever found in the deep quicksand.

Chapter 11. John J. Long was a quiet unassuming man with a wealth of pioneering experience. A close friend of Bat Masterson, he was Mobeetie's biggest booster. Though a young man, he earned the "Uncle" with the help and gifts he gave to other people. He worked on the U. P. Trail when the Union Pacific railroad was spanning the country. As a civilian, his freight wagons transported supplies for General Nelson Miles, General Custer, and Col. Ranald Mackenzie. His wagons freighted in the first wagon-loads of the designated 1,000,000 pounds of grain, and 650,000 pounds of goods, for Fort Elliot—including a saloon he set-up close to the Post. He cut the flagpole for Fort Elliot on the Canadian River, and it stands today at the Mobeetie jail museum—the only remaining flagpole of the era.

Eight hundred buffaloes said to have been killed by Dick Bussell in a one day stand at the site of present day Canadian, Texas.

Chapter 12. King slashed a mule skinner's throat that smiled and tipped his hat to Molly Brennan.

The O'Loughlins' were truly plains pioneers. The Indians burned them out in Kansas. They loaded up what they had left to come to Texas. About ready to leave with their two boys, Miles and Willie, and their two year old daughter, a skunk came in the yard and bit the little girl. They thought it wise to leave her in Kansas with relatives to be near doctors. Three months later, in Hidetown, Texas, they received word she had died with hydrophobia. They moved from Hidetown and squatted on a section of land a mile northwest—halfway to the Fort Elliot location. They gave 100 lots to start the town of Mobeetie. The O'Loughlins' first opened up their home as a cafe/boarding house, but later built the Grand Central Hotel. The hotel register shows many famous Western characters as their guest, including Billy the Kid, Luke Short, Ben Thompson, Wyatt Earp, Mysterious Dave Mather, Bill Tilghman, and others. Tom O'Loughlin was a hide hunter too.

Bat was hired as the town surveyor for Mobeetie. Boundry markers included, skunk dens, buffalo chips, sagebrush, buffalo heads, whatever was handy.

Henry Dittmos, Bat's surveying partner, recorded it—Bill Sty, Red Day, and Henry Dittmos saw it, the lightening fast pistol whipping Bat gave "Dogface" Melvin King. These, along with others, including Henry Fleming and Johnny Long, saw Bat work King over the second time.

Chapter 13. Oldtimers believed Mysterious Dave Mather killed a man in Mobeetie over a horse, one put up for a gambling debt.

Temple Houston, lawyer son of Sam Houston, came to Mobeetie in the late 1870's and built a home, across the street, west of the jail and courthouse.

Bat Masterson and Ben Thompson were in a saloon fracas with a loud mouth woman. Billy Joe Carter was there.

Chapter 14. European syndicate land buyers flocked to the Texas Panhandle in the 1870's. They bought millions of acres of land and established big ranches.

Chapter 15. Bat Masterson as the offical town surveyor boasted, in fun, "Nobody's ever gonna check this surveyor." However, nearly 100 years later when oil companies drilled in the area they almost went crazy trying to figure out Bat's surveying. The town paid Bat $10 in gold every night plus drinks on the town; he was the boss. Henry Dittmos, his helper, only got $10. Bat was Henry's idol.

Chapter 17. A Kentucky school teacher and her husband acquired several sections of land in the Mobeetie community.

The buggy incident created lots of laughs.

Chapter 18. Henry Cresswell laid out one of the first ranches in the Panhandle, a 2,100,000 acre spread in the north Panhandle. To stock it, he began with 25,000 head of cattle he trailed from Colorado. The Panhandle's XIT ranch had 3,000,000 acres.

Chapter 20. Bat and Billy Dixon scouted under Lt. Baldwin.

Chapter 21. At the Salt Fork River crossing, Texas U. S. highway 83, the historical marker shows outlaws were in the area later, too. Bonnie and Clyde, of ill-fame, pistol-whipped and threatened a ranch couple there for hours.

Chapter 23. Mary Long was a prime mover in Mobeetie church work.

Clay Allison, called "The Wild Wolf Of The Washita," acquired sections 18 & 20, Block M, H & GN R. R. survey, near the confluence of the Washita River and Gageby Creek, 12 miles northeast of Mobeetie, in what is now Hemphill county. He occasionally rode his horse down main street wearing only his hat, boots and six-guns, shooting out lights. People thought he showed an odd streak of religion while at Mobeetie. His argument with his neighbor rancher, Johnson, over a water hole, ended in a fight. They dug a pit, agreed to get in it, and fight to a finish with Bowie knives—the winner bury the loser. Then, Allison left for New Mexico.

Mark Huselby came from England then to Fort Elliot as a soldier. He later had extensive holdings.

Chapter 24. Ben Thompson was in Mobeetie on visits with his brother, Bill, co-owner of the Lady Gay saloon.

Chapter 26. Dutch Henry was an uncanny operator. He stole horses from Emanuel Dubbs, and others, before Dubbs came to Mobeetie. In Kansas, a posse went after the thieves, killed some of his sidekicks, but Dutch got away. In Texas, he was caught up in the Adobe Walls battle. His name is on the monument marker in

Hutchinson County, along with Bat Masterson and others. Years later Dutch and Dubbs became friends, visited each other.

Charles Goodnight and Dutch Henry made a pact to respect each other's territory in the Texas Panhandle.

Chapter 27. The four John German girls, held by the Indians, were found in the Texas Panhandle. Years later they had a reunion in Pampa, Texas.

Chapter 29. Wyatt and Jim Earp figured on buying a ranch in the Texas Panhandle. Wyatt visited with Bat Masterson in Mobeetie on different occasions. Later Henry Fleming ran Wyatt out of Mobeetie for selling "gold bricks," (painted). Also a lawman, Jim McIntire, run Wyatt out of town again for trying to pull the same old gold brick swindle with gunfighter, Mysterious Dave Mather.

Chummy Jones was a notorious horse thief. Mothers simmered down their misbehaving kids with just the mention of his name. He and another horse thief, Charley Morrow, were hung somewhere between Fort Elliot and Fort Sill.

Many Texas land surveyors were killed by Indians.

The Casner Brothers were big sheep operators in the Panhandle. Two Casners' were murdered for the gold coins they carried in a leather pouch—nine killings over this one incident.

Chapter 31. Charles Goodnight trailed cattle through Mobeetie. After The Panhandle Stock Association of Texas was organized for protection against cattle rustlers Mr. Goodnight was chosen president—a prominent figure in Mobeetie and the Panhandle.

Jim and Bob Cator came over from England in 1871 and settled in the Panhandle in 1873 to hunt buffaloes. Their knee pants amused Billy Dixon, Bat Masterson and others, however they have the oldest White linage in the Texas Panhandle. And it's still a mystery, even to family and friends, how Jim and Bob Cator survived in hostile Indian country, 20 miles north of Adobe Walls...'didn't even know of the raging battle until they went for supplies the next day. Then they fell into the job of burying the dead—white people, Indians and horses. The Zulu post office was opened at their stockade on Palo Duro Creek in Hansford county. Nephew, Marshal Cator, and other relatives of Jim and Bob Cator ranches' in the same vicinity today near Sunray, Texas.

Granger Dyer, Mrs. Goodnight's brother, was killed in a Mobeetie gunfight. Goodnight handled his brother-in-law's death like his partner's on a trail-drive to a Wyoming Indian Agency. Oliver Loving caught an Indian arrow trailing across New Mexico. He died from complications. Goodnight kept his promise to carry him home to be buried—the same with Granger.

When Jim Springer brought in 300 head of cattle to range near his saloons. It was said by many oldtimers to be the first ranching in the Panhandle, however Charles Goodnight established the first continuous operation; it exist today. Springer's main ranch saloon was located on the bank of the Canadian River. His ranch saloon on the Washita north of Mobeetie catered to thirsty buffalo soldiers and hide hunters. Jim, an expert poker player, was killed during a drunken brawl in his saloon.

Chapter 31. Frenchy McGraw, Mobeetie dance hall girl, came to Mobeetie during the early days of the settlement. There she met Mickey McCormack and they fell in love. Finally, they left Mobeetie and went to Tascosa, Texas, married, and lived there the rest of their life. He died October 7, 1912, and she died Janurary 12, 1941, and was buried, "Next to my Mick," in Tascosa.

A family was decimated by Indians east of Mobeetie on Sweetwater Creek. The family was waiting in the wagon for the 12 year old girl to bring the baby. The girl heard screams and looked out the window. She saw Indians swinging tomahawks, massacreing her family. She ran and hid under a creek-bank with the baby and they survived.

Chapter 34. Mobeetie boasted 500 prostitues on Featherbed Hill. Never questioned.

Chapter 34. Fort Elliot's garrison was around 1000 soldiers.

Chapter 35. A prairie chicken hunt east of Mobeetie that ended with a walk home.

Chapter 36. A skating rink was put in for the soldiers'.   Dr. Evans was stationed at Fort Elliot. He doctored the cowboy that got snake bit. Soon Dr. Pryor Shelton, a civilian doctor, injured in the Civil War, arrived. His specialty, wrapping up gunshot wounds.

Chapter 37. The popular Lady Gay saloon was rivaled only by the Shores-Of-Hell. As related by Johnny Jones, and J. J. Long, the Shores-Of-Hell was the wildest and wickedest place in town. Barney and Buzzard Breath's sham battle brought in many customers.

J. J. Long helped bury the men that got their throats slashed by King.

Chapter 41. Curry County New Mexico was named for George Curry.

Chapter 42. Ben Thompson threatened King's sidekicks after the gunfight, "I'll blow the first son-of-a-bitch to hell that lays a hand on Bat Masterson." Ben stayed in Mobeetie with Bat until he was able to get on his feet— eight weeks later.

Chapter 42. For years Bat Masterson wore a red rose in his lapel on the anniversary of Molly Brennan's death...the day she laid her life down for him.

Molly Brennan, Johnny Long, Rip Nesbit, John Corcoran, Mark Huselby, Capt. Arrington, Sam Morris,

Johnny Jones, Willie O'Loughlin, and two men that were hung are buried at Mobeetie, Texas—Billy Dixon is buried at Adobe Walls—Tom, Ellen, and Miles O'Loughlin are buried at Miami, Texas—Amos Chapman died July 18, 1925 at Seiling Oklahoma—Charles Goodnight is buried at Goodnight, Texas—Robert Baley is buried in Spearman, Texas—Judge Emanuel Dubbs and Grainger Dyer are buried in Clarendon, Texas—Mickey McCormick is buried in Tascosa, Texas—Frenchy McGraw McCormick is buried at Tascosa, Texas— Melvin King was buried at Fort Elliot in an unmarked grave, according to oldtimers. It was rumored and talked for years Clay Allison was secretly buried in the little Elam cemetery 12 miles north of Mobeetie, in present Hemphill County. There is no legible marker.